THE UNITED FEDERATION MARINE CORPS

BOOK 8: COMMANDANT

Colonel Jonathan P. Brazee
USMC (Ret)

Semper Fi Press

A Semper Fi Press Book

ISBN-13: 978-0692608395 (Semper Fi Press)

ISBN-10: 0692608397

Printed in the United States of America

Acknowledgements:

I want to thank all those who took the time to pre-read this book, catching my mistakes in both content and typing. I want to thank Christina Cutting, my editor, for her help in the book and for catching my many typos and mistakes. Any remaining typos and inaccuracies are solely my fault. Finally, I want to thank those in my mailing list who gave me invaluable advice and insight concerning this book.

Original cover art by Jonathan Brazee and with the background photo by NASA's Hubble telescope.

Dedicated to Corporal Jonathan Yale, UCMS, and Lance Corporal Jordan Haeter, USMC, who on 22 April 2008, in Ramadi, Iraq, sacrificed their lives by taking down a heavily-laden truck driven by a suicide bomber. While local police at the checkpoint ran for cover, the two Marines stood their ground and took the truck under fire, killing the driver and detonating the truck. By destroying the truck at the cost of their own lives, they saved the lives of over 150 of their comrades.

Their actions were the inspiration for Chapter 24 in this book.

And in remembrance:

Staff Sergeant Thomas James, USMC
Guadalcanal and Chosin Reservoir Vet

Corporal Tomtom Copperwait, USA
Vietnam Vet

RIP

FS ADMIRAL KRAVITCH

Chapter 1

Major General Ryck Lysander sat in the ground commander's chair in the back of the bridge, fingers white as they pressed hard into the seat's arms.

Only a dreadnaught the size of the *Kravitch* had that small courtesy to the senior Marine on board. Usually, the senior Marine either had a station in CIC[1] or just occupied the desk in his stateroom. But a dreadnaught was a completely different creature, resplendent with pomp and circumstance, from the gold inlay on the bridge and in the wardroom to the requirement of six Marine guards in dress blues standing at attention while awaiting the admiral's beck and call.

The admiral in this case was none other than Vice Admiral Marc Kurae, the CO of the *Ark Royal* when Ryck was a captain and who had ridden Ryck's fight with the Confederation in the Cygni B system into his admiral's stars. Ryck had thought Kurae was a flaming asshole then, and nothing he'd observed over the last two months had changed his opinion of the man. And the fact that Ryck was, well, Ryck Lysander, the only living man with not one, but two Federation Novas, the subject of three Hollybolly flicks, and now only one rank below the admiral seemed to grate on the man to no end. He might be the commander of Task Force 31, but Ryck was the star, the person the newsies wanted to interview.

Not that Ryck wanted to do much in the way of interviews, not on this mission. The *Kravitch*, along with two frigates and the *Ballston Shore*, a *Falklands* Class Integrated Assault Transport with

---

[1] CIC: Combat Information Center. The hub of a ship's communications and data gathering from which a naval battle is fought.

a battalion of Marines and a battalion of FCDC troops aboard, was stationed off Ellison, the homeworld of Ryck's parents before they had emigrated to Prophesy before Ryck was born. Unrest had been growing on the planet over the eight years since the government landed first the Marines, then the FCDC to break the impasse with the planet's two main unions. The official numbers were never released, but close to 13,000 Ellisonians had been killed by the FCDC troops.

Ellison had long been one of the few planetary or national governments within the Federation not controlled by the People's Rights Party, but the ruling Democratic Voice Party had always kowtowed to the federal government, and the Federation even pointed to the party's power as proof that the Federation was, in fact, a free democracy. With the overwhelming election of the Freedom First Party, however, the new Ellison government had become decidedly an opposition party and a thorn in the side of the Federation. A plebiscite had been scheduled with the question of whether to cede from the Federation, a vote that was canceled by the Chairman of the Federation Council—and whose decision was backed by FCDC troops—when polling showed the vote might swing to leaving the Federation. Riots had broken out, and 52 troops were killed in the fighting before they pulled back off-planet to await reinforcements.

Task Force 31.

Not that a single battalion of Marines and a battalion of FCDC troops could quell the unrest on a planet of 12 billion souls. But it was the specter of the task force, sitting off the planet and untouchable by the Ellisonians that was supposed to knock some sense into the people.

Ryck's sudden assignment to the task force, pulling him out of his assigned billet as Junior Military Aide to the First Minister, had been a transparent effort to use his fame and public perception as a shield against what could be a messy operation, one that had already lit the ethersphere with criticism. He resented the assignment, but as always, he'd saluted smartly and reported for duty.

He'd hoped that the mission would end as it had with the prior year's mission to Teller's Reef, where a much smaller Navy-only task force had convinced the Judgment Movement to stand down. But no FCDC troops had been killed on Teller's Reef, and there was an undercurrent of, well, revenge, as Ryck considered it, within the admiral's staff as they planned for this mission. After a week of fruitless back-and-forth, Admiral Kurae had issued his ultimatum: a dissolution of parliament and the arrest and surrender of all individuals who had participated in attacks on FCDC troops.

The deadline for the ultimatum was in a few short minutes, and Ryck waited anxiously to hear the premier's response. Ryck thought the ultimatum went too far and left no room to maneuver. A dissolution of parliament and new elections set were a possibility, but the arrest and extradition of what had to be thousands of Ellisonians, most of whom would probably be executed, would be too much for the government to bear, on both political and moral grounds. Several thousand Ellisonians had already been killed during this round of fighting, and any more being sent to their fates would seal the fate of the Freedom First Party, something Kurae and those giving him his orders undoubtedly realized. To Ryck's growing suspicion and concern, the ultimatum could just be a sham and an excuse for a Federation response.

Over on the *Ballston Shore,* the embarked First Battalion, Tenth Marines, was ready to land and secure Jorgenson Hill, the Ellison government complex. Ryck didn't like the mission one bit. Civil unrest was not in the Marine Corps' charter. *Posse comitatus,*[2] or rather the proscription of granting it to a military force, had been embedded in federal doctrine since the Federation was formed, even if it had been routinely ignored and bypassed over the last century or so.

The battalion was commanded by Lieutenant Colonel Naranbaatar Bayarsaikhan, "Genghis," one of Ryck's posse and one-time fellow recruit. Only this time, for once, Ryck had nothing to do with them working together. His late orders to the task force would

---

[2] Posse comitatus: the authority to use others to assist in enforcing the law.

have precluded that, but it was a happy coincidence that Genghis had been in command of 1/10 for close to two years already, and the battalion had already been deployed on the *Ballston Shore* for a training mission and was ready to be absorbed by the task force.

Ryck had spent much of the last week on the comms with Genghis, and Ryck had stressed that if the battalion landed, extreme care would be taken to minimize violence. Ryck was damned if he'd let Marines be killed under his watch, and if the Ellisonians resisted, Genghis was to reply with as much force as was needed, but the Marines would not initiate a heavy-handed response unless absolutely required to save life and limb.

This was not in line with the many briefs Ryck had attended aboard the *Kravitch,* but if they didn't want him to put his own thumbprint on the actions of his Marines, they should not have assigned him as commander. Ryck was a pretty well known quantity, and they had to have understood that he was not just going to be a smiling figurehead.

Ryck looked around the bridge as the deadline approached. Admiral Kurae had taken over the captain's command chair, which was somewhat of a breach of Navy tradition. Captain Brian Plummer, the ship's CO, had moved to the navigator's console while the admiral's senior staff grabbed whatever seat they could find or simply stood. Other than routine reports, no one said a word. There was an open line back to Brussels, and for all anyone knew, the chairman himself was listening in.

"Captain, we've got an energy bloom, coordinates 10243 by 73527. It looks like a launch!" one of the junior officers shouted out from his console to Ryck's left.

"Spook, give me a visual!" Captain Plummer shouted out.

Before the words were out of the captain's mouth, the Intel chief had already switched Surveillance 2 to the coordinates. The nose of a chemical rocket was clearly visible to the ship's hi-res cameras, a cloud of exhaust following the rocket as it climbed.

"It's a Blackbeard Buster," the same junior officer shouted out in a less-panicked voice. "Probably a Gentry V-22 or clone."

Ryck let out the breath he hadn't realized he'd been holding. A Blackbeard Buster was the slang for any number of low-tech chemical rockets that served as point defenses for a planet, able to reach into low orbit to take out satellites or ships. They could be effective against pirates or jumped-up converted freighters, but they posed absolutely no threat to Navy ships-of-the-line.

There were more than a few chuckles from around the bridge as the men realized what had been fired at them.

"Guns, take it out," Captain Plummer ordered his weapons officer, almost cavalierly.

Within five seconds, the ship's meson cannon reached out, and the screen displayed a flash of light as the rocket was destroyed.

"Well Admiral, I guess they answered your demand," Plummer said with a chuckle, joined by most of the bridge.

The Ellison government knew that their Blackbeard Buster would stand no chance against any of the Navy ships, but by sending it off, they were giving the Navy—and hence the Federation itself—the proverbial finger.

Ryck hadn't joined in any of the derisive laughter. He knew now that he'd have to send in the Marines to seize Jorgenson Hill and secure the two main spaceports in the capital. He pulled out his PA to glance over the planned course of action, despite having the thing pretty much memorized. He'd hoped for a better outcome, but it was what it was.

Ryck looked up at the admiral, only the back of the man's head visible above the back of the command chair. He hadn't moved. Ryck figured that the admiral was taking this as a slap in the face.

Well, don't give out ultimatums you know won't be accepted, he thought.

He shook his head and started to look down at his PA, when quietly, almost too quietly, the admiral said, "Initiate Option 109."

What the fuck? Ryck asked himself in shock. *Did I hear that right?*

The genial mood in the bridge vanished as everyone in it went deathly still.

"Sir?" Captain Plummer asked, rising out of his seat.

"Initiate Option 109," the admiral repeated as if asking for a second cup of coffee.

"But sir!"

"But nothing. They have attacked a Navy vessel. There are consequences for that."

Ryck stood up, his mind reeling.

"With a Blackbeard Buster, sir! Nothing that could hurt us. It was a message!" the captain continued.

"And I am going to send a message back. Initiate Option 109," the commodore repeated.

Captain Plummer looked over at the cam pick-up that was broadcasting back to Brussels as if waiting for a reprieve. Ryck waited, too, waited for the voice of reason to cancel the admiral's orders.

"Sir, I can't—"

"Captain, you are relieved. Commander Xhosa, you now have command. Initiate Option 109."

"Yes, sir," the XO, no, now the ship's CO, said. "But we will need a Level 6 release."

"You'll have it. Initiate the sequence," the admiral told him.

"Aye-aye, sir," Xhosa said as he moved to the weapons officer's console.

He looked into the pickup, had his eyes scanned, and then spoke, "This is Commander Lester K. Xhosa, P92845566, Commanding Officer. Initiate Option 109."

Ryck hoped the ship's AI wouldn't accept the order. But it had heard the admiral assign the commander the ship's command, and it started the process, the lights in the bridge slightly dimming momentarily as the ship's systems were shifted to power up the weapon in its bay.

Option 109! For what? Ryck asked himself, taking several more steps forward.

Option 109 was the code for a planet buster. One had been used on G. K. Nutrition Six after the Trinoculars had taken over the planet, but none had been used against a human foe for over 30 years, when the Federation and Brotherhood had jointly interdicted what was then the SOG homeworld. The Brotherhood had since sworn off their use, as had more than half of humanity. The Federation had retained the right to use the weapons, but supposedly only as a weapon of last resort. It was supposed to be deterrence, not a weapon to use against Federation citizens.

Twelve billion Federation citizens!

"Admiral Kurae!" Ryck shouted out.

"At ease, General," the admiral said, not bothering to turn around.

Ryck looked around the bridge. Half of the officers and ratings seemed shocked. The rest? Those from the admiral's staff? They did not look surprised.

Grubbing hell! They knew this was going to happen!

"Initiation complete," the AI's flat voice filled the bridge.

Ryck looked to main hadron comms speaker, almost willing the voice of reason to come out and order the admiral to stand down.

"Admiral, about that release?" Commander Xhosa asked.

"Green 7659807-tack-88 rose petal," the admiral said, still sitting in his seat.

"Acknowledged," the AI intoned. "You are cleared to launch."

"Admiral, you can't do this!" Ryck shouted again, stepping up to the center of the bridge as several of the Navy officers mumbled their agreement.

"This is beyond you, General. It is beyond me. This has been made at the highest levels, so it would be better if you just shut up and sit down," Admiral Kurae said, finally turning to look at Ryck, his eyes blazing.

As Ryck shifted to look at Commander Xhosa, trying to will the man to refuse, the XO shrugged, and then turned the red key that had risen from the weapon's officer's console.

"Admiral?" he asked, stepping back.

The Admiral leaned forward into the console pickup and said, "Vice Admiral Marc V. Kurae, L77549201, Commanding Officer."

Ryck wanted to rush the man, to pound him into a pulp, anything to stop what was about to happen.

"Corporal, your sidearm," he said to the Marine guard who'd stepped forward as well.

Ryck hoped the Marine hadn't stepped forward to stop him, and he was relieved when the worried-looking Marine readily handed over his Ruger.

"Gentlemen, this is a grave decision, but one brought on by those down on the planet's surface. They've killed Federation troops, and now they've fired upon the Navy. We have no choice. May God have mercy on their souls," the admiral said to the rest of the bridge before starting to turn around to reach the second key, the one that would send the planet buster on its way.

"Don't move, Admiral, or I will kill you where you stand," Ryck said striding forward, finger tightening on the trigger of the corporal's Ruger.

He knew he should just shoot. With the admiral down, it would take some time for someone else to be authorized to turn that last key. But years of ingrained behavior kept him from killing his commander.

Ryck almost laughed at the thought. He was already a dead man. He'd just threatened his commanding officer, and that was a capital offense. And now he was worried about pulling the trigger?

But the admiral froze, still a couple of meters from the planet buster's trigger. He put up his hands, and then slowly turned to face Ryck.

"I think you need to put that weapon down," he told Ryck calmly.

After I shoot your condescending face I will, Ryck thought.

"I'm not going to let you kill 12 billion people," he said instead.

"Ryck, put the gun down," the familiar voice of Hopkins Garrison, the Federation First Minister and Ryck's boss, filled the bridge.

"I can't do that, sir," Ryck answered, his eyes and Ruger never wavering off Kurae.

"I told the chairman it was a mistake putting you on this mission. You're too moral for your own good," the first minister said. "Look, there are things in motion about which you have no idea. This is the way things have to be. It's bigger than you. It's bigger than me. It's bigger than the chairman himself."

"Is it bigger than 12 billion Ellisonians? That's 12 billion, sir!"

"Yes, it is, it pains me to say," the first minister answered.

"The Brotherhood won't stand for this, you know," Ryck said, switching tack.

"We've taken that under consideration, Ryck.

"Look, put down the gun, and we'll forget all of this happened. Come back here to Earth, and I give you my word that I'll explain it all to you. You'll see that this is the right choice, the only choice," the first minister said.

Ryck hesitated, the muzzle of his Ruger wavering ever-so-slightly.

What if he's right? What it there is something I don't know?

Movement caught the corner of his eye. Without thinking, he whirled and fired, sending three darts into the chest of Captain Lief Klinger, the admiral's chief of staff, as the man rushed him.

Ryck immediately swung back, his two darts zinging off the console stopping the admiral who had started to reach forward.

"Ryck, this pains me. Really it does. But Admiral Kurae, do what you have to do," the first minister said.

"Marines, arrest General Lysander. That is a direct order coming from the chairman himself."

Lying piece of shit, Ryck thought. *The chairman might want me arrested now, but he hasn't given any such order.*

"I'll kill you first," Ryck told the admiral.

"Maybe," the man said with a laugh. "But that'll only delay the inevitable. You've killed Captain Klinger, but with me gone, it will take, what, ten minutes to elevate Captain Jestonia to command? And you'll be on your way to be hanged in disgrace.

"Marines, I gave you your orders. Arrest the general."

He's right, Ryck thought as he contemplated just shooting him anyway.

He could fight, but to what avail? And he wasn't going to kill a Marine just for obeying his orders.

He stared at the admiral as he felt more than heard several of the Marines step forward. He waited for their hands on his shoulders. It was over, and there was nothing he could do, he realized in despair.

"Sir, what do you want us to do?" Sergeant Parker asked him as the sergeant of the guard stepped beside him, shoulder to shoulder.

"I said arrest him!" the admiral shouted, for the first time losing his composure. "That's an order!"

"Do you know what you're doing," he asked the sergeant quietly. "This is your career, and probably your life."

"We're Marines, sir, and we've got your back," the sergeant answered.

"And your oath?" Ryck asked.

"We swore an oath to protect the citizens, not sit back and let them get all blown up and like."

"You too?" he asked the corporal whose Ruger he'd taken, a Marine whose name he didn't even know.

"Me and the sergeant, and the rest, sir, like he said, we've got your back. You're General Lysander, and that's good enough for me."

"No!" Admiral Kurae shouted, wheeling to lunge at the planet buster's trigger.

Without thinking, Ryck fired off four quick shots, the hypervelocity darts reaching the man in an instant and piercing his body before the fins at the back of the dart twisted, causing horrendous internal damage. The admiral was dead before his body started to fall.

Ryck didn't watch the body slide to the deck. His eyes were on the rest of the men on the bridge. Most were in a state of shock, some were angry, and only a bare few seemed relieved. He half-lowered the Ruger, not pointing it at anyone, but still keeping it at the ready.

"Well, gentlemen," Ryck asked calmly. "It seems we have a situation here. Now what?"

Chapter 2

"We have to surrender. We can return to the Doughnut and turn ourselves in," Commander Hector Bortello pleaded. "They'll accept that."

The commander was not alone in his opinion among the staff gathered in the wardroom. No one there had wanted to interdict Ellison, but now that that threat was over, temporarily, at least, the realization of what they had done was sinking in. More than a few of the men wanted to return to *Prometheus Station*, the "Doughnut," and the homeport for the ships in the task force.

"Water under the bridge, Hector," Captain Plummer said. "Or that saying about the horses and the barn door. We've already committed mutiny, and the consequences of that are death, whether we return the *Kravitch* or not."

"We didn't commit mutiny! He did!" the commander continued, pointing at Ryck.

Corporal Glukhov, the Marine whose Ruger Ryck had taken, took a step forward to stand at Ryck's shoulder, hand on his holster. Ryck waved him back.

"The general may have pulled the trigger, but not one of us objected. I personally applauded his action, something I hadn't had the guts to do myself. But according to the FCMJ,[3] our inaction, much less sitting here discussing the situation, is compliance, and that is still a capital offense. Right, Commander Quintos?"

"Right, sir. I'm afraid we are all complicit in this from a legal standpoint," Lieutenant Commander Quintos, the task force staff judge advocate agreed.

"Gentlemen, I appreciate the situation I've put you in. And if you arrested me," Ryck said, as all six Marines converged behind him upon hearing that, "I would not resist. I may not be the expert

[3] FCMJ: The Federation Code of Military Conduct

that Lieutenant Commander Quintos is, but I imagine that would stand all of you in some good.

"We have saved Ellison for now, at least. And as Commander Fields has told us, the Ellisonians picked up the emissions as the planet buster powered up and have raised a hue and cry to the Universal Assembly. I would have to think that an interdiction is off the table for the moment. So I've done what I needed to do and am willing to face the consequences. I can't think of any reason why all of you should suffer the same fate as me."

A number of faces in the wardroom looked like they wanted to take him up on the offer.

"Bullshit, General. You had the guts to do what was right, and I cannot stand by and let you hang for that. And I am not willing to accept that the hangman's noose is, in fact, inevitable. We simply need to get to neutral space until this shakes out. You are a hero, and I, for one, am proud to be here with you now," Plummer said, his voice heated in his excitement.

"And if you are wrong?" Ryck asked, his voice calm.

"Would you do it again, sir?" Plummer asked.

"Yes."

"And so would I. We saved 12 billion people today. That's 12 *billion*! And if I do have to hang for that, well, I swore an oath to protect the Federation, and that's what we did. Not those politicians who ordered the interdiction, but the real Federation, the citizens."

"And for those here who disagree with you?" Ryck asked.

"We've already got 14 men in the brig. If anyone else wants to join them, I'll swear that they resisted us, and when we figure out how to transfer the prisoners off the ship, they can join them," the ship's CO responded.

Ryck looked around the room. All eyes were on him, waiting for what he had to say. Ryck had been resigned to the fact that he would be arrested and ultimately executed. He'd committed the cardinal sin for the military: he'd mutinied. But now he'd been given a glimmer of hope. His mind churned with ideas on how he could get the Brotherhood involved, how he might save not only his skin but also the skin of the men sitting around him.

Is it worth it, though? he wondered for a moment. *What if things blow up and get out of control?*

His life, even the life of those here on the bridge, were really meaningless in the grand scheme of things. Yes, Hannah and the kids would grieve, as would the families of the men with him. They would all be branded as traitors, bringing shame on their families. But what were the lives of the 30 or so officers and senior staff gathered there with him? Were they worth the potential disaster of a full-fledged mutiny?

Then he thought of those 12 billion people, and a government, his government, that was willing to wipe those people out of existence.

Things need to blow up, he thought with growing conviction. *Something has to change.*

"I am willing to take this further, whatever that might be," he told the gathered men. "But this is not my decision, nor yours, Captain. This is an individual choice, for each man, each officer, chief, petty officer, and rating. And Marine," he added, nodding to the six who were still behind him. "So, for all of us here, who wants to join the prisoners? No harm will come to you, and we'll get you off the ship as soon as possible."

The men looked at each other nervously. One hand went up, followed by three more. Ryck was surprised that Commander Bortello's hand was not one of them.

"Sergeant Parker, please escort these gentlemen to the brig. They are not prisoners, though, so treat them with respect," he told the sergeant of the guard.

Ryck didn't resent the four men's decision. It was asking a lot of all of them. And there was the matter of their oath. Frankly, Ryck was surprised that so few had taken him up on the offer. He watched as the men left the wardroom and the hatch closed behind them.

"Well, Captain Plummer, the die is cast. We need a course of action, and we need it quickly if we are going to get out of this mess."

JULIETTE STATION 2

Chapter 3

"Did you get a hold of my wife?" Ryck asked as First Lieutenant Kerry Feinstein leaned over his shoulder.

"Not yet, sir, but I've left several messages," his junior aide answered.

Hannah, Esther, and Noah were on Earth, and Ryck was beside himself with worry that they could pay the price for his actions.

While a ship was in bubble space, its communications were limited to her hadron comms and message torps, but those were official Navy comms, and Ryck couldn't use them for obvious reasons. As they left the Ellison system, he'd asked Kerry to try and contact his family any way he could the moment the ship emerged from bubble space on the other side and tell them to take the first transport off-planet. Now that comms were available again, he just hoped Kerry could contact Hannah before the government decided to act against them.

At least Ben was still on Tarawa where he was finishing up his senior year at school. Ryck was pretty sure that no matter what he'd done, the Marines on Tarawa would not let Ben bear the brunt of any Federation retribution.

"Keep trying, Kerry. I need you to get it done."

"Aye-aye, sir," his aide said, straightening back up and leaving the conference room.

"Sir? About Major Gustavson?" Captain Plummer asked after the hatch closed behind the lieutenant.

Ryck turned back to look at the gathered men sitting around the large, ornate conference table. Like everything else on the *Kravitch*, it was over-the-top: five meters of expensive inlaid wood with gold trim. On other ships, meetings like this were held in the wardroom, a separate conference room being a waste of space. But this was a dreadnaught, the pride of the Navy.

Captain Plummer had been requesting a decision on what to do with Major Gustavson and the 23 FCDC troops he'd brought along with him to the *Kravitch.* Before departing Ellison, the loyalist sailors who'd been put in the ship's brig, along with more than 300 other sailors and civilian staff, had made the transfer to the *Ballston Shore.* Some 200-plus sailors and Genghis, along with 1,943 Marines transferred to the *Kravitch* to join Ryck. Only 19 Marines chose to stay on the *Ballston Shore.* Surprisingly, to Ryck, at least, Gustavson and his 23 troops had requested to join the *Kravitch.* Plummer was sure they were plants and should be held in the brig, especially as they approached *Juliette Station 2.*

Ryck understood the captain's concern. FCDC troops were noted for their almost fanatical devotion to the central government, and to the council in particular. The fact that any of them wanted to join what was essentially a rebel group was somewhat surprising.

"They're all snakes, sir. Every one of them, and you know it. They live and breathe for the council," Plummer insisted.

Ryck felt an urge to point out that the Navy itself was the long arm of the council, and more than half of its members were former admirals. But he couldn't afford to alienate the captain. The *Kravitch* and the accompanying *Temperance* were all Ryck had to keep him, and those who'd joined him, alive. A dreadnaught and a frigate, along with 4,000 sailors and half that many Marines, against the entire might of the Federation.

But he couldn't just lock up men without cause. It wasn't morally right, and Ryck's only defense of his recent actions was that contravening the orders from the Federation had been justified on a moral basis. Ryck had to maintain the moral high ground, for both personal reasons and for justification of his actions.

The thing was, the captain was probably right. Ryck didn't doubt that at least one of the FCDC troops was a plant, and that could have drastic consequences down the road.

"Captain, I understand your concern—believe me, I do. But we cannot go locking up men without probable cause. Let's see how things shake out on the station, and meanwhile, let's keep our FCDC guests away from anything vital."

"Aye-aye, sir, we'll do it your way," Plummer said, obviously not mollified.

The authority of command still works, even among a bunch of mutineers, Ryck mused. *And I hope it lasts.*

"So, Commander Bortello, nothing has changed from the station?" Ryck asked, changing the subject.

"No, sir. Upon dropping out of bubble space, we confirmed with Meister Hendricks-Pata that we would be allowed to dock. We're still to remain in the ships until given further notice, though. And we need to come in weapons cold."

Before leaving Ellison orbit, Ryck had ordered a tight-beam comms link with *Juliette Station 2*, an independent station out in the Far Reaches. Run by the notoriously dictatorial Meister Glenda Henricks-Pata, granddaughter of Juliette Hendricks-Pata herself, Ryck was taking a huge chance. *Juliette Station 2* was heavily defended, and with the *Kravitch* and the *Temperance* coming in weapons cold, the station could easily blast both ships into their component atoms. Hendricks-Pata, though, hated the Federation (and the Confederation, and most of all, the Brotherhood, who she called medieval monks). Whether she would risk the might of the Federation or not over a dislike of the council was a good question, one for which they would soon receive an answer. But to Ryck, it was their best chance to regroup and formulate a plan.

The problem was that what that plan might be, Ryck didn't have a clue in hell.

Chapter 4

"Atteint!" Genghis said, slapping the five cards down on the table and raking together the chips.

Ryck folded his cards in disgust and dropped them face down. They'd been playing for only a little more than an hour, but he was already down over a hundred credits to the other three men. Ryck didn't even like playing cards that much. Hannah was into bridge, and he'd played with her, but he'd rather be kicking back in front of the holo with a Corona in hand. But with the *Kravitch* in a Mendoza Cage, there wasn't much else to do.

The Mendoza Cage was not a physical cage but rather an impenetrable array of pulsating electromagnetic waves that covered the ship. As long as the station provided power to the cage, the ship had no way of receiving or sending comms other than a single optical cable now connected to one of the ship's docking hubs. When the station wanted to contact them, it would. Until then the ship might as well have slipped into an alternate, unpopulated universe.

Only they were still in their universe, just blind. For all they knew, the Federation could be gathering a fleet of ships, ships that could be orbiting the station right then, weapons trained on the *Kravitch* and the *Temperance.* Not knowing what was happening was excruciating, and Ryck's imagination had taken a turn to the worst possible scenarios.

It wasn't just Ryck. After the thrill of breaking away from the Federation, reality had begun to rear its head among the Marines and crew as the gravity of the situation sunk in. Men started thinking of home, of family. Thoughts drifted to the penalty for mutiny. And isolated, without knowing what was going on, the negative thoughts fed upon each other, growing into a tsunami of self-doubt. Add the fact that it was crowded, with Marines and sailors hot-racking[4] it, fights broke out every few hours, and the chiefs and SNCOs had their hands full.

With two days in the cage so far, Ryck was second-guessing himself to death. He'd hoped that Meister Henricks-Pata would grant them a safe haven, but the longer they were held in the cage, the more it seemed as if the choice had been a bad one. The *Juliette Station 2* might be an amazingly powerful bunker in space, and the Juliette Group controlled important mineral resources that the Federation needed, but the station could not stand up militarily to the Federation. Self-preservation might be trumping the reasonable-to-expect kindred spirit connection Ryck was hoping to exploit.

Ryck had accepted Genghis' offer for a game of lances more just to be doing something, anything but the planning sessions that had taken up most of his time since arriving at the station. Along with Captain Plummer and Lieutenant Commander Xanci, the ship's chaplain, the four went through the motions of playing. Ryck's thoughts kept straying to Hannah and the twins, and his lack of concentration had cost him a full day's pay so far.

Shit. A day's pay? Who do I expect to be paying me now? he asked himself.

The dealer duties rotated to Ryck, so he collected the cards, fed them into the shuffle-master, and dealt them out to the other three. Lances was pretty much poker, to Ryck's inexperienced mind, not much different than seven-card chutes or Texas hold 'em, but it was the current flavor of the month that periodically swept through human space, only to fade away as a new fad took hold. Ryck might not be as big a fan of bridge as his wife, but at least that game had remained basically unchanged for centuries.

Captain Plummer took one look at his hand and immediately folded, a look of disgust on his face. Ryck took a peek at his; not bad, and something with which he could work. He hesitated only a moment before hitting the double-down button.

"Levée," he said after momentarily forgetting the proper term to send the hand into mêlée.

"Oh, feeling frisky, eh, General?" the chaplain asked. "What could you have, there?"

---

[4] Hot-racking: a process where up to three men share a single rack for sleeping, each man being allotted an eight-hour window to use the rack.

"Well, Father, you're going to have to play to find out."

"So says the man who's lost about every hand so far this evening," the chaplain said to the laughs of the other two.

With the captain out, Ryck dealt two cards to Genghis and three to the chaplain before dropping one and dealing himself another.

Damn! That's what I'm talking about, he thought, trying to keep his face devoid of visible emotion. *Time to get some of those credits back.*

Ryck was just about to double down again when there was a knock on his hatch, followed immediately by Lieutenant Feinstein sticking his head in the stateroom.

"General, the station is requesting your presence. Yours, Captain Plummer's, and Commander Kaawa's."

Ryck dropped his game control, his bet forgotten.

"How much time do I have?" he asked, jumping to his feet.

"There will be a guide at Starboard 3C in 20 minutes—uh, 18 minutes now."

"Hell, they could have given us a little warning after having us sit here for two days. Brian, let's get moving. Service dress, OK?"

"Roger that, sir. I'm on my way," Captain Plummer said, bolting for the hatch.

Ryck had a private head, and he was tearing off his shorts and shirt as he told his AI, "Water, fine mist, 45 degrees."

By the time he slid into the shower, the water was already at temperature.

"Genghis, can you get out my alphas?" he shouted out as he triggered the soap.

Thank God some things never leave you, he thought as he jumped out of the shower a minute later, thinking back to his recruit training and the "Navy showers"[5] he'd had to take then.

Genghis had laid out his alphas. It wasn't a lieutenant colonel's job to dress a general, but the ancient practice of having an orderly had disappeared ages ago, and time was a-wasting.

---

[5] Navy Showers: slang for quick showers, limited to 60 seconds in duration.

It took another minute-and-a-half to slam on his uniform. Ryck opened his sea locker, and there on the top shelf, his two Federation Novas glinted in the LED lighting over his desk. The Novas were worn on ribbons around the neck. Ryck handed the medals to Genghis, and just as Ryck helped Hannah with her pearls, the lieutenant colonel played husband and fastened the clips. Ryck was facing the desk, and as Genghis finished up with the medals, Ryck's attention was caught on the sea locker. Almost without thinking, he reached out and took the small PA that he'd had for close to 15 years, a PA he'd never used, and slid it into his trousers pocket. He turned around, and with Genghis running alongside and still adjusting the hang of Ryck's Novas, the two Marines were out the hatch in just under five minutes.

"Get your ass in gear, Captain!" Ryck shouted through the ship's CO's closed hatch as he hurried down the passage.

The *Kravitch* was a huge ship, and while elevators plied the engineering and weapons spaces, there were none in officers' country. Ryck checked his watch; he should make it in time, but it would be close.

With two minutes to spare, Ryck reached the designated hatch. Genghis fussed over his uniform like a mother hen, which annoyed Ryck to no end, but he did want to make a good impression, so he stood there and endured it. With only 30 seconds to spare, Captain Plummer showed up, breathing heavily.

"You ready?" Ryck asked.

Plummer took a deep breath, then said, "Doesn't matter if I am or not. I just want an answer."

Commander Bortello showed up huffing and puffing and immediately bent over to catch his breath. Captain Plummer leaned over to give the commander some last-second guidance.

Ryck looked to Genghis. Ryck's inclusion in the task force had been purely political, and he'd never had a real staff with him. Genghis was the next senior Marine. Both of them had enlisted at the same time, so they were the same age. But it was asking a lot of a lieutenant colonel to shoulder the burden of a mutiny should something go wrong out in the station.

"Look, Naranbaatar," he started, for once addressing Genghis by his real name. "If something, well, if things don't go right out there, well, it's your call. Do what you think is right for the men."

"Hell, General, we're in this together. Whatever happens, it happens to all of us."

"I'm not holding you to that. Do what's right, that's all."

Genghis didn't have a chance to respond as the bosun mate in charge of the hatch called out, "Opening S-C3. Stand by."

With a whoosh, the hatch swung back. Air rushed in, the breeze cooling the slight sweat that had formed on his face in the rush to the hatch. Exotic smells almost assaulted his nose after the sterile air of the *Kravitch*. Like all stations, *Juliette Station 2* used overpressure to keep from being invaded by pathogens from visiting ships, but unlike most stations, open-air markets, replete with food stalls, kept the air full of aromas that were not scrubbed. The Juliette Group liked it that way, and it gave visitors a feel of how Ryck imagined an ancient casbah might strike people for the first time.

Ryck didn't have time to contemplate the sociological implications of how the Juliette Group ran their holdings, though. Waiting outside the hatch were four well-armed police, their faces hidden by helmets and dark visors. A lone young man in a silk suit stood one step in front of the muscle.

"This way, please," the man said.

Ryck stepped through the hatch, followed by Captain Plummer. A technician punched something into a control box, and with an audible snap, the Mendoza Cage snapped shut around the opening that had allowed them to open the hatch.

Ryck felt an emotional connection severed as the cage closed. He and Plummer were cut off. If something happened to them, no one on the *Kravitch* would ever know.

Without a word, Ryck and Plummer stepped off on the heels of their young escort. With two of the police leading, the other two fell behind, effectively keeping the two mutineers surrounded.

For a fleeting second, Ryck was tempted to spin and jump one of the two men behind them and then make a break for it. But to what end? Even if he could immobilize one of them, something that was not a sure thing given their air of deadly competence and Ryck's aging body, there would be three others. And if he did get away, he was in a space station. Hollybolly flicks notwithstanding, people just cannot hide on a station where every living being is monitored 24/7.

The sheer size of the *Kravitch*—which would normally keep it off-station, but with the need of a Mendoza Cage requiring station-provided power, it had to have a physical docking—kept the ship at the very end of the terminal arm, a huge ball stuck on the end of a tube. That made it about as far away from the main station as was physically possible. The walk down the terminal arm, however, was shorter than Ryck had expected; as was logical, a small cart was waiting for them at the security checkpoint for the gate, and all seven men clambered aboard. The shuttle took off smoothly, whisking them to the end of the terminal. After two right turns, the shuttle sped down the adjacent terminal arm, stopping at a security point outside Gate B6 and where Commander Kaawa, the Temperance's CO, stood waiting, along with four more police guards. At least those guards did not get on the crowded shuttle as it turned around to take them into the heart of the station.

At the end of the terminal arm, *Juliette Station 2* boasted a large window, some 40 meters long. This was a favorite spot for locals and visitors alike as it offered a view of three of the station's four terminal arms, and when the orientation was right, of the enormous hulk of the gas giant Gardenhaupt.

Ryck was no different, and he looked out the window to try and spot the *Kravitch*, which was pretty hard to miss. Something else caught his eye, though, and it tickled a warning.

"Is that—" he started to whisper to Captain Plummer.

"Yes," the captain whispered back quickly, cutting him off.

Far off in the distance, probably 30 or 40 kilometers, a vast sphere caught the sun's rays. The unique outline, even at that distance, left no doubt. Another *Admiral Neung*-class dreadnaught was out there. And where the Navy sent a dreadnaught, other ships would accompany it.

The Navy only had five of the *Admiral Neungs*, the *Kravitch* being one. The *Kravitch* would be an even match for the ship out there, but the *Kravitch* was in the Mendoza Cage. Even if the cage were shut down, the *Kravitch* would be a sitting duck for the other dreadnaught even without considering the other ships that had to be accompanying it.

Ryck turned to look back forward, his stomach in his throat. With the Federation Navy there, his options were limited. While he'd known their chances were minimal, to have that confirmed was heartbreaking. This wasn't some flick where some improbable miracle and feats of derring-do could extract them. The jig was up. And now, he could only offer himself as a way to save the 6,000 men on the two ships.

The Federation had him, no matter what. And they could eliminate him and execute the rest of the men as they chose. They'd been willing to murder 12 billion, so what was a mere 6,000? But the Federation was aware of the media and public opinion (although that hadn't seemed to enter into the equation when deciding to interdict Ellison). If Ryck would publically admit to his sins, he might be able to negotiate at least exile to a prison planet for the enlisted. It was worth a try, at least.

Ryck took a deep breath and sat up straighter. He knew they were being watched as the cart carried them along, and he was not going to look defeated, at least. What he'd done had been right, and he'd be damned if he'd look guilty—unless that is what it took to save some of his men.

The shuttle bounced over a kill bar and entered a wide avenue, the landmark of each Juliette station. Trees lined the median as throngs of people walked to and fro. Only official vehicles were allowed on Center Boulevard; the kill bar would stop any other vehicle as it tried to pass. People stopped to stare as the shuttle made its way slowly to—and then past—the large gothic-looking building that Ryck assumed was the station headquarters.

At the far end of the avenue, the shuttle pulled in front of a nondescript building that spanned the entire height of the main chamber. Where the other central buildings stressed appearances and architecture, this was a no-nonsense, utilitarian structure. A side-door opened, and the shuttle drove inside and up to what looked like a commercial loading dock as Ryck might find in the industrial sector of Tarawa. Four more guards awaited them; the only difference between them and the police in the shuttle was their well-tailored suits, complete with muted teal cravats. Teal might not instill fear, but the four could have been dressed in pink tutus and still no one would doubt their lethality. Their skin color ranged from almost black to a very light and pale pink, but still, they could have been clones in posture and movement.

At least they aren't FCDC, Ryck thought. *Although that might be next.*

"This way, gentlemen," a fifth man said, possibly physically larger than the four guards, but much smaller in presence.

Ryck, Plummer, and Kaawa stepped out of the shuttle, and then hopped up to the platform. Their guide waited only a moment before stepping into the brightly lit corridor. Ryck didn't need the muscles' urging to follow. He kept his head high as if being there was at his request and not a summons.

To Ryck's surprise, the three were led to a small room not far from the service entrance. There were no windows, not even an eWindow. It wasn't a jail cell, but with only a couch and a table with a pitcher of water and three glasses on it, the room was pretty Spartan.

"If you will wait here, gentlemen?" their guide said, his voice rising in a question while still leaving no doubt that they really had no choice.

To Ryck's surprise, their guards left the room, too, leaving the three alone.

"So, what do you make of this?" Captain Plummer asked, his voice a measured calm, but with an underlying note of apprehension still evident.

"Until I see fuckdick security, I'm OK with anything," Ryck said.

Commander Kaawa laughed at that. "'Fuckdicks?'"

"Yeah, fuckdicks. As in FCDC. Fuckdicks," Ryck said, looking at the commander.

Where have you been all your career? Or is that only a Marine term? Ryck wondered. *Can't be.*

"Pretty funny, sir. And appropriate," the commander said before all three fell into silence.

Ryck looked around the room, trying to spot the surveillance devices that had to be there. He couldn't see them, but then again, he was no countersurveillance expert.

His hand brushed the hard lump in his pocket. Reaching in, he pulled out the old PA, holding it at arm's length, thinking back to when he'd received it. For the first time, he contemplated activating it.

He doubted it would do any good. How could it? Things had changed since then, especially as all humans were supposedly bonded in the effort against the Klethos. He looked around the room again, once more trying to spot the surveillance.

What the hell? I've got nothing to lose, he told himself.

He half-expected the PA to remain dead, but when he hit the power button, it powered right up, green lights flashing.

"What's that, sir?" Captain Plummer asked.

Ryck ignored him. Pushing the connect could be considered an act of treason, after all.

And that made him laugh out loud.

This would be treason? What the grubbing hell have I been doing up until now!

He was still laughing when he hit the connect to the only saved number in the memory.

After one ring, a familiar voice came on the line.

"General Lysander, it's good to hear from you," Titus Pohlmeyer said as if this were a normal call between friends.

Ryck was surprised that first, the call had even gone out. All comms from the ship had been blocked, but now he was free to call? And second, that Pohlmeyer had answered so quickly. He had no idea as to the time back on New Mumbai, and even then, interplanetary calls had to be queued and slotted.

Suddenly, Ryck didn't know what to say. He almost cut the connection.

"Uh, is it Colonel now?" Ryck asked, stalling.

"Just major, General. I'm glad you called. You're in quite a predicament," the Confederation major said matter-of-factly.

"So you know about all of this?"

"I wouldn't be very good at my job if I didn't, now, would I?"

"I guess not," Ryck admitted.

"So, what can I do for you?" the major asked.

"I. . .uh, I really don't know. I just, well, you said—"

"I told you we had our eyes on you and to call me if there was anything we could do for you."

"Uh, right. That's about it, I guess."

"And you want to know if we can do anything."

Ryck hesitated. He may have disobeyed orders, but he was still Federation. Asking for help from a foreign government was a huge step in a different direction.

"Maybe," he equivocated.

"Well, the fact of the matter is I don't know if there is anything I can do. You've got 42 capital ships orbiting the station right now, a good chunk of the Federation Third Fleet. We don't know their intention, to be honest."

Ryck's heart fell, and he wasn't sure why. Forty-two was a lot, but in his situation, forty-two or five didn't make much of a difference in the long run.

Ryck used his hands to indicate 42 to both sailors who were watching him closely. Commander Kaawa slumped back in the couch, eyes closed and head up as he realized what Ryck meant.

"You've got company arriving now. I imagine the meister will see you first, and then, well, we'll see what happens after that. Call me again if you can, General," Major Pohlmeyer said.

If I can, Ryck thought. *Not too much of an endorsement, is it?*

"How do you know all of this?" he asked.

"As I said, I wouldn't be very good at my job, now, would I, if I didn't know. And you are my job. You have been since you were our guest on New Mumbai. But to answer you, I am sitting in a café about 120 meters from your position now. I have eyes on the building."

"You're here? On *Juliette Station 2*? How?" Ryck asked, surprised.

I guess that's how my call got through immediately.

The major said nothing, and Ryck added, "Oh, your job."

Still, it astounded him. They'd gone straight to *Juliette Station 2* from Ellison, and they'd been docked here for not even three full days yet.

How the grubbing hell had he made it here already?

Ryck didn't know what one Confederation major, albeit one whose abilities and pull undoubtedly surpassed that of most majors, could help. Still, it was a hope, and at this point, Ryck would grasp and claw at any life ring thrown his way.

"Gentlemen, the meister will see you now," their guide said after sticking his head in the door.

"I've got to go," Ryck said over the phone. "I'll call you if I can when I find out what's going on," he said hurriedly.

He cut off the responding "Go with—" and slid the PA back into his pocket. With the other two in tow, he followed their guide (and four guards) to discover their fate.

Chapter 5

"Shit does really follow you, General," Meister Glenda Henricks-Pata said as Ryck and the two sailors were escorted into the room.

Ryck held his face steady, fighting to keep from rolling his eyes. In *The Warrior*, the flick about his fight with the Klethos *d'relle*, or "queen" as the populace had started to refer to the Klethos champions, that accusation had been repeated several times to the point that it had almost become his motto, and then time and time after that, usually by people trying to be clever. Meister Henricks-Pata didn't seem to be trying for clever at the moment, though.

The meister waved a hand, more of a flick in the air, and the two muscles and their guide quickly left, closing the door behind them.

"The problem is that you brought your shit along with you to my station, something I don't appreciate."

The meister was a large woman, easily 120 kgs, and somewhere in her upper middle ages—exactly where, Ryck couldn't tell as her turquoise-spiked hair, currently a fad among young teens, threw him off somewhat. She was seated in a large hoverchair, her sturdy legs spread, feet planted firmly on the deck. For a moment, Ryck imagined her springing forward to take down the little gnats who had dared to interfere with her small kingdom. She stared at Ryck, ignoring Plummer and Kaawa, her light blues eyes piercingly intense. Ryck stared back while trying to maintain a neutral expression. In the grand scheme of things, a major general in the Federation Marine Corps had more power than a station meister, but this wasn't the grand scheme of things. Ryck didn't have the backing of the Federation behind him, and on her station, Meister Henricks-Pata had full control over him.

She finally wrinkled her upper lip in an expression Ryck couldn't interpret and leaned back. The hoverchair gave a little mechanical squeal as it valiantly tried to compensate for her shifting weight.

"So what do I do with you and your merry band of men?" she asked rhetorically, pausing for dramatic effect. "The Federation has offered a nice—well, no use playing coy—a *substantial* reward for your arrest and return to their tender embrace. They are sending a fleet here to facilitate your transfer."

"Seems to me that they're already here," Ryck said calmly.

His voice might have remained calm, but his thoughts were bouncing around his head like a songbird in a cage.

"Ah, yes, them. I should have realized that you probably had ways to pierce your cage."

"Not really," Ryck said nonchalantly. "I saw them as we passed your observation window."

He neglected to mention Major Pohlmeyer, although he was sure she'd be told that he'd been in contact with someone.

She leaned back forward and stared hard at him before bursting out in a peal of laughter.

"I guess we forgot about that. Good on you," she said as she fought to get out the words through her laughter.

"You know, General? In another day and age, I could like you. And I don't mean the you portrayed in the flicks. For all I've heard, you can be somewhat pompous, and you act like you have a stick up your ass, but you are also an honorable man. And that is rare in this day and time.

"But this shit sandwich, this is beyond me. My little station—all of the Juliette Group, for that matter—we can't stand up to the Federation, even if we wanted to."

Behind him, Ryck heard Plummer stir.

I should have figured it'd come to this. What the grubbing hell did I expect? Ryck asked himself, his face outwardly emotionless. *Their vaunted defenses can't stand up to an entire fleet.*

"So for me and mine, we need you off the station. Sorry, but your request for asylum is denied."

Well, that's that.

Ryck had a momentary thought of rushing the meister, of holding her hostage. And judging from the sound of a step from behind him, either Plummer or Kawaa had the same thought. But to what good? The meister was only looking out for her people, and even if the three of them somehow managed to gain control through Henricks-Pata, then what? There were still 42 Federation ships out there, and the *Kravitch* was a sitting duck while docked.

No, it was better to sacrifice himself and others in the leadership and try and save as many of the Marines and crew as they could.

"I understand, Meister. Your hospitality has been appreciated, as has your consideration. So, I'm sure you've been in contact with the fleet out there. How is this supposed to work?"

"General!" Captain Plummer said from behind him.

Ryck held up one hand, stopping the captain.

"Meister?"

"Well, there are two officers in the next room waiting for you. They would like to talk first."

Ryck gave the meister a curt nod, then spun around so quickly that he almost collided with Captain Plummer.

Plummer's eyes were wide, and he had that twitchy motion of someone about to swing into action.

"Captain, we are guests here. We will cooperate," Ryck said, with as much authority in his voice as his 36 years of service could muster.

This was a turning point. Ryck's mind was on the men waiting in the ships. Plummer's mind was undoubtedly on how to fight, how to extricate themselves from the situation.

He could have been a Marine, Ryck thought.

But there comes a time when no action at all is the correct choice.

Plummer seemed to be at war with himself, but within moments, he calmed down. He nodded, then turned around as the door opened.

Their guide stuck his head in. "Gentlemen?"

"Go with God," Meister Henricks-Pata said as the three men left the office.

"Not much chance of that, thanks to you," Plummer muttered, too low for the meister to hear.

Ryck sucked in a deep, calming breath as he followed their guide about 15 meters down the passageway to another door. The muscle had disappeared, which seemed odd, given the circumstances. But there were probably armed guards waiting inside the room. For personal reasons, Ryck hoped they would be FCDC, not Marines. He wasn't sure he could take getting arrested by Marines.

Their guide knocked several times on the door, a ratatatat that seemed too loud. He turned the knob, pulled the door open, and motioned to the three men.

Ryck took another deep breath, stood up straighter, and marched into the room. . .

. . .to see General Hank Ukiah, the 91st Commandant of the Marines, and Rear Admiral Lester Linney, alone and waiting for them.

Ryck stopped dead, looking at the two men. For a split second, he felt a surge of hope. General Ukiah was his rabbi,[6] his mentor. Rear Admiral Linney had been the CO of the *FS Brandenburg* while Ryck had been embarked, and the two men had formed a strong friendship over the ensuing years.

That hope quickly turned to anger as he realized what was happening. The Federation had sent two men, two friends, in the hope that Ryck wouldn't fight back, that he'd go quietly. For a moment, he *wanted* to fight back, to punch the Federation in the jaw one last time.

Ryck had sent his own brother-in-law on a suicide mission, so he'd absolutely fight his two friends if he had to. But once again, to what end? That was just his hubris trying to force him into action. If his goal now was to save as many of the men as possible, that would be a good way to sabotage that effort.

"General, I see they've sent you to do their dirty work," he said, his voice dripping with scorn. "Glad you could make it, too, Lester," he added.

"What? Who sent me?" the commandant asked. He shook his head in confusion, and then continued, "Look, we don't have

---

[6] Rabbi: slang for a mentor, someone of higher rank who can help in promotion, billets, and in the advancement of a Marine or sailor's career.

much time. The task force from First Fleet is on its way here, and we've got to be long gone by then."

What?

Now it was Ryck's turn to look confused. His scorn evaporated as he tried to process what the commandant had said.

"I . . . what? You're not here to arrest us?"

"Arrest you? Hell no! We're here to rescue you. You think I'd agree to arrest you? Me?"

"But, the meister, she said the Federation was here, and she would not grant us asylum, so, well—"

"General?" Lester Linney asked, tapping on his watch.

"Ryck, we've really don't have much time," the general said, turning to Ryck. "And we are not prepared for a fight yet when the First Fleet's task force arrives. We've got to get the *Kravitch* and *Temperance* fired up and moving, then all of us need to diddiho out of here.

"Going where?" Ryck asked, his mind still reeling.

"To Tarawa, of course," the commandant answered.

What? Tarawa? But—

"Unless you want to stay here," he continued.

"Ryck, we really have no time. I don't want to be caught in orbit when the task force arrives. I know you've got questions, and we'll answer on the *Kravitch*, but now, we've got to get onboard. Unless you have a better plan, I really, really suggest we blow this joint and get out of the meister's turquoise hair," Admiral Linney said.

For a moment, Ryck's suspicious mind wondered if this was some elaborate trick to get the two ships off station where they could be easier dealt with while not risking damage to the station. He pushed that thought away. He was being thrown a lifeline, and only a fool in his position would wonder who was doing the throwing.

"Lead on, Admiral Linney. We are at your command," he said, his heart suddenly lighter.

FS KRAVITCH

Chapter 6

"The Third Fleet?" Ryck asked, trying to get his mind around it.

"Not 100%, but enough so that every ship is with us, except for the *Pieter Smolev*, which was loaded with the 2,800 dissenters who wanted to remain with the government and then sent back to marry up with the First Fleet," Lester Linney said.

Ryck, Captain Plummer, Genghis, and Commander Bortello were with Lester, the commandant, and Colonel Prince Jellico in what had been Ryck's stateroom until he'd insisted that General Ukiah take it over. Over the last thirty minutes, Ryck had been bombarded with facts, too many to absorb. And he was still in shock that after essentially giving up and being ready to sacrifice himself in an attempt to save most of his men, he'd been given a second chance.

As the task force commander, Rear Admiral Linney and the 42 ships of the Third Fleet had "accepted the transfer" of the "prisoners" from Meister Henricks-Pata and *Juliette Station 2*, thereby giving her reasonable deniability. She was turning them over to the Federation Navy, after all, and how could she know that the Third Fleet had joined the mutiny? It made no sense, and no reasonable person could have assumed that she'd been in on the plan.

She'd been standing in her doorway as the five men were being escorted back to the *Kravitch*, her slight smile all Ryck had needed to see. She'd done what she could to protect him and his men without endangering her station, and General Ukiah had been more than willing to play along and give her the cover she needed. She could have refused, and the Third Fleet would have done nothing. And she'd get the reward from the Federation along with its gratitude. But she'd gone with her conscience and her dislike for the Federation.

Picking up Major Pohlmeyer as they left the building, the now six men had been whisked back to the ship. The cages were dropped, and within what had to be a record time of 37 minutes, the engines were fired up and the two ships pulled out of their berthing. An almost unbearably long 98 minutes later, with Ryck expecting the arrival of Task Force 1.1 at any moment, the Third Fleet task force was sliding into bubble space. It was only then that Ryck could start to relax and find out just what the heck was going on.

And what was going on boggled his mind.

First and foremost was the fact that there had been a cabal of Navy and Marine officers and senior enlisted, along with some members of the bureaucracy and even at least one ex-minster-level official, who were unhappy with the federal government and its increased suppression of the citizens, using the war with the Klethos as an excuse, much less the growing, but business-as-usual, revolving door between the top government officials and big business.

Numbers within the loosely organized cabal had increased over recent incidents. The "accident" that had claimed the *FS Justice* two years ago had been a summary execution ordered by the chairman himself when the ship's CO, Commander Kurt Nilsson, refused to fire on striking workers on Rainment Haven (Brian Plummer swore out loud when Lester mentioned Commander Nilsson's name, slamming his fist on the small conference table). The *Justice* was a Third Fleet frigate, and when Admiral Chandanasiri had conducted an investigation, he'd been told to stand down by the chairman and why. Only instead of bringing Chandanasiri into the fold, the Admiral had been alienated. That was his crew that had been vaporized, his men.

The problem with this cabal, if it even rated the term, was that it was powerless. It had no organization, no focus. While those who wanted a change were numerous, they didn't know who else felt that way. With the FCDC spies everywhere, to say anything to the wrong person would be a death sentence.

But Ryck's open defiance had been too big to ignore, and the genie could not be shoved back into the bottle. The government had to act quickly, and that meant arresting and putting Ryck on trial with a quick conviction followed by an equally quick execution and then worrying about damage control later. There could be no *Justice*-style accident to take care of this problem.

With the facts out in the open, Admiral Chandanasiri had taken a huge gamble. Instead of surreptitiously feeling out his fellow fleet commanders or the Chief of Naval Operations, he'd placed a call to General Ukiah, knowing Ryck to be one of the commandant's posse. This was a huge leap of faith, and he was rewarded when General Ukiah expressed similar concerns about the Federation. After the admiral had sent the commandant the evidence about the *Justice*, the general was fully on board. The admiral put his handful of confidants into motion, disseminating the same *Justice* evidence, along with other documents he'd gathered over a long and distinguished career, and presented it to the fleet. To his surprise, over 95% of the Third Fleet followed his lead, declaring themselves for, well, just for what wasn't exactly delineated yet. It was to save the *Kravitch* and the *Temperance*, and to rescue not only the sailors but also the famous Ryck Lysander and his Marines. But the words "mutiny," "coup," and "revolution" were never mentioned. It was a "rescue."

It was a clever sleight-of-hand, though. Whether the words were used or not, that was exactly what it was. With 25% of the Federation Navy suddenly refusing to follow orders or acknowledging the central government, it was a mutiny. And when Ryck mentioned Major Pohlmeyer, that upped the ante. With the Confederation potentially on their side, the fledgling movement actually had a chance to succeed—once they figured out just what they wanted. But accepting any help from a foreign government now meant they were treating with the enemy, and that was treason. After that, there would be no turning back even if it weren't already too late.

There were undoubtedly more people out there who were unhappy with the government. But just how far they would go, or if they would even declare themselves, was a question that none of them could answer. What was pretty clear, however, was that Ryck's unique position in the public eye, and the fact that he'd kept a Federation planet from being vaporized, had galvanized a huge segment of the population. But while important, what they really needed were enough of the power brokers to join with them. And no one in the stateroom knew how to do that. None of them had ever run a revolution before.

"What about the other fleets?" Ryck asked.

The fleets were the source of the Federation's power, and while having the Third Fleet for protection was welcomed, that still left three others of equal strength.

"First has declared for the Federation. We had nothing from Second and Fourth before entering bubble space," Lester said

"And the Brotherhood? The other governments? Other than Major Pohlmeyer, and we don't know how that will pan out."

"Nothing yet. At least that we know of," the commandant said. "I imagine we'll get more when we reach Tarawa."

Ryck shook his head. He hadn't planned on starting a revolution. Hell, he'd sworn an oath to the government, and he'd done some pretty dicey things in his career at the behest of it. All he'd wanted to do was to save the citizens of Ellison and keep the government, his government, from making a huge mistake. Now, it seemed as if he'd been a catalyst in bringing forth what had been an underground feeling of dissatisfaction.

He felt no pride in that. Chaos could destroy the people of the Federation, something the government, despites its many faults, had held at bay. If he could nudge the government in some way, that would be fine. What he didn't want, however, was a war. But the die was cast. He'd been caught up in the growing maelstrom.

"Well, sir, for the men of the *Kravitch*, the *Temperance*, and 1/10, we owe you our lives. And to Admiral Chandanasiri, too, of course," he added, addressing Lester. "And whatever you decide, we are there for you. I am, at least. Let me know what you want, and I'll do it."

That got a quick exchange of looks between Lester and the commandant.

"Uh, that's the thing, Ryck. You see, this entire groundswell of support is based on the fact that it's you and what you did. So you have to be the focal point of the movement," the commandant said, avoiding any stronger word than "movement."

That took Ryck aback. He'd taken one simple action, that was all. He wasn't yet experienced in the big strategic arrows needed to manage anything as potentially complicated—and political—as what this might become.

"Well, if you need me as a figurehead, of course, I can do what's necessary."

"I don't think you understand. You need to lead this. Not me, you. Admiral Chandanasiri agrees."

"But you're the commandant, sir. Not me," Ryck protested. "And we're Marines, not the Navy. We're ground pounders."

"Ryck, I'm old, and I'm tired," the commandant said.

Which was probably half true, at least. General Ukiah should have been the 89th commandant, not the 91st. But politics had raised its ugly head, and he'd been kept around in billets back on Earth before he could slide into the position. Old, yes, but tired?

"And I just don't think I have the heart for this, or what this could become. I'm resigning as soon as we get back, and you need to step up into the position."

That hit Ryck hard. Ever since Ryck was a lieutenant, Hank Ukiah had been there, his rabbi, his protector, his guide. He'd been Ryck's safety blanket. Now Ryck wouldn't have that anymore, and he felt suddenly vulnerable.

"What about Fred Nottingham? Eric Yeong? Bert Nidischii'? They're all senior to me. Hell, there are 15 officers senior to me."

"Yes, and Fred is going to be a problem, I know. But Bert is marshaling the troops while I'm gone. We'll find out when we land if we have the support for you. If we do, then you need to accept it. If we don't, then it's back to square one, and I don't know what Admiral Chandanasiri will say. His plan was dependent on you being not only the commandant, but also the face of the movement."

"Sir, I think you'll be surprised. The Corps will follow you," Genghis said, the first time he'd opened his mouth since the meeting started.

Ryck turned to look at his friend. They'd been recruits together so many years ago, back at Camp Charles. They'd gone through a lot, and Ryck trusted Genghis explicitly.

"I, uh—" he started.

"Look, Ryck. This has all been thrown together at breakneck speed. For all I know, General Huckmaster will have deposed me and have the MP's formed up to arrest us," the commandant said, referring to the assistant commandant. "But if we find out that the Corps is behind us, then you've got to take the position. It's our only hope."

Whose hope? Yours and mine? The Corps'? The Federation's?

"Sir, let's see then. There's not much we can do right now except go along for the ride. We'll be back in Tarawa soon, and we can decide what to do then," Ryck said.

"But if you are drafted, will you accept the position?"

Ryck hesitated. It was one thing to save a world. There was a moral imperative for that. But lead a revolution? He'd go down in history for that, and history might not look too kindly on him. And in the end, 12 billion souls could have been a lighter butcher's bill compared to what could happen.

Ryck looked up at his old friend and could read the hope in his eyes. He owed the man too much to refuse.

"Yes, sir, I will."

God help me!

TARAWA

Chapter 7

"I'm so sorry about this, Ryck," Rear Admiral Dearborn Knutson, the Chaplain of the Marine Corps, said, his hand on Ryck's shoulder. "It's a lot to take in, I know, but I'm sure they're safe."

Ryck leaned back in the overstuffed chair, shock taking over his body.

Hannah!

Ryck and Prince Jellico were in the commandant's inner office, waiting to find out which way the Corps would go, but now, the importance of that decision was lost to Ryck as he felt as if chunk of his heart, of his very being, had been ripped from him.

He'd only been back on Tarawa for less than an hour. The *Kravitch*'s command shuttle had brought him, along with Prince and the commandant, down at 0200, and the three Marines had been hustled to Headquarters where General Ukiah had gone immediately into Conference Room A. The Headquarters was fully staffed despite the hour, and Ryck has asked Vivian Queensbury, the commandant's secretary (and the secretary for the previous five commandants as well), if Hannah and the twins had made it off Earth and back to the comparative safety of Tarawa. Vivian hemmed for a moment, something out of the ordinary for her, and said she'd get right back to him. When the chaplain had entered the room five minutes later, Ryck should have realized something bad had occurred, but it hadn't dawned on him at the moment. When the chaplain gave him the bad news that Hannah and the twins had been intercepted at the spaceport, it hit him right in the solar plexus, robbing him of air as if he'd been physically punched.

The Federation didn't care about Hannah and the twins, but they cared about Ryck, and without the slightest doubt, Ryck knew they would use his family to get to him. He fought to keep his mind from listing all the possibilities. His one hope was that the Federation would realize that hurting his wife or kids would bring them extremely bad press. Not that they cared about bad press, but unless it served an end, it still wasn't something to seek out.

"You OK, sir?" Prince asked, his face full of concern as the chaplain left.

"No, I'm not," Ryck answered with enough vitriol to make the colonel blanch and sit back.

Fuck, sorry about that, Prince, he thought as he struggled for composure. *Not your fault.*

He took several deep breaths, purging his body of carbon dioxide, wishing he could purge his mind as well.

"No, I'm not," he repeated to his old friend in a much calmer voice. "But there isn't much I can do at the moment."

Prince Jellico had never been a star in the Corps. He and Ryck had been commissioned together, but their paths had diverged almost immediately. Prince was probably pretty lucky he'd made it to colonel, and he'd never get a star, but he had a good heart, and at the moment, Ryck needed the support. He reached out and patted Prince's shoulder.

"Don't worry about me. I'm functioning. If they hurt her, though. . ." he said, leaving unspoken what he'd do if the worst happened.

Prince was saved from responding when they heard the conference room door open. Both Marines looked out the open office door, and in a moment, Lieutenant General Fred Nottingham strode past, followed by someone else Ryck didn't recognize.

What does that mean? Ryck asked himself.

More than a few moments later, Major General Tomtom Copperwait stuck his head through the open hatch and said, "Ryck, if you can come in, we're ready for you.

"Uh, Colonel Jellico, if you could wait here," he added apologetically.

Ryck stood up, gave Prince a pat on the shoulder, and said, "Lead on, Tomtom."

The conference door was only a few steps away across the passage, but it seemed to take forever to get there. A lieutenant colonel was holding a door, a mere peon amongst the number of stars in the room. All eyes were locked on Ryck as he struggled to center himself and remain calm. Whatever they had decided, he was going to face it as a Marine should.

"General," the commandant said to Ryck, indicating a position at the foot of the huge laminated wood table.

"This is a very hard thing for me to say," General Ukiah said, clearing his throat. "All of us here, each and every one, have made an oath to the Federation, to serve it to the best of our abilities."

This doesn't sound too promising.

"But the question is just how do we serve the Federation? Is the Federation the Council? Is it the people? This is a horrible spot you've put us in, having to make that decision. And I am being blunt here when I tell you that not all of us are in agreement. What we are doing is splitting the Corps, our Corps, something that hasn't happened in the 367 years of our existence.

"But the majority of us have decided that our oath is to the people we serve, not the Council, and certainly not a council that can summarily execute a Navy frigate without due process, a council that can order the extermination of an entire world over minor protests. Some of us did not agree, though, and they will be leaving, unmolested, for Alexander."

Fred Nottingham, Ryck realized, letting out a breath he'd been holding.

He felt relief, but he also felt a huge weight settling on his shoulders.

"And as I told you on the ship, you need to agree to take over the leadership. Either way, as of 0001 Tarawa time, not GMT, I am resigning, not just the billet, but my commission, too. I have no ill will for you, but I am one of those who cannot break my oath, for good or bad."

That took Ryck by surprise. General Ukiah had flown out to rescue him, and he'd been the one who'd convinced him to accept the mantle of the commandant. And he was against this? It didn't make sense.

"So, do you accept the position?"

Ryck looked around the table, meeting each Marine's eyes, even if only for a moment. Fourteen general officers and eight sergeants major, all those who could make the meeting, minus Nottingham and whoever else had left with him, stared back, some with hope, some with resigned acceptance, some with what looked like they were chomping at the bit. The last eyes he met were Bert Nidischii's. Ryck knew Bert would make a better commandant than him. Ryck was a fighter, and men followed him, but Bert coupled personal courage with the organizational skill that would be needed going forward.

Bert pursed his lips in the Navajo way with which Ryck had become familiar. Bert was at his back, Ryck knew.

"General Huckmaster?" Ryck asked, leaving the rest unsaid.

"I understand the necessity of this, and I am ready to continue as the assistant 'dant. If you'll have me, of course. If you want to bring in someone else, I will retire along with General Ukiah," the general said, giving a quick glance to where Bert sat.

Ryck was tempted. He'd never really gotten along too well with Huckmaster, unlike the close relationship he'd had with Bert. But Huckmaster was an able administrator, and Ryck was under no illusion that he was really up for the job of commandant. He'd never even commanded a division yet, much less the entire Corps.

"I'd be honored if you would stay on. I welcome your experience and guidance."

From the ever-so-slight relaxing of the big Marine's posture, Ryck knew he'd hit the right chord. His first act as commandant, even if he wasn't officially in the position yet, had been a good one.

"And Bert, seeing as how General Nottingham has decided to vacate his position, would you step into the Chief of Staff's billet?" Ryck asked, turning to his friend.

"I'd be honored, sir."

"Well, I guess it's settled. If you would come up here, Ryck, let's get this over," General Ukiah said.

Ryck marched to the head of the long table and stood at attention facing the commandant.

General Ukiah, suddenly looking old and frail, reached under the podium and brought out a set of collar insignia. Ryck couldn't help but break his position of attention to glance at each bar, four silver stars joined in a row. The commandant looked at them for a moment before straightening up and gathering himself, shouted out, "Attention to orders!"

"Raise your right hand and repeat after me," he told Ryck, his voice becoming fuller.

I, state your name, do solemnly swear that I will support and defend the United Federation of Nations. . .

I, Ryck Lysander, do solemnly swear that I will support and defend the United Federation of Nations. . .

Ryck almost choked when he said "United Federation." It felt wrong, but it was to the people he was swearing his oath, he reminded himself, not to the men serving on high.

. . .against all enemies, foreign and domestic. . .

. . .against all enemies, foreign and domestic; that I will bear true faith and allegiance to the same, that I will well, faithfully, with honor, and with humility, discharge the duties of the office of which I am about to enter. So help me God.

General Ukiah unfolded his left hand, which had been holding the stars. He reached up and took off both sets of two-star insignia on Ryck's collar.

"I hope you understand, Ryck. I love you like a son, but I cannot in good conscience join in this. I cannot be part of a revolution, and I'm afraid that this path will lead to the destruction of all we hold dear," the commandant whispered as he took off Ryck's major general's stars. "I'll leave quietly tonight and get out of your hair."

"Sir, you've been a mentor to me, and I owe you so much. If you cannot offer your guidance, then I understand. You are an honorable man, and I will not hold that against you. And no hurry, if you are going to leave. You and Fiona are welcome on Tarawa for as long as I'm in charge," Ryck whispered back.

A single tear formed at the corner of the commandant's left eye as he pinned the first bar of four stars on Ryck's left collar.

"Uh, I'm dreadfully sorry that Hannah isn't here, but who do you want to pin on your other stars?" the commandant asked. "Bert?"

Ryck wanted to say yes, and he broke his position of attention to glance at Bert, who was already starting to move forward. His friendship with Bert was strong, and it would mean a lot to him. But Ryck had to think beyond personal interests now. Whether he liked it or not, he had to learn politics and learn it fast.

"Sir, I'd be honored if General Huckmaster would pin them on," Ryck said with a sure voice.

The assistant commandant was taken by surprise, if the look on his face was any indication. He gathered himself and hurried forward.

For a moment, Bert also seemed surprised, and the look on his face was not as pleased.

Please understand me, Bert, Ryck silently implored.

Whether the ESP vibes were working that day or not, Ryck didn't know, but Bert seemed to stop, and with a grudging smile and nod, settle back into his position of attention.

Within moments, both sets of stars were on his collars.

"Congratulations, General," the commandant said as the others in the room broke out into loud "ooh-rahs."

"Wait, there's one more thing," General Ukiah said as Marines started to move forward to shake Ryck's hand.

"Attention to orders!" he said, stopping the men in their tracks.

From: Commandant of the Marine Corps

To: General Ryck Lysander, United Federation Marine Corps

Subj: Marine Corps Special Order 4-21, effective immediately, you are ordered to report to duty as the Commandant, United Federation Marine Corps.

Signed, Hank K. Ukiah, General, United Federation Marine Corps, Commandant of the Marine Corps

The order should have come from the chairman of the Council, but that wasn't likely to happen, so Marines adjusted when they had to.

"It's official, Ryck. You are the 92nd Commandant of the Marine Corps," he said, shaking Ryck's hand.

Once again, the men started pushing forward as General Ukiah held up his hand.

"You need to relieve me, Ryck."

"I don't have any orders."

"Just say it. You're the commandant now."

Ryck cleared his throat and said, "General Hank K. Ukiah, I hereby relieve you of your duties."

Nothing then could have stopped the press of men coming forward to shake Ryck's hand.

"Good move there, sir," Bert whispered as he shook his friend's—his commandant's—hand.

Ryck was relieved to know that Bert understood why he chose the assistant commandant to pin on his stars.

After the last hand was shaken, the last congratulations given, the 92nd Commandant of the Marine Corps cleared his throat and shouted out, "We'll have a wetting down when all this is over. But right now, we've got work to do. Lieutenant Colonel Trondheim, please get Major Pohlmeyer and have him in my office in 20 mikes. The rest of you, get home, get fed, and get cleaned up. I want all of you back here at 0600, and plan to stay for a long time. Thank you for your confidence, but let's get our butts in gear!"

Chapter 8

"So you're feeling strong?" Ryck asked Sams.

"Like an ox, sir. I'm ready to come back."

Ryck looked at Master Gunnery Sergeant, (Ret) Bobbi Samuelson as the man sat nervously across from him, hand fidgeting along the brim of his bush-cap. Sams was one of his closest friends in the Corps, a man he trusted implicitly. But after so many years together, he knew Sams was lying.

Like Ryck, Sams suffered from BRC, Boosted Regeneration Cancer, the bane of too many Marines who'd undergone regen. Ryck had only had two bouts and was in remission, although no one was ever completely cured of the disease. Sams, however had had three bouts within the last four years, the last one so severe that it had resulted in his medical retirement. And he didn't look good, Ryck saw. Sams was haggard and gaunt, a good 15 kgs less than what he was at his fighting weight.

What was equally as evident was that Sams needed this. His nervousness couldn't hide the hope he held in his eyes, the hope that as commandant, his old rabbi could overrule the Navy medical staff.

Ever since the conclusion of his 0600 meeting, he'd had a steady stream of men seeking his time. He'd already welcomed Sergeant Major Phantawisangtong and Gunnery Sergeant Hans Çağlar into the fold, Hecs from his position as the Senior Enlisted Monitor and Çağlar from the First Marines Three shop, and he'd given Hecs a list of names of men he wanted on his staff, but he'd been surprised when Sams had shown up. Surprised and not sure what to do. His old friend was suffering, that much was plain, and the pace of what was to come might be too much for him. But Ryck also knew that Sams didn't have much of a life now. His ex-wife, Tara, after keeping him company for so many years after their divorce, had finally left once the Brick had robbed Sams of his ability in bed, and from what Hecs told Ryck, Sams was pretty much alone.

Ryck was tired, and he wanted to go home and see Ben. As he looked at Sams, he hoped he was not making a decision while his mind was clouded by fatigue. But even if Sams was weak, it wasn't as if Ryck needed him to be kicking down doors and taking names. Sams' mind was still sharp, and despite his irreverent attitude, he held a wealth of knowledge. And something told Ryck that by giving Sams a purpose, he might be saving the old grunt's life.

"I want you to report in at 0700 tomorrow, Master Gunnery Sergeant. You're going to be my special advisor on enlisted morale," Ryck said, quickly picking the first thing to come to his mind.

"Master gunnery sergeant? You mean?"

"Get your ass in gear, there, Marine. You're back in, and I expect I'll work you to the bone. I'll have Hecs work up the paperwork, but I think I have the pull now to get this done."

"Oh, shit, sir! I was just hoping to do something. I never thought I'd get back into uniform. Thank you, sir!" Sams shouted, jumping up to take Ryck's hand, shaking it madly.

Sams seem to fill out and come to life. Ryck could have sworn that his friend gained five kgs right then and there.

"OK, get out and get your kit back in shape. Some of us have work to do!" Ryck said with a laugh. "I'll see you tomorrow."

Sams thanked him several more times as he backed out of the office.

Well, I've made at least one person happy, Ryck thought to himself, relaxing for a brief moment.

Then the situation caught up with him. Both his secured and personal PAs were flashing for his attention. He took a quick glance at the personal—there were four messages now from Ben. Ryck felt a wave of guilt wash over him. He wanted to respond—hell, he wanted to go home and hug his son right then—but he kept hesitating. With Hannah and the twins in the hands of the Federation, Ryck wasn't sure how to handle things with Ben. He knew they needed to support each other, but something was keeping him from confronting the reality that it was only the two of them now.

Grubbing hell, just do it!

"Vivian, I'm going home. Please have my driver ready," he said out loud, the office AI picking up his voice and sending his statement to his secretary.

"I'll have him ready, but there's one more person waiting for you. A Colonel Sandy Peltier-Aswad?"

Oh, shit! Sandy! I should have contacted him earlier, Ryck told himself as he wondered where he wanted his protégé.

Sandy was still too junior for one of the major billets where he could really help Ryck out, but maybe junior aide would be appropriate. Sandy was buried in a staff job in J1,[7] and Ryck knew he'd jump at the chance to get into a position of more impact. And Ryck looked forward to it. Ryck and Sandy had not served together since the first battles of the Klethos War, and their relationship since then had been slightly strained. Ryck had given Sandy room after that, out from under his shadow so the younger Marine could make a name for himself. It hadn't quite worked out that way for Sandy, but he'd made colonel, at least, based more on his past history of performance than on his more recent billets. But if they got out of this mess in one piece, after serving as an aide to the commandant, Sandy should be able to convey that into a command, putting himself back into the running for a star.

Ryck stood up as Sandy came in, moving to meet him in the center of the office, hand outstretched. Sandy had come to a position of attention, but then he broke that to take Ryck's hand and shake it.

"Sandy, it's good to see you. Really good."

"Thank you, sir. And I guess I should offer my congratulations on your new position," Sandy said formally.

Sandy's distant attitude took Ryck by surprise, but he was now the commandant, he knew, and that changed things. Sandy might be an old friend, and he was Ben's godfather, but he was still a Marine, and Ryck was the commandant now. Ryck knew it would take the by-the-book prim and proper Sandy a while to come to terms with that.

---

[7] J1: the administrative division within headquarters.

"Well, I'm glad you caught me. I was just on my way out to see to Ben. I haven't seen him yet, and with Hannah and the twins. . ." Ryck said before trailing off.

"Yes, I heard, sir. I'm sorry about that, but I imagine your family will be fine."

"Well, yes, I hope so," Ryck said in a subdued voice. "Well, anyway, I don't have much time right this moment, but I'd like you to come onboard and be one of my aides. I know what you think of riding my coattails, but I could really use you, and I think that after all of this is over, you can work your way into a regiment.

"In fact, why don't you come with me now. We can discuss this on the way, and you can be there in case Ben doesn't take what's happened to his mom and the twins all that well."

"Sir, I don't think I can do that," Sandy said.

"Oh? Well, of course, this is short notice, and you can't just leave your office without telling them what's going on. I'm not sure if I'll make it back tonight. I don't have all of this scheduling down, and I've been running on fumes for about 30 hours now. So why don't you take care of things on your end, and we can start fresh in the morning?"

"No, sir, with all due respect, I can't."

"What? Are you still worried about those coattails?"

"It's not that, sir. I'll be leaving in two hours with General Nottingham and the rest. To Alexander. I just wanted to tell you that personally, face-to-face."

Ryck stood looking at Sandy stupidly for a moment until what he said registered.

"With Nottingham? You're for the Federation?" he asked, astounded.

"And so should you be, with all due respect. We swore an oath, you and I, to the Federation. And I thought men of honor upheld their word," Sandy said, more than a hint of anger seeping into his voice.

"Honor? Honor, you say? You do know the Federation was going to murder 12 billion citizens, don't you?" Ryck shouted back. "And you think I should have let that happen?"

"No, sir. That order was a mistake, and you did what you had to do. But that's in the past, and now, to lead a revolution, to break your oath?"

Ryck just stared at Sandy, at a loss for words as his protégé, or what now looked like former protégé, stared back at him defiantly.

Finally, Ryck quietly asked, "So, after stopping the genocide, what was I supposed to do?"

"Surrender, sir, and defend yourself within the system."

"And you think that would have worked? Did it work with the *Justice*? Did they even get a trial?"

Sandy had the grace to look troubled at that, but he took a deep breath, and then said, "If it's for the good of the Federation, then any sacrifice must be accepted."

"And just give up the Marines of 1/10, and the sailors of the *Kravitch* and *Temperance*? Genghis was one of those Marines, you know."

"Nothing would have happened to them, sir. The Federation does not punish subordinates for the actions of their seniors," Sandy said, seemingly more in an attempt to convince himself rather than Ryck.

"Once again, like the *Justice*?" Ryck said, scorn evident in his voice.

Sandy stood at attention, his face getting redder and redder.

He started to say something, stopped, took a deep breath, and then said, "The *Justice* was a sacrifice to law and order, to keep chaos at bay. Sad, but shit happens, sir, and they knew the risk when they enlisted," he said, his anger rising to the surface and spilling out. "But what are the consequences? How many people are going to die now because of your ego? How many people are going to die because you wanted to save your own ass, and so you broke your oath?"

Ryck stared at Sandy in shock. He couldn't believe what he was hearing, and a purple rush of his own anger threatening to take over him. He balled his fists as he took a step closer to Sandy, ready to lash out and crush the little cockroach onto the ground. He felt himself starting to lose it as he imagined his fist smashing into

Sandy's face when the slightest change of expression in that face stopped him. It wasn't fear; it was almost satisfaction.

And Ryck left his hands at his side. Sandy wanted him to hit him. Whether that was so that he could feel the righteousness of him abandoning Ryck, of choosing to oppose him, or if this had been planned out by Nottingham as just one little piece of evidence that Ryck was out of control, a madman bent on violence, Ryck had no idea. He suspected the latter, but regardless, he wasn't going to give Sandy the satisfaction.

He slowly leaned in until his face was centimeters from Sandy's, then just as slowly, he said, "Colonel, I believe we are done here. You are dismissed."

With that Ryck spun around and marched back to his seat. He sat down and picked up his PA.

"I said, you are dismissed," he repeated when Sandy didn't move.

Ryck didn't even look up, his eyes on his PA, even if he didn't take in a single word of what was written there. With his peripheral vision, he watched Sandy slump ever-so-slightly.

"Aye-aye, sir," Sandy said before conducting an about-face and marching out of the office.

"Vivian, please have Gunnery Sergeant Çağlar escort Colonel Peltier-Aswad to the gym," he said. "The colonel is not to deviate from the direct route there."

"The traitors are already being bused to the spaceport," Vivian said. "Should he still go to the gym, or do you want him on one of the buses."

"Get him on a bus. And if the last bus has gone, get him to the spaceport by donkey cart, if necessary. I want him off this planet now."

"Yes, sir. I understand."

Ryck stared blankly at his PA before throwing it against the wall, its almost indestructible body bouncing back to take a chip out of the side of his desk. His anger was still seething, but another emotion was starting to make itself felt. He'd lost his friend, someone he trusted. Hannah and the twins were being held by the central government. And now, he had a revolution on his hands, one where people were depending on him to bring about a successful conclusion, something that he hadn't a clue yet as how to achieve.

He might be the Commandant of the Marine Corps, something to which he'd long aspired, but he'd throw all of that away if he could just turn back the clock and get his family—and yes, Sandy, too—back.

Chapter 9

Ryck stared at the simple plastisheet on the table in front of him. It looked innocuous, just another routine piece of admin requiring a physical signature, but it caused a pounding in his head, a narrowing of his vision.

Slowly, the signature "Amarin Frederick Kean Chandanasiri" appeared on the paper. A moment later, the retinal scan was shown as accepted. Light-years away on *Prometheus Station*, the home of the Third Fleet, Admiral Chandanasiri signed his copy of the *Articles of Assumption*, which were molecularly linked to the copy in front of Ryck.

There were few documents that have stood the test of time as turning points in human history: the *Summa Theologica*, the *Magna Carta*, the US *Declaration of Independence*, the *Federation Charter*, the *Munich Accord*, and the *Writ*, coming to mind. Ryck didn't know if the short declaration on the plastisheet in front of him would hold the same weight or if it would be relegated to a footnote in history about a foolhardy and failed attempt at fundamental change.

"Sir, Admiral Chandanasiri has signed his copy," Major General Talliman Hayes said needlessly.

Ryck picked up the stylus and looked at the gathered men around him. All of the flag and command sergeants major at the Headquarters, Sams, Hecs, Jorge Simone, and five randomly selected junior Marines were there to represent the Corps. Brian Plummer and his senior staff from the *Kravitch* were there as representatives from the Navy. The governor and his staff were gathered together, representing the civilian population. And Major Titus Pohlmeyer, the Confederation of Free States Army, was the loan witness from a foreign government.

The news teams, three in all, couldn't be ignored as they jockeyed for position to best record what was about to happen; whether for posterity or a future trial, Ryck didn't know.

Ryck hesitated. Up until now, there had been no direct action between the loyalist Federation forces and the new government, or "Evolutionary forces," as they were now calling themselves. ("Not revolution, evolution!") Signing this document, though, was essentially a declaration of war. There would be no turning back. And Ryck didn't want war. He knew the consequences of war, the horrors, far more than most, and he knew, without a shadow of a doubt, that people were going to suffer, and people were going to die.

Most of all, though, Ryck didn't want to lead a revolution, for that was what it was, despite all the play on words the experts were bandying about. He could fight battles. That was what he had been trained to do throughout his career. But being the co-head of a government scared him shitless.

What do I know about government?

Just 30 minutes before, he'd received a briefing about the banks. Most of the largest banks in the Federation had their headquarters on Earth, and they had already cut off funding to the planets that had come out siding with the new provisional government, or what was about to become the provisional government as soon as Ryck signed the document. The few banks that had promised to work with the new government did not have the financial wherewithal to support them, to fund a revolution. The whole thing made his head ache.

He took a quick glance and Titus Pohlmeyer. Ryck was going to have a one-on-one with the major right after the signing ceremony—they needed Confederation support.

He knew he had to sign, but his brain screamed at him "No!" The consequences were just too great. Part of him realized that his hesitation as he looked at the gathered men had a dramatic effect for the news teams to record, showing the import of the act, but any more hesitation could turn that into someone unsure if this was the right step.

Which was true. He was unsure. But the die had been cast, and he couldn't reverse course. It was too late for that. He had to forge on, seemingly positive that this was the right—and legal—course of action.

"In accordance with Section 3(a), paragraph 1 of the Federation Charter, whereas the current government has contravened Section 1, Paragraph 1 by ordering the murder of the planet Ellison and all Federation citizens therein, and as the co-representative of the people's military forces, I am ordering the dissolution of the Federation Council and the imposition of martial law and formation of a provisional government until a new government can be formed," Ryck said in the speech crafted by the Third Fleet staff judge advocate.

Ryck lowered the stylus and signed his name, knowing that his signature would be appearing simultaneously on the second copy at the Third Fleet headquarters. He leaned forward to the small pick-up in the lower right-hand corner of the sheet, and a small light flashed green indicating his retinal scan was accepted.

Ryck lowered the stylus and tried to look confident in front of the news teams.

The federal government had just been toppled by a coup d'état. That was the easy part.

Now if they could only get the old government, along with the bulk of two Navy fleets, most of the FCDC, and the 13% of the Marines who sided with them to go along with it.

Chapter 10

"They're in good health and are not being mistreated," Major Pohlmeyer told Ryck as the two sat alone in his office. "But they're still not being authorized any communications."

The Confederation had pushed the Brotherhood to force a Red Cross visit to Hannah and the twins, who were being held in a secure location that the Red Cross could not—or would not—reveal. Ryck had hoped to be able to make a call, but he wasn't surprised. The feds were not about to give Ryck that peace of mind, but they couldn't really defy the Brotherhood request given that the Federation, which they obviously claimed was still them, had signed the UAM[8] Retained Persons Convention which required access to prisoners.

"I wish I could give you more, and we will continue to work on it, sir."

"Thanks, Titus. I really do appreciate it, and I am glad to know they're not being mistreated, at least," Ryck replied.

"Vivian, please send in the rest," Ryck said aloud, anxious to move on to something else.

Bert, Prince Jellico, Hecs, Jorge, and Tomtom Copperwait came in and sat down. Ryck had sent General Huckmaster and an ad hoc staff to *Prometheus Station* for a series of meetings with Admiral Chandanasiri (who was sending his own team to Tarawa), so this was the brain trust of the Marines at headquarters, and Ryck wanted them to hear what Major Pohlmeyer had to say.

"The first order of business, sir, concerns planet busters," the major began.

That's the first order of business? We don't control planet busters, Ryck thought.

---

[8] UAM: United Assembly of Mankind, an organization of the various governments of man.

"We are letting the Brotherhood take the point on this. . ." the major began.

Which is what you have been doing with almost everything, Ryck thought. *Keeping yourself somewhat neutral. I hope that is a ploy and not fact.*

". . . and they have given the Council what could be an ultimatum that no planet busters will be used in any potential conflict."

"That's fine with us," Ryck said. "We're not the ones who were about to kill off Ellison."

And Ryck was fine with that. The Council controlled far more planet busters than what were in the Third Fleet Armory, and as a ground pounder, Ryck had a particular aversion to a weapon that could wipe out Tarawa, for example, with the Marines powerless to stop it

"We need your agreement to that, sir. In writing."

"But I don't control any planet busters. We're Marines," Ryck said. "You need to talk with the admiral."

"We did, but you are the face of the revolution, I mean *evolution*, sorry about that. And we need you to take the lead on this. The Council is balking despite some heavy-handed threats from the Brotherhood, saying that you have not agreed yet."

"What, they think we'll interdict Earth?" Tomtom asked with a snort.

Major Pohlmeyer said nothing, but the expression on his face was a giveaway.

"They're saying that?" Bert asked incredulously.

"Let's just say that they are using that threat as a reason not to sign any binding agreement to that effect," the major said.

"But—" Tomtom started only to be cut off when Ryck held up his hand, palm out.

"It's ridiculous and pure Council gamesmanship, but we would never use them, so I don't have any problem with it. Major, give me what you want, and I'll sign. I don't want to waste any more time on this sideshow."

The major smiled and held out a docpad. Unlike the Articles of Assumption, this was not something that needed to be in a physical form. Ryck took two minutes to read over the document. He knew that he should give it to the SJA to review, but he didn't want to waste any more time on something that would never happen anyway. He signed and scanned, and it was done.

"With that out of the way," the major said, bringing up something on his PA, "I'd like to confirm just who has declared for the provisional government. If I may?" he asked, pointing to the screen on the wall just past the end of the table.

Prince reached under to toggle the screen open, and the major's list popped up with all the Federation planets and military units. They were listed in four columns: Loyalist, Provisional Government, Undeclared, and Neutral.

Ryck couldn't help but grimace at the list. The Loyalist tally was the largest, with 128 planets and major stations as compared to 87 planets and stations declaring for the provisional government. Most of the planets, though, to be blunt, would have no vital impact on the conflict one way or the other.

The final disposition of the naval forces, which did have the potential to turn the tide one way or the other, still hadn't become completely clear, even four days after the Articles of Assumption. First and Third Fleets, the two largest and most capable, had split largely along geographic lines, with First, which was headquartered at *Station One* in Earth orbit, supporting the Council and Third with the provisional government. Second had declared support for the Council, and Fourth had issued a strong condemnation of the schism and vowed to remain neutral, focusing on their task to defend the Federation from a possible change in strategy from the Klethos. But while the commanders had issued statements, individual ships and forces had been breaking away and making treks to join whichever side they felt was right. Currently, that meant 410 naval combatants supported the Council while only 283 were for the provisional government, but those numbers constantly shifted as individual ships broke away from their fleets and showed up with either force.

Even the ground forces favored the old government. Some 6,000,000-plus FCDC troops and, to Ryck's chagrin, 69,212 Marines declared their loyalty to the Council. Facing them, on the provisional government side, were about 35,000 FCDC troops, and the bulk of the half-a-million-strong Marine Corps.

The major's list showed 36 planets as still undeclared, and under the neutral column were 26 planets and 238 ships. One of those 36 planets was Ellison, which frankly made Ryck's blood boil.

Just the evening before, Ryck had called the president of Ellison to plead for the planet's inclusion. Ellison, with 12 billion people, would easily be the largest planet from a population standpoint to declare for the provisional government. But while the president expressed his sincere gratitude for Ryck's actions in saving the planet, he said his people were done with the Federation no matter who won out. Ryck asked him to declare for the provisional government until after things were settled, and then declare for independence, which Ryck would support. The president laughed at that, saying that assumed the provisional government would prevail, something he thought was a long shot.

"This is what we've been able to compile, and we would appreciate your input as to its accuracy," Major Pohlmeyer said.

The list was very accurate, at least as far as planets, stations, and ships. The numbers of ground personnel were not 100% accurate, but they were close enough for government work. Whatever else could be said about the Confederation, their intelligence gathering was top-notch.

"That's about right, Major. We're still hoping to sway most of the undeclared, and we are still in talks with the Fourth Fleet. . ." Ryck said.

Not that we are gaining any ground with them, he admitted to himself.

". . .and that can swing the balance of power somewhat."

"With all due respect, sir, we don't think Admiral Tinsley is going to change his mind. He's had some very high-level contacts with other governments who do not want that sector left open to the Klethos—"

"Who are still abiding by the agreement," Ryck interrupted, "Even if they changed the rules."

"Be that as it may, an unprotected frontier could be an invitation that is too sweet to ignore," the major said. "As you said, they've already changed the rules once, so who's to say they won't again?"

Ryck knew the major was right, but he didn't want to concede the point. After four years of almost complete domination by Marines in PICS over the Klethos *d'relles* in their gladiatorial combat for planets, the Klethos had demanded that humans meet them without armor, hand-to-hand. Unable to face a full-out war with the still unknown Klethos order of battle, the combined governments had to acquiesce, although they had been able to extract a two-year cease-fire agreement to enable humanity time to genmod fighters to match the Klethos in size and strength. Given the Klethos sense of honor, Ryck was not surprised that they had agreed. There was no pride in beating someone unless they posed a reasonable challenge.

"I might add that the Confederation of Free States feels it is vital that your Fourth Fleet remain in place. But we do understand the inequality this creates with your forces, so I am pleased to tell you that the president has authorized the deployment of our own naval forces to these locations—at your invitation, of course."

The major was still using the screen, and it took Ryck a few seconds to take the 2D image and get it straight in his mind as to the sector of space controlled by the provisional government. Then it became pretty clear. The naval forces would be deployed along several axes, and those centered along some vital commercial routes, routes that were vital to the Federation, true, but also for the Confeds themselves. If they did deploy, this would free up some of Admiral Chandanasiri's forces, but it would also serve to ensure there was no interruption of trade vital to the Confederation.

Ryck kept his expression neutral as he felt a small rush of satisfaction. The Confeds needed this, too. Ryck would accept it as a starting point, and he thought Chandanasiri would, too, but if the Confederation needed it, then Ryck hoped to extract more in exchange for the "invitation," as the major put it.

"Well, Major, we do appreciate your offer, but I was wondering if perhaps a better place for your ships, if they came, might be in the Franzonni Group. . ." he began as he settled in for some old-fashioned horse trading.

Chapter 11

Ryck hit the rewind and ran the clip one more time.

"This is the man who claims to be fighting for the common man? I think not," the talking head said as an image of Marines rising out of the water and opening fire on the people hugging the two-meter-high berm played behind him. Bodies were blasted apart in high definition, brought into the living rooms of billions of households. "Over 2,000 citizens of Kakurega, slaughtered, just because they were protesting work conditions, conditions, I might add that were voluntarily changed by Propitious Interstellar once those conditions became known."

The carnage of Charlie 1/11's fight outside the old powerplant continued for a few moments, the editing skillfully removing weapons from the hands of the rebels who were attacking Ryck's company. Then the view switched to another scene and to a close-up of a Marine in a PICS, "Captain Rick Lysander, UFMC" captioned beneath him. The recording, taken at Prosperity Square in Tay Station, panned out as the Marines of Alpha Company advanced into the crowd, which had been unarmed, trampling many of them as they marched forward.

"Turn it off," Ryck ordered.

"So you see, sir, we've got a problem. But it is a good problem," Deke Montero, the civilian advisor on loan from LRP Marketing, said.

"How can this be a good problem?" Ryck growled. "It isn't even true. I mean, those people were armed, and I stopped the fight as soon as they broke!"

"Truth doesn't matter. It's the perception that counts. And if they show you as a murderous psychopath, then who will trust you when you declare yourselves to be their real government?"

"And just where does the 'good' come in with this problem?"

"It means they're panicking. They need to smear you, which is going to be hard considering they've given you two Novas, not to mention *The Aliens Are Here* and *The Warrior*. And if those people were armed, we can prove the images were manipulated. Believe me, sir, we can smash them on this. I can't believe any PR firm would let this weak shit out," he said, his voice rising with excitement.

Knowing the Council, Ryck doubted very much that any PR advisor was in a position to "let" or not let something go out if the chairman thought it was a good idea. Montero had a grandiose sense of the importance of his field, a field that Ryck sometimes despised. But maybe the guy was right in that truth mattered little in the long run. It reflected a sad state of affairs, though.

"Mr. Montero, why don't you come with me," Hecs said. "I'd like a full briefing on how you want to address this."

The PR flack looked to Ryck, obviously wanting to speak with the big man himself, not a sergeant major.

"That's a great idea, Sergeant Major. You can give it your undivided attention. I want this a top priority," Ryck said. "And Zeke, I trust you on this. You let the sergeant major know what you need."

Montero looked unsure, but with Sams assisting, he and Hecs escorted the man out. Ryck mouthed "Thanks" to Hecs as he left.

Ryck leaned back in his chair, closing his eyes for a moment. He snapped back up and asked, "OK, what's next?" of Bert who brought up his PA to check.

"What's next, sir, is your son, whose been sitting in your outer office for the last 90 minutes," Vivian's voice filled the room.

Shit! How the grubbing hell did I forget that!

Ryck hadn't been home in two days, and he felt guilty for that. He was just having a hard time facing a house that almost screamed at him that his wife and two of his children were gone. But Ben was still there, and he needed support. And Ryck was abandoning him.

"Gentlemen, if you would give me a few moments," he said, dismissing the men sitting at the table.

"Vivian, please send him in," Ryck said as the men filed out and he started to move to his desk.

He thought better of it and stood in front of the couch in his sitting nook. He put his hand in his pocket, then took it back out, suddenly unsure of himself.

"Hi Dad," Ben said as he came in the door.

Ben seemed a little nervous himself as he started to raise his arms for a hug, then change it to a shake.

"I'm sorry I haven't been, home, son. You know," Ryck said, sweeping an arm around the office.

"Oh yeah, I know. Of course," Ben said.

"Let's sit," Ryck told him. "Are you doing OK? I mean, with . . ." Ryck asked, not even able to vocalize the fact that Hannah and the twins were prisoners.

"Yeah, I am. No. Fuck no. I'm not. I'm pissed at those bastards," Ben said, his voice rising with pent up emotions. "I'm not going to lie, Dad, but I want to hit back at them. I want to kill them."

"Me, too. I feel the same. But like I told you, they're safe."

"For now."

And there was the rub. "For now."

"I'll be doing everything I can to get them back, I promise," Ryck said.

"And I want to help, too," Ben said.

"I appreciate that, and knowing you are here with me is a big help."

"No, more than that," Ben said, pulling out a rolled up plastisheet from his back pocket and handing it to Ryck.

Ryck took a quick glance and almost dropped it. It was an enlistment contract.

"But, you're still in school," was all he managed to get out.

"I'm almost done, and I can finish in the Corps. You need more Marines, and I want to do it."

The Corps did need more Marines. With those that declared for the old government, and the projection of a possible shooting war, Ryck has instigated a directive two days earlier to actively seek out recruits and not just wait for them. He had also authorized a waiver for non-high-school grads if they could pass the entrance exams.

"Yeah, but, you should finish," Ryck said automatically.

"Why, Dad? You know I'm going to be a Marine. You've always known it."

Which was true. Unlike Noah and Esther, Ben ate, drank, and breathed Marines. There had never been any doubt in Ryck's mind that his son would follow him into the Corps, something that caused no end of pride in him as he watched Ben grow. Fathers were not supposed to have favorites, but deep in his heart, it was this connection to the Corps that made Ben his favorite—not that he would ever admit that.

But now? He wants to enlist now?

Ryck looked down at the contract. The name on it was not Benjamin Lysander, but Benjamin Hope-of-Life, which was a gut shot. He quickly looked back up at his son.

"I, uh, I want to go in as myself, not as the son of the commandant," he said nervously, not meeting Ryck's eyes.

And Ryck felt a surge of pride sweep over him. He had imagined the Lysander name carrying on, but his son had just validated the high opinion Ryck had for him. Ben was his son in spirit as well as in blood.

"You know, some people will make the connection," he said without conviction.

"Some, maybe, but not most," Bens said.

The Federation allowed minors to choose either their father's or mother's last name, a change that was implanted with the admission into the Federation of several planets where property was passed down along the matriarchal line. Choosing a fake name would invalidate the enlistment contract, but using Hannah's family name was completely legal. And while he might not have considered it, choosing the Hope-of-Life name could also be a tribute to his uncle, Joshua.

"You could just wait for seven more weeks, you know. You wouldn't need my permission, and you could change your name to anything you want."

"I know, but I want . . . I'd really appreciate it if I had your blessing, Dad. And I want to keep my family ties. I'm proud of being a Lysander, but—"

"No buts. I understand."

"And I don't want to wait."

Ryck laughed out loud at that. Yes, Ben was his son, all right. Impatient to get on with his life, just as Ryck had been back on Prophesy so many years ago.

"You know, your mother will kill me if I sign this. You're still her baby."

"So you're going to sign it?" Ben asked hopefully.

"And say no and have to live with your pouting for seven weeks? I'd rather be going back to boot camp all over again!" Ryck said with a laugh. "Give me a stylus."

Ben whipped one out and gave it to Ryck, who without hesitation, signed on the parental consent line. Under the second line, Ryck signed for Hannah, and added as a lump in his throat formed, "POW, not available for signature."

"When do you report?" he asked, handing the form back to his son.

"On Tuesday. They've got to clear the new barracks at Camp Charles, but we'll be the first accelerated recruit class to form."

With the current situation of the conflict coupled with the loss of about a fifth of the Corps who opted for the loyalists, each recruit class was expanding four-fold for the duration. Ryck hoped that this would only be a very temporary measure.

"Tuesday? So soon? Hell, I can't let my son go off without a send-off. Sunday, come hell or high water, you and I are going out on the town."

"I'm still only 17, Dad. I can't drink."

"I've got connections to people in high places, Ben, or so I've heard. I think I can get that rule bent just this once," Ryck said, punching his son in the arm.

"Hah! I guess you do," Ben said. And then, more soberly, added, "And Dad, uh, you know, Camp Charles is only an hour away, and I don't want, I mean, I don't think it would be good if you, like, show up? With the accelerated camp, I won't have time to see you, I mean."

And you don't want anyone to know you're the commandant's son, Ryck thought.

"I'll be pretty busy here, fighting the war and all, so you're going to have to be on your own, son. Get used to it."

"Thanks, Dad."

"Well, poolee,[9] get the hell out of here. I've got work to do!" Ryck said.

Ben came to attention, and beaming a huge smile, did a credible about-face and marched out of the office.

Grubbing hell! My son's going to be a Marine!

---

[9] Poolee: a term for someone who has enlisted but who has not yet reported for boot camp.

Chapter 12

Ryck leaned forward, his elbows on the table, his forehead cradled in his hands. Dres Lemon, one of the many former Federation bureaucrats to offer his or her services and now Ryck's trade advisor, blathered on, mindless of Ryck's complete lack of interest.

Just get it over with, Ryck pleaded before he sat back up and tried to look engaged.

He had never really imagined what it took to run a government. As a Marine, even a high-ranking Marine, he had to worry about more than just the X's and O's of battle, to be sure. But basically, what the Marines did was request funding and equipment, then given what they received, decided best how to train and conduct missions.

The Federation, even just the part under Marine Corps and Third Fleet control, was a far more intricate beast, and one to which Ryck was taking a strong dislike. It was a yammering, greedy baby, constantly demanding more and more. Ryck was almost tempted just to surrender and give it all back to the Council—not as a reward, but as a punishment.

"So you can see, sir, that given the embargo and our lack of major industrial players committed to us, we will begin to run out of Class A materials within approximately four months. I've highlighted the most vital to the war effort in green, the most vital to the subsistence of the civilian sector in purple for easy reference," Lemon went on.

He's enjoying this shit, Ryck realized in amazement. *He's in hog heaven.*

General Copperwait interrupted the advisor with "I don't see iridium on the list. Certainly that's a Class A. We can't fight without it."

Shut the hell up, Tomtom. You don't need to bullshit me that you're up on all of this, Ryck thought, trying not to groan aloud.

"Certainly, iridium is a Class A material," Lemon said with just a hint of condescension in his voice. "But we have all the sources for it within our control. It is the loyalist forces that might run out, especially if no one else trades with them for it."

Over 80% of the iridium was mined by the Federation and the Confederation, and Ryck made a mental note to bring the matter up with Major Pohlmeyer later that afternoon. There were other sources of it throughout human space, but no other government had yet developed the processing needed to actually make use of it to any great extent.

"Now, on this next slide, I've listed some of the possible trading partners to acquire some of the vital materials, but as you know, the central bank's freezing of funds means barter might be the only way for us to pay for them, and that assumes we have the goods another government will want. It's a predicament."

No shit. A predicament, he says, Ryck thought sourly. *And that's another thing to go over with the good major. Will the Confederation give us the bridge loans?*

"Excuse me, sir," Vivian said, actually sticking her head in the door instead of announcing whatever it was over the intercom. "You have a call I think you should take."

"Who is it?"

"I think you need to hear that privately, with only General Nidischii', Colonel Simone, the sergeant major, and Top Samuelson," she said with conviction, naming the only other four in the room that were in Ryck's personal circle.

"OK, all of you, you heard her," Ryck said, trying to keep the happiness out of his voice that the mind-numbing brief would be over, at least for him. "General Copperwait, if you could take over the meeting and move it to Conference Room C, I would appreciate it."

Tomtom's looking pissed, Ryck noted as the general and the rest filed out. *I'll need to smooth out his feathers later.*

"Well, Vivian, who is it?" he asked when the rest were gone.

"Governor MacCailín, sir. On the green phone."

The green phone was the most secure form of communications in his office. Only the comms in the vault were more secure.

Ryck jumped up and bolted for the desk. Michiko MacCailín, Governor MacCailín, was the head of the local government on Kakurega, and she had led the forces on the attack on Camp Joshua, the same attack that the loyalist PR dicks had used to try and smear him.

Ryck hit the accept while toggling the relay so that the governor's image appeared on both his personal screen and the large screen at the end of the conference table. He held up his hand, palm down, to the other three, telling them to keep quiet.

"Governor, to what do I owe this pleasure?" he said, taking in her image.

The last time Ryck had seen Michiko MacCailín, she had been naked, bloodied, and battered on the torture table of some fuckdick interrogator, a preening rooster of a warrant officer whose name Ryck had long ago forgotten. Ryck had stopped the fuckdick from giving her Propoxinal, the drug that would have opened up her secrets while destroying her mind.

The younger version of the governor had not been a beautiful woman, but she had an impressive physique that had nicely filled out the superhero costume she'd originally worn for the first holos she made for the rebels. Now, some 20 years later, her curves had somewhat faded as she filled out with age, but she had gained an impressive air about her, a gravitas that had been lacking in the rebel leader.

Ryck had followed the governor's career given their brief but important connection, so he'd seen holos of her. But as she stared at him from light years away, he felt a force of presence.

She'd have made a great Marine, the thought came unbidden.

"So, General. Or do I call you Great Leader?" she asked wryly.

"General will do. Or Ryck. Whatever you want."

"I thought I'd touch base with you, given a certain set of transmissions by the Federation."

"We are the Federation, Governor. The loyalists, as we call them, are the holdovers from the previous criminal government," Ryck said, keeping the governor's image under a steady gaze.

"Of course," she said, breaking out into a laugh that hinted at the happy-go-lucky girl she must have been once so many years ago before she was caught up in the maelstrom of modern politics. "But we here on Kakurega are not overly fond of the Federation, so is that still you?"

"You are not fond of the previous government. You should be joining up with us to change history as we go forward."

"Ah, the invitation to the dance. But do I want to go?" she asked. "Ellison decided not to attend your dance, even if you did all of this for them."

"I didn't do it for them. I did it for the Federation, for all of mankind," he asserted, knowing that what he said might be a little over-the-top.

"Right. Spoken like all good little revolutionaries."

Evolutionaries, not revolutionaries, he wanted to shout even if he was not married to the movement's pet phrase.

"We are what we are, Governor. And I hope you will join us. Given your past, I would think it would be a no-brainer."

"Don't take me for granted, General," she said, steel back into her voice.

Ryck knew he'd taken it too far, but screw it. Either Kakurega would join or not, but he was not going to beg this woman.

"But, as it happens to be, we do seem to have some common ground. I am ready to officially debunk those Federation—excuse me, *loyalist*—vids. I was there, after all. And I can sweeten up the pot to where you are the hero of the people, saving us from brutal annihilation.

"And I can deliver Kakurega to your cause of merry revolutionaries. But I have a price. Well, two prices."

Here it comes, Ryck thought, but calmly asking, "And what might those be?"

"The first is suffrage."

"What? Suffrage? Of who?"

"Of women, of course," she answered. "Or are you complicit with the plight of women in Federation society?"

"But women are free. They are citizens, right?"

"Your wife, Dr. Lysander, is she free? Can she ascend to an EP[10] within the federal government?"

"Well, no."

"Can your daughter, Esther, the sports star, join your own Marine Corps?"

"No."

"Then are we equal to men?"

"No, not when you put it like that," Ryck admitted, not that he hadn't considered the issue time and time again as he met capable women who were limited by Federation policy.

His own Hannah was one of the most capable women—no, most capable person—that he'd ever met. But her rise in the government had stalled as less capable men had been promoted over her. He'd been present when the Greater France Admiral Celeste DeMornay had soundly defeated the stronger Federation fleet under Admiral Starling. And back before women were stripped of many of their rights, Major Melissa "Missy" Walters was one of only two people up until then to be awarded two Federation Novas (and before Ryck made it three). Certainly the governor herself, and even Meister Hendricks-Pata had proven that women were equally as capable of leading as men.

And Ryck realized that he was a feminist, to use an ancient phrase. He wanted his Esther to have every opportunity available to her as Noah or Ben. He may not have openly come to terms with it before, but it had been there all the time.

"Done," he said. "What's next?"

"Done? Just like that?"

"Yes. Done."

The governor leaned forward into her cam pickup and stared at Ryck for a long moment, expressionless.

Then she raised her eyebrows, shrugged, and said, "OK, done."

---

[10] EP: Executive Placing, the highest class of government workers in the Federation.

"And the second price?" he prompted.

"I want to be on your civilian advisory council."

Ryck actually sat back at her words.

How the grubbing hell did she know about that?

"Uh, the what?" he asked lamely, despite knowing that denying it would be a lost cause.

"The CAC. The little council of civilians, currently made up of Terrance Gnatson, Lin Hao Bi, and Patrick de Misterie. You are going to end with five members, and I want to be one of them."

Bert had initially come up with the idea, and Admiral Chandanasiri had eagerly come onboard when Ryck had broached the subject with him. The idea was two-fold: to gain legitimacy with a promised future turnover of the government back to civilian control and to give the headache of actually governing to someone who actually knew what they were doing. Terrance Gnatson, an obvious choice, had been approached only eight hours previously, and he had immediately agreed. Patrick de Misterie had only agreed two hours ago.

No one actually knew what the CAC would do yet. That would be developed. But now the governor was petitioning herself to be on it? One of the other three must have told her about it, at least that is what Ryck hoped. If she had a mole in their inner circle, so could anyone else.

She looked at him expectantly, and Ryck had to consider it. Kakurega was not the most populous planet, but the governor had been in office for 16 or 17 years and had been proven quite effective. They could do worse with her in charge. And having her refute the propaganda smear campaign against him was an added bonus.

"It's not just up to me, you know. I'll have to broach this with Admiral Chandanasiri," he said, sure though that the admiral would not balk, especially if he had someone for the last position and wanted Ryck's concurrence on that.

"You do what you need to. But to sweeten the pot, tell him I'll bring along Propitious Interstellar with me."

The elicited a gasp from the other four eavesdropping Marines. Ryck was floored as well. No major Federation-wide corporation had come in on their side yet. Most were not even neutral but firmly on the side of the loyalists. PI was not only legally headquartered on Earth as were most of the large firms, but it was the third largest fabricator in the Federation and the fifth largest anywhere. With the company supporting them, their dire position vis-à-vis supplies and materials would immediately improve tremendously.

"I think that will catch the admiral's attention, governor. But may I ask, how—" he started.

"No, you may not. Just trust my word, General."

There had been a few tabloid rumors every now and then that the friendship between the governor and David del Solar, the PI CEO, was a little more than platonic or a friendship of political convenience. Ryck had never paid attention to that. They might cooperate due to mutual expediency, but still, PI security goons had killed the governor's activist fiancé. That would seem to be a pretty big hurdle to clear.

Looking at her image, though, Ryck began to question that conclusion. Maybe there was more to it that he'd thought. If Ryck and the governor could cooperate, given their one-time adversarial relationship, why not her and del Solar?

And if PI were going to come onboard, it could be for selfish reasons. They were number three now, but if the provisional government prevailed, then they would be in perfect position to ride their support to be the largest fabricator in human space. They were taking a chance, one for which Ryck was grateful, but they stood to gain if things went their way.

"Well, Governor, this has been a rather interesting, and can I say, welcome call. If you will excuse me, I'll get on the hook with the admiral. If you'll stand by, I'll try to get back to you within the half hour."

"Fair enough, General. I'll be waiting. Let's hope we can come to an accommodation," she said before cutting the connection.

Ryck lowered his green phone screen to look up at the other four Marines.

"Holy fucking shit," Sams said. "That Lemon geek is going to cum in his pants when he hears this. Propitious Interstellar? Who'd have thunk it?"

"Not to mention someone to refute the propaganda," Bert said dryly.

"Yeah, but PI?" Sams said, a huge smile on his face. "Holy fucking shit!"

"Well, gentlemen, my dad used to say it was not polite to keep a lady waiting, so I'm going to the vault and make the call to the admiral. Why don't the four of you wait here, and Jorge, get ready to ask General Copperwait and our pet economist to come back in here to get caught up on what just happened," Ryck said, standing up.

"Vivian, I'm on my way to the vault. I want to speak with the admiral," Ryck said as he passed through his outer office. "Good things are happening," he added, unable to resist.

Sams, in his indubitable manner, had once again nailed it.

"Holy fucking shit" was right.

Chapter 13

Ryck stared at the holo that was projected above the main conference table in the MCCC, or the Marine Corps Command Center. The MCCC was the heart and soul of Marine Corps combat operations, but this time, no Marines were involved in the upcoming battle.

It had been two weeks since Ryck returned to Tarawa, and the schism between the old council and the provisional government had not broken out into fighting—yet. With the Brotherhood spearheading a combined effort to keep what would be a civil war from breaking out and getting more UAM proclamations passed that limited the use of ship-to-ground weaponry, both the loyalists and evolutionaries had been hesitant to initiate hostilities. That had been fine with Ryck. He didn't even know yet just who was in their camp, and it was hard to plan a course of action without knowing the extent of both the friendly forces and the "enemy," as much as Ryck still had a problem with that term for the Federation loyalists.

That lack of action was about to come to an end. The Federation had sent a small task force of 14 ships, none larger than a frigate, to take out the GT-3 Hub, which was the nexus of most of the communications for the broad swatch of planets that seemed to be coalescing with the Evolution forces. The loss of GT-3 would not be a death blow. There were always workarounds, from hadron communicators to convoluted routings, but this would mean comms would be degraded, and that could make a difference in any conflict. So Admiral Chandanasiri had dispatched a 20-ship task force, with two cruisers in the lead, to defend it. Conscious that the attack could be a feint, he kept most of his ships around *Prometheus Station* and Tarawa. A scattering of ships was dispatched to several planets that had weighed in on the Evolution cause, more for show than for any militarily strategic decision.

His task force should be able to fend off the Federation task force, but the Federation did not have to defeat the Evolution ships. It just had to get one missile through them to take out the station.

Ryck thought back to the last time he'd watched a naval battle, while on the *FS Ark Royal* during the war with Greater France. During that battle, the Greater France spoofing and Admiral DeMornay's battle plan had carried the day, with the dreadnaught *FS Bismark* being destroyed by the smaller and technically less-capable *Jean d'Arc*. This time, it was Third Fleet ships against First Fleet, and so the battle display holo was an accurate depiction of the ships as they maneuvered. During the battle with the Greater France navy, Ryck had been a mere spectator to the fight, and now, even though he was the commandant, nothing had changed. He could watch, but he had no input into the fight. Even being able to watch it was a courtesy, relayed to him through a Navy corvette in orbit over his headquarters.

As Ryck watched the slowly moving avatars, a small bloom of light appeared beside the *FS Dundee*. The loyalist ship had fired a torpedo, and the fight was on.

"That's it then. It's war," Bert said.

The torpedo was quickly knocked out by several provisional government ships, but the damage was done—not to GT-3, but as Bert said, this was now a shooting war. Any hope of a negotiated settlement had almost disappeared, not that Ryck had expected anything different. But to expect fighting was not the same as having it thrust at you.

At least they started it, Ryck thought to himself. *History can't accuse me of that.*

For the next 20 minutes, the loyalist ships feinted and maneuvered, keeping at the edge of the defending ship's range. Ryck kept expecting the more robust Third Fleet task force to charge and scatter the attackers, but they held fast in a geometrically designed formation. Ryck thought that was too passive, but it seemed to be working for the moment. None of the loyalist volleys had managed to pierce the shield of ships, and two of the attacking ships had to withdraw due to damage.

Ryck was beginning to hope that the loyalists would withdraw with no loss of ships and possibly no loss of life when half of the loyalist ships darted forward, shields on high as they charged at the heart of the Third Fleet ships.

Ryck stood up, hand on the table as he watched the fight unfold. Rear Admiral Housa shifted his cruiser's fire to concentrate on the lead attackers, and Ryck could see the shield strength on the attackers degrade by the second under the withering energy weapons. The *FS Dundee*, the same ship that had fired the first volley, took the brunt of the evolutionary fire, and suddenly, her shields collapsed, and the ship was vaporized.

There was a collective gasp around the room as the ship, with over 200 men aboard, ceased to exist.

At the same moment, the loyalist ships not in the attack split into three axes, each arching around and firing what had to be their full load of hyper-velocity torpedoes. Under pressure from the initial assault force, only a handful of the evolutionary ships were able to switch over to the new threat. It only took those ships a few seconds to target the incoming torpedoes, but that was a few seconds too long. One Gangee torpedo, a small, 8cm wide inert missile, boosted to .42 of light speed, made it through the defending fire to hit and pierce GT-3. The torpedo only massed 35 kg, but the energy released upon impact was over 4,000,000 Newtons, and that was enough to destroy the hub. There was no catastrophic, slow-motion explosion common in the Hollybolly flicks. There was a large flash of light as the missile hit and parts of the hub were instantly vaporized, but the missile itself punched completely through the hub. The damage inside the hub, however, was extensive. GT-3 was dead.

The attacking loyalist ships immediately broke off the engagement to scatter. Admiral Housa chose to let them go. The loyalists had lost a ship and had two more damaged. Not a single evolutionary ship had been lost. But the loyalists had won.

Ryck slowly sat back down before he looked at the gathered men around him, men now looking to him expectantly.

"Well, gentlemen, we knew it was coming. Now the genie is loose, and the only way to get him back in the bottle is to defeat the Council. And that is just what I plan on doing."

Chapter 14

"Gunny, please get Colonel Edison," Ryck told Çağlar. "We might as well get this done."

Hans Çağlar tried to withhold a grimace as he rose and left the room.

"He don't like our pet fuckdick none," Sams remarked as the hatch closed.

"Would you?" Hecs asked, throwing a pen across the table, hitting Sams in the chest. "He's always felt it was his job to protect the general, and now we've got an FCDC officer in charge of that? I don't blame him."

Ryck simply shook his head at their bickering, which had lately risen in intensity. Jorge caught Ryck's glance and rolled his eyes. The two of them had spoken about the two senior SNCO's. Hecs and Sams had known each other for a long time, but a small schism had begun to develop between them. Jorge thought that it could be because neither had a real job. Sams was on a temporary recall to active duty, assigned at-large to the office of the commandant. Hecs had been slated for assignment in Brussels at the Government Center, which was still technically his billet, but as going to Earth was more than a little problematic at the moment, he'd been pitching his tent in Ryck's office as well. Jorge also thought that with Ryck's ascension to the position of commandant, Hecs felt he should have been made the Sergeant Major of the Marines Corps.

If that were the case, then Hecs would have a long wait, Ryck had decided. He and Hecs went back to when Ryck was in recruit training, and Hecs was firmly in Ryck's posse, but that didn't mean that Ryck was going to boot out Sergeant Major Ito just to stroke Hecs' ego. Plus, Nils Ito was doing a bang-up job as the point man in building up the newly expanded recruit training program at Camp Charles as well as preparing for the introduction of female recruits—

which was part of the promise Ryck had made to Michiko MacCailín.

With Ito an hour away, Ryck had hoped that Hecs and Sams could provide a sane enlisted point of view to the daily issues that cropped up, but if they were going to be having kitten fights, one—or both—of them would have to go. Ryck had a government to run, and he didn't have time to play daddy to the two older men.

Çağlar came back into the office with Colonel Nils Edison in tow. Edison was a career FCDC officer and had been in command of the barracks on Tarawa. Given the Marine Corps presence on the planet, the barracks had been small at fewer than 300 troopers. But when it came time to choose sides, Edison had brought over all but 16 of his men to join the provisional government. This was the highest percentage of any FCDC unit, where less than six percent Federation-wide had joined the cause.

Anxious to show that all were welcome in the evolutionary movement, Edison was given a key position in Ryck's headquarters. Given the nature of the FCDC, the troopers were put in charge of security. At Bert's insistence, Marines were also part of the detachment, but Colonel Edison was the public face of the security detachment.

"Colonel, please take a seat," Ryck said. "And thank you for coming.

"I want to give you a head's up. In three weeks, more or less, I will be attending a conference off-planet, along with Admiral Chandanasiri, the CAC, and various heads of states. There will also be neutral observers."

"You are going off-planet, sir?" Edison asked.

I just said that, Ryck thought, but he said, "Yes. I'll give you the location later, but I need you to start planning the movement. The Third Fleet will be officially hosting, so overall security is their responsibility, but I will be going with approximately a dozen or so Marines, and Governor Franzetti will hitch a ride with us. Our transport will arrive six hours before we embark so you won't have much liaison time."

"Sir, is this a good idea?"

"We can't cower on our bases, Colonel. We're asking the civilians heads of state to stick their necks inside the noose, so to speak, and we have to make a show of confidence and power. So yes, it is a good idea."

"I understand, sir, but I have to go on the record as opposing this. It's hard enough to guarantee your safety here, but going to some planet? And I don't even know where? I'm afraid the risk is too high," the colonel said, worry evident in his voice.

"I can appreciate that, but that's how it's going down."

"Can I, at least, ask where and when?"

"I'm afraid not, Colonel," Ryck said, then quickly adding when he saw a cloud take over the colonel's face, "I don't know the details myself, and I won't know until our ride appears. This is highly classified, as you can imagine, and I don't yet have the need to know."

That seemed to mollify the colonel.

He wrinkled his brow, and then said, "Roger, sir. I'll put something together that we can implement at short notice. I still think the risk is too great, but I'll soldier on and get it done."

"Thank you, Colonel. I have full confidence in you."

"Well, Colonel, I imagine you'll want to get cracking," Jorge said, standing up and indicating the meeting, short as it was, was over. "Let me escort you out. And if you need anything, I'll be your point of contact for this."

"Don't get your panties in a twist, Hans," Sams said as Jorge and the colonel left. "You're still the chief bottle-washer and personal bodyguard for the general here. That there, with the fuckdicks, that's just politics."

"Not just politics, Top," Ryck said to Sams. "The FCDC troops have shown us nothing but loyalty, and we are doing this for all citizens, not just those who're lucky enough to be on planets following our lead."

Sams seemed to want to say something, and a few years back, he probably would have. But as a consequence of Ryck becoming commandant, even Sams had tempered his irreverent nature. He just nodded and said nothing more.

"But he's right, Gunny. I can't think of anyone I'd rather have at my side," Ryck told Çağlar.

And that wasn't a line of BS. The big Marine, who rarely spoke more than a few words at a time, had a presence about him that calmed Ryck. And with Hannah and the twins still incommunicado and prisoners on Earth, with the stress of trying to run a government and a war, Ryck needed all the calming he could get.

Chapter 15

"No friendly KIAs?" Ryck asked. "And she's fully operational?"

"Yes, sir," Vice Admiral Jeremy Mendez, the Navy liaison to the Marines, said. "Our techs think that with the ship's shielding, which affects the general detection capabilities out of the ship as well, the crew didn't know the SEALs were there before they breached the hull."

Given the explosive nature of a hull breach on a ship that size, unless the crew had been suited up, there would have been no survivors. Ryck didn't know if the little spy ship had a crew of two or twenty, but as there were no reported POWs, he knew the loyalist sailors had all died.

It had been a miracle that the spy ship had been spotted in the first place. Only 25 meters long and crammed with every anti-surveillance piece of gear known to the Federation, it should have remained invisible as it kept a watch on the Doughnut, undoubtedly monitoring the comings and goings of all the ships from the station. But the ship's skipper had made a small, but ultimately fatal, mistake. While keeping within a celestial blind spot of the homeport itself, he had let his ship occlude the light from a far-off star that an observant petty officer aboard a picket ship had caught. Running it through the picket's AI, it was quickly apparent that something was out there. They didn't know what, but given the situation, Admiral Chandanasiri rightly concluded that it had to be a loyalist ship and had authorized the quick reaction force into battle.

Using stealth techniques about which even Ryck and the Marines were kept in the dark, the SEALs had approached the ship unnoticed, placed a breaching device on her, and detonated it. With the crew dead, the ship was in the provisional government's hands, a prize of war.

"And we think we can hack the system. The loyalists wouldn't be expecting comms back unless necessary, so we believe we can feed them bad intel."

The admiral looked quite pleased with himself. And Ryck had to admit that this was a welcomed piece of news, even if he felt somewhat embarrassed that the Navy had been the tip of the spear so far. With three operations—one loss and now two successes—it was the Navy crossing swords with the loyalists. The Marines had yet to fire a shot in anger. If he could get the Marines through this with no loss of life, he'd be quite happy with that. But that sense of hubris that still lurked inside his heart created a desire that it would be the Marines carrying the day, not the Navy. It was stupid and childish, he knew, but that didn't make the desire any less real.

He wished he could be the one bloodying the Council's nose.

They've got my wife, for grubbing's sake, he thought, his blood pressure rising as he gripped the edge of the conference table.

If he'd been alone, he knew he'd slam his fist on it as he'd done more than a few times each day when he thought of his family.

He tried to force an image into his mind of a calm tropical ocean wave, picturing it enveloping him, relaxing him. He'd read about the technique in a self-help book. But when he tried to force calmness, it usually had the opposite effect.

Ah, fuck it, he thought, abandoning the wave he'd imagined. He'd just act calm, even if his insides were roiling.

"Well, Jeremy, that's great news. Please relay my congratulations to the admiral and the SEAL team itself," he said, putting a smile he didn't feel on his face.

"Why don't you hang around for lunch. Major Pohlmeyer's coming over for an informal, and Top Ekema's ginned up his famous Hawaiian medallions. I'd like you to hear what the good major has for us today."

A smile broke out over the admiral's face—not for the meeting, Ryck knew, but because Marten Ekema's skill in the kitchen was half legend already. One of the perks of being the commandant was a full-time kitchen staff, and Ryck had brought the master gunnery sergeant along. Top Ekema knew Ryck's tastes, so Ryck hadn't had to break in anyone new. And just the thought of those glazed medallions was beginning to calm him down where his imagined gentle tropical waves had failed.

Hah! Ryck thought as he realized the unintended connection. *Tropical meal, one; tropical waves, zero!*

Chapter 16

"Vivian, where's Montero? He's late, and we're running out of time!"

"He's still five minutes out," Ryck's secretary informed him.

"Make a note of it. If I've got to clear things with him, he needs to be here in the headquarters. He can sleep here if need be."

Ryck had agreed to follow Admiral Chandanasiri's request that any unilateral action concerning the political situation be vetted first by his PA office, and that meant Zeke Montero for Ryck. With only an hour before embark, Ryck was running out of time. He was sick and tired of Hannah and the twins being used as pawns, but pawns about which the public was unaware. Ryck wanted to issue a press release, but that fell under his promise to the admiral to run it by his PA advisor. Actually, Ryck had a brigadier general, Rapiko "Rapper" Weisener, as the Marine Corps spokesman. Rapper was the face of the Corps for the press, but this went beyond the typical Marine Corps fodder. As a provisional government issue, even if a personal one for Ryck, the Office of Information—and on Tarawa, that was Zeke Montero—had to weigh in.

"What about Colonel Edison?" Ryck asked.

"He's here," Vivian's voice filled the office.

"OK, send him in."

Within a few heartbeats, the FCDC colonel rushed in, coming to one of the disjointed positions of attention peculiar to the FCDC.

"At ease, Colonel. Are you and your men ready?"

"Yes, sir. We still don't know to where we're going, though, right?"

"Not until we get on the ship, which will be in . . . Vivian, how long before we leave?"

"Your driver will pick you up in 52 minutes," she immediately responded in her calm voice.

"Well, sir, we've got five contingencies that we've rehearsed, from an open field planetside to a ship to a station. I'll trust you to ensure that all hands obey my commands upon arrival, sir. I mean, as a colonel, and as, well—"

"As an FCDC colonel among generals and admirals, you mean."

"Well, yes, sir. You know how it can be sometimes."

"Don't worry. I'll make sure everyone toes the line."

"And one thing, sir. As soon as possible, and before we arrive, I need face-to-face comms with whoever is leading the overall security. I need to make sure our side isn't at odds with whatever they've set up."

That seemed reasonable, so Ryck said, "OK, you've got it. As soon as we've got comms, you'll have priority."

"General Lysander, Mr. Montero is here," Vivian announced over the intercom.

"Well, Colonel. I'm sure you're busy, and I sure am, so you take care of your business.

"Vivian, send him in."

It took Montero more than a few heartbeats to walk into the office, and Ryck was getting impatient. Time was short, and he'd gotten used to the deference people gave to him as the commandant. Maybe that's why he didn't like Montero, he knew. Montero didn't even come close to acting as someone under Ryck's authority.

"I'm ready to release the statement to the press," Ryck said without preamble.

"About your wife?" Montero asked.

No, you grubbing idiot! I meant how big of a shit I took this morning. That should interest them!

"That's the only press release, to my knowledge, that I have sent to you over the last 24 hours, so yes, that one."

"Well, sir, after careful consideration, I can't really endorse that."

Why the hell doesn't that surprise me? Ryck wondered.

"And why not? They've got my wife and children as hostages, and no one knows about it. And that directly contravenes the Universal Charter, right?"

"Well, yes, it does. And that's the problem," Montero said as if lecturing a child.

Why isn't anything clear with this guy? It's "good news" when the Council slams me as a war criminal, and now that he admits the Council is breaking the charter, he says we can't act?

"And why might that be?"

"Well, General, right now, your wife and children are, well, sort of 'guests' of the Council. There are no charges against them. But if we force the issue, do you really think they are going to relinquish this advantage over you?"

This "advantage" is my wife and kids you're talking about!

"I think not. So what are their options? Well, limited. The most logical one is to charge your wife and children with treason so that their arrests are legal."

That hit Ryck with a gut shot. He hadn't considered that, nor had his SJA.

"And what is the penalty for treason?" Montero asked.

"Death," Ryck said hollowly. "But they wouldn't do that, would they? Think of the bad press they would get."

"Really? They were ready to interdict a planet of 12 billion people. Do you really think they'd hesitate to kill three more?"

Ryck knew the answer to that, even if he didn't want to admit it. The Council would murder hundreds, thousands, hell, millions to get what they wanted.

"With that in mind, I can't sign off on this. I can't be parcel to the executions of your family."

Ryck stared at his advisor. Part of him wanted to scream that it wasn't up to him to decide what would happen and what wouldn't. Ryck was the commandant, the co-head of government. Montero was just some jumped-up bureaucrat.

But he was right, Ryck knew. When Ryck, Jorge, and Major General Devarja, his SJA, had come up with the plan, they really hadn't considered the ramifications. As military men, they tended to think in simple terms of right and wrong, of maneuver and outcome. Montero, however, was one of those slimy men who couldn't be trusted farther than they could be thrown—which is why he was able to understand how the Council would react. Slimy or not, he'd probably just saved Hannah and the twins from Ryck's rash actions.

"Look, I'm running out of time. I'm leaving for the conference shortly, but we'll discuss this when I get back."

Which he wouldn't, he knew. The man was right, but Ryck didn't want to admit defeat to a man he didn't respect. Ryck did shake his hand, however, and escorted him to the hatch.

"Sir, Major Pohlmeyer left this package," Vivian said, spotting Ryck in the doorway. "And you have one more visitor."

"No time for anyone else," Ryck told her, accepting the small package.

"Sir, it's Corporal Hailstone," she said.

Ryck stopped, taking a moment to recall just who Corporal Hailstone was and why a corporal would be calling on the Commandant of the Marine Corps.

Shit! Of course. The Wall.

Corporal Peyton Hailstone was the first Marine assigned to the UAM, the Universal Assembly of Man, as one of its new genmodded gladiators, as they were commonly called. He'd undergone extensive genmodding, regen, and training, and only two months ago, under his nickname of "The Wall" and as the human representative, had defeated a Klethos queen on Isseret. The previous two fights had resulted in human defeats, so his win had been highly heralded.

Ryck checked his watch. He had a few moments. Çağlar would have his kit and get him in time.

Ryck walked into the outer office. Corporal Hailstone was impossible to miss. Standing almost four meters tall, or hunching in this case, he was simply huge. Ryck had watched some of the training sessions of the candidates, but from bleachers. This was the first time he'd been so close to one of them.

"Welcome, Corporal," Ryck said, walking up, hand outstretched.

Corporal Hailstone tried to come to attention the best he could in Ryck's three—and-a-half meter office. He reached out, and Ryck's hand completely disappeared in the big man's horny and huge paw of a hand.

"Thank you for seeing me," the Marine stuttered out, his voice surprisingly normal given his bulk.

"I'm about ready to leave, but I've always got a few moments for one of humanity's guardians. Um, shall we go into my office?"

Ryck turned and led the way back into the inner office. Hailstone followed, ducking through the front hatch.

"I, well, I'm not sure I have furniture for your size," Ryck said, unsure of himself and proper protocol.

"If you want me to sit, sir, I can sit on the floor. I'm used to it. And maybe it will be easier to talk," the corporal said.

"Uh, sure, if you think so."

Corporal Hailstone smoothly lowered himself into a cross-legged seat, his head now even with Ryck's.

He moves like a cat, Ryck noted.

Not for long, though, Ryck knew. The extensive genmods and regen, all accelerated, would have drastic consequences. Ryck, with his relatively innocuous genmods and more intensive regens, had twice come down with the Brick, or Boosted Regeneration Cancer. The gladiators had undergone vastly more invasive procedures, actual genetic modification, and then forced regen. Whatever Peyton Hailstone had been as a boy, he was no longer that person. His body had undergone huge transformations, more than it could possibly accept. Doctors gave this generation of gladiators fewer than four years before the Brick would claim them. And two of those years were in the medical transformation, then the therapy and fight training. This huge, immensely powerful Marine sitting in front of him had probably less than a year to live.

"And what can I do for you, Corporal?" Ryck asked, unsure why the Marine had requested a meeting.

"Sir, I'm sorry to bother you. But I want to come back. I want to be a Marine again and fight the Federation."

We are the Federation, Ryck thought, but kept quiet.

"But you are serving all of humanity, son. You've gone beyond the Marines."

"There's no such thing as an ex-Marine, right sir? I'm still a corporal."

"Well, yes. You're still a Marine. You are carried on the rolls."

"And I want to fight with you, sir. I can help," he said, a hint of pleading in his voice.

"I'm sure you can, Peyton. Can I call you Peyton?"

"Yes, sir, but I'm rather proud of my rank. I earned it."

"That you did, Corporal. And I know you can help. But you can't. I mean you could if it was allowed, but even a Marine has to bow to the treaty. All governments have to contribute gladiators, and no one can interfere with any of you."

"But you aren't interfering. I want to," Corporal Hailstone protested.

"And I know you want to. But this is bigger than us. It is bigger than the Corps. We've got an agreement with all of humanity."

"You fought a *d'relle*, and you're still in the Corps," the corporal said quietly.

"Yes, I did. But I'm not . . . a . . . I'm not—"

"You haven't been made into a freak," Corporal Hailstone finished for him.

"Right," Ryck answered, not bothering with the facade of disagreeing with the corporal's blunt description of himself. "I'm still mostly me, at least the physical me. A few new limbs, some fiddling around with my hippocampus so I can navigate, but out of uniform, no one would give me a second look. And you, I can't know what you are feeling, but I can guess."

"I've probably got one more fight left in me. Even if I win . . ."

"Do you know when you fight next?"

"No one knows. It's up to the Klethos' challenge. Rock is next, but the schedulers tell me I might be after that, given the last fight."

And if he lives, the Brick will be about ready to take over, Ryck thought sorrowfully.

"Well, sir, I thought I'd try. I'm on home leave now, so I came in. Rock said you couldn't take me, but you know."

"Home leave? But you aren't from Tarawa."

"All Marines are from Tarawa, sir. And Alexander, but, you know. I'm from Respite, but my grandfolks were from Vandum.

Grubbing hell. Vandum? No wonder he wants to fight.

"Were? They're on Respite now?" Ryck asked hopefully.

"No, they were killed in the fighting. FCDC troopers got them."

Ryck shook his head. Twenty-some-odd years ago, there had been one of the periodic strikes on Vandum. The FCDC was sent to suppress the strike, but fighting broke out, and the FCDC went berserk, killing indiscriminately. Some 30,000 civilians, out of a total planetary population of only a million, were killed.

A thought hit Ryck. He couldn't take the corporal back into active duty, but maybe he could do something.

"When is your leave over?"

"Sir? I've got about three weeks left before I'm back into training."

I can't take you back in uniform, not that we have any big enough to you," Ryck said with a lame-sounding laugh. "But if you want to go with us to a conference as an independent observer, I think we can swing that. There will be other observers from the other governments. I have to check with my SJA, but I think it would be OK."

"A conference? About what?" Hailstone asked.

"I can't really say. It's pretty classified. But if you're ready to go now, why not? We'll be gone for only two days. Are you interested?"

"And I'd be traveling with you and other Marines?"

"That you would."

"Yes, sir, thank you, sir. I'd love that. You can count on me," the corporal said, excitement evident in his voice.

Ryck called General Devarja, who while he thought it was a bad idea, couldn't think of why it would be forbidden. Hailstone couldn't be part of the official Marine party, but he could hitch a ride and observe as an independent at the request of Ryck as the co-head of the provisional government.

"General, you've got 20 minutes," Vivian reminded him.

Ryck tilted his head to the speakers and whispered, "She's worse than my mother."

"That's because you need it, sir," Vivian's sharp voice filled the office.

That elicited a laugh, a surprisingly girlish giggle from the big Marine.

"Ears like a bat, too," Ryck whispered even quieter, leaning into the gladiator.

"Vivian," Ryck spoke out, returning to his normal voice. "Corporal Hailstone will be hitching a ride with us to wherever we're going. Please let the Navy know. I'm sending him out now, so please ask the Gunny to take him under his wing."

Ryck watched Corporal Hailstone stand up in one smooth motion, come to a hunched position of attention, then duck out through the hatch. Ryck knew he couldn't take the man back into serving as a Marine. He could make sure Hailstone was promoted to sergeant, though, before the Brick or some unknown Kelthos queen claimed him. He probably deserved some sort of medal, too. Ryck had received his second Nova for his fight, after all, and he'd just been reacting to the situation. Hailstone, along with the other 100 or so gladiators undergoing genmodding or training, had volunteered, knowing that even if they weren't killed in training, fighting, or genmod rejection, they would die a pretty horrible death as the Brick ate them alive. And for them, unlike for Ryck and Sams, there was no more regen to keep the Brick at bay.

He glanced back at the desk to make sure he hadn't left anything and spotted the package. He was tempted to leave it until he got back, but he still had a couple of minutes, so he pulled the release and the package unfolded, revealing a small case. Flipping open the case revealed a small Bianchi 6mm and a handwritten note:

Thought you might need this again sometime, and it was taking up too much space in the evidence locker.
Titus Pohlmeyer, Major, Confederation of Free States Army.

Ryck picked up the small Bianchi, remembering its feel. It had been given to him by FCDC Major Faustus Rychmont while on New Mumbai. As a diplomat, it had been highly illegal for him to carry it, but it had saved Ryck's life when he was attacked by two assassins. It had been confiscated by the Confed police, and Ryck hadn't given it much thought since. But having it in his hand brought back a rush of memories.

He still didn't know what game the Confeds were playing. Obviously, they were out for themselves. But did that include helping the provisional government? Pohlmeyer was more than a mere major. Ryck had known that for years. But in his gut, Ryck trusted him. He hoped the Confederation had their back

And Ryck appreciated the gesture. It wasn't a game-changer as none of the Marines were going into the meeting unarmed. They were in a state of war, and Marines were always armed during wartime. Even in his office on Tarawa, Ryck had an M99 and his larger 8mm Ruger within a step or two from his desk. Montero had argued incessantly that going into this meeting armed sent the wrong message, but Ryck overruled him. This was a military matter, and Marines went armed, period. The main security would be from his FCDC troops and the admiral's own security force, but still, every Marine would have his sidearm with him—with live rounds.

Ryck knew history, and Marines from Beirut to Hades had been sent in by politicians with weapons and no ammunition—with disastrous results. So when Montereo had suggested that, Ryck had immediately cut the man off, restraining himself from leaning over the table to punch him.

No, the Marines would be armed, and Ryck's 8mm was far more powerful than the little 6mm in his hand. Still, it felt good there. He slipped it under his blouse and into the small inner pocket. He patted down the spot on the outside, feeling the slight bulge.

"Gunny Çağlar, you out there?" he shouted, looking at his profile in the mirror. "We need to get moving. We've got a mission to accomplish!"

STUDEVAANT 3

Chapter 17

Ryck watched the screen that showed the outside view as the shuttle descended to the planet's surface. Studevaant 3 was a lifeless, airless planet, and the surface below them was barren and almost featureless. As a "dead" planet, there was no volcanism nor tectonic shifts that would create landforms, and as an orphan, there were few objects in that little bit of the galaxy that could hit it creating craters.

As a choice for a clandestine meeting, it wasn't a bad one. It wasn't the best, either. Ryck could name several better venues, but the loyalists would know of those, too. And the restriction against interdiction foisted on them by the other governments did not hold for stations, only planets.

The landscape 30 kilometers below the shuttle was colorless given the minimal illumination from the nearest star, but that had its own kind of beauty, Ryck thought. But he knew that on the planet's surface, it would be a pretty bleak place. A flare below and ahead of them indicated another shuttle was landing. Ryck absently wondered who it was carrying.

It was ten minutes later before it was Ryck's shuttle's turn.

"Please prepare for landing," the pilot passed over the intercom before he flared the shuttle to touch gently down at one of three snake causeways that quickly reached out to latch onto the shuttle's hatch.

Within 20 seconds, the hatch light showed green, indicating the causeway was pressurized.

"Let's move it," Bert Nidischii' said as he stood up. "We've got a limited time here, so no use wasting any of it."

Ryck pulled out his Ruger, checked the load, and re-holstered it before stepping up to the hatch. Bert, Hecs, Çağlar, and he comprised the official Marine Corps party from Tarawa to the conference. Colonel Edison had twenty-two troopers and three Marines for security. And then there was Corporal Hailstone scrunched up in the back of the shuttle, although he was there not as a Marine but as an independent observer.

"Do you know where to go?" Hecs asked Hailstone.

"Yes, Sergeant Major. In the back and out of the way, in Row F."

And then the hatch opened, and whatever else Hecs had to say was lost as Ryck stepped forward into the cool causeway. The center was at a reasonable temperature, but Ryck could feel the cold emanating from the causeway's walls. Ryck had used the snakes only a few times in his career, given that they tended to be temporary, and the unfortunate name, in Ryck's opinion, brought to mind images of crawling down some huge serpent's throat to its stomach. He hoped the image would not prove to be prophetic.

A moment later, Ryck was passing through the inner airlock, which was already open to the station. Two Navy ratings came to present arms as a civilian functionary rushed forward to guide Ryck and the others to the elevators.

The Studevaant 3 station was located some 70 meters underground where it was better insulated from the bitter cold of the planet's surface. That depth coincidently shielded the station from almost any shipborne weapon, Ryck knew. Perhaps it was not so coincidental. Ryck had no idea as to the station's scientific purpose, but it made a pretty good bunker.

The elevator came to a stop, and their guide hurriedly led them down a passage to a guarded set of double doors.

"The conference will start in a few moments," the guide said as he stepped aside.

The conference room was surprisingly large. There was a stage in the front, then at least 500 chairs arranged theater-style. Why a simple research station needed something like this was beyond Ryck, and he became convinced that the science was just a cover for whatever purpose the station really held.

That was all well and good, but if the Third Fleet knew this place had another purpose, then so would the First Fleet. That would elevate it as a potential meeting site, raising it on the list of potential loyalist targets. It would have been impossible to completely hide that something was going to take place, no matter how tight the security had been. Despite only four men knowing the details of the meeting beforehand, there were other ways for the loyalists to gather information. Loyalist AIs could monitor comms patterns and movement of people well enough to surmise that something was going on. The security of the conference relied on keeping the Federation in the dark as to just what was taking place and where.

Given that half of the Third Fleet was around and near the planet, it wouldn't take very long at all for the loyalists to determine just where the event was taking place. It may not be the entire Third Fleet gathering around, but still, the loyalists would soon know that something big was up, and with the number of people now involved, leaks had to have occurred. And now that foreign governments had been invited only two days ago, with reps to be picked up by Navy ships, that word had to have reached the loyalists.

Many people were already in their seats, but more were milling about the aisles, shaking hands and chatting. One man saw Ryck and immediately approached him.

"Prime Minister de Misterie, it is good to meet you," Ryck said, extending a hand to the Civilian Advisory Council member from the Kingdom of Hiapo.

With their economic might and their history of four Federation chairmen, the Kingdom held a pretty powerful position within the Federation. Having them supporting the provisional government had been a coup, one rewarded with the prime minister being offered the position in the CAC. He wasn't the king, who traditionally never left the planet and who would have been even more impactful, but as a career politician, the prime minister was a good second choice.

"And it's good to meet you, too, General. I'm sorry we won't have time for socializing, but I think a person can tell the mettle of a man even in a short time."

The conference was scheduled for six hours. That was because of security concerns. The loyalists would be able to discover where the conference was taking place, but by the time the loyalists could hope to launch some sort of strike deep within evolutionary territory, the participants would be long gone.

"Admiral Chandanasiri and I will have a short meeting with the five of you before we kick out of here, so I hope we've formed a lasting bond before we part," Ryck said.

Boy did that sound lame, he thought. *I never said I was a good smoocher.*

"Yes, let us hope. Well, I think we're about to kick this off, and there's no time to waste, as they say," the prime minister said, giving a little half bow, then making his way around Ryck to his assigned seat.

He was followed by his personal *kao'o'e,* or King's bodyguard, a huge man wearing traditional Hawaiian clothing and carrying a *lei-o-nano,* or war club, complete with real shark teeth, if Vivian's brief had been accurate. The prime minister had two more conventional bodyguards as well, but Ryck thought that the *kao'o'e* might be able to make himself noted should it ever come down to an assault on his charge. For a non-royal to have a *kao'o'e* was considered a sign of direct royal favor.

"I think that has to be the second biggest man in the room after Corporal Hailstone," Bert whispered in Ryck's ear as they made their way forward to their seats. "He could probably fight a Klethos queen without modification."

"He probably *is* modified," Ryck said.

Several more people offered a quick handshake and hello as Ryck moved forward. At the start of the second row, Michiko MacCailín was standing and speaking with two others.

"Governor, I'm glad to see you made it," Ryck said, catching her attention.

"After all I put you through, I wouldn't miss it, General."

Ryck took her proffered hand, but the tough-looking bodyguard-type standing next to her caught his attention. Something about the man tickled the recesses in the back of his mind.

"And I believe you know my chief of security, Seth MacPruitt?" she added.

Grubbing hell! It is him!

"Uh, yes. Mr. MacPruitt and I go back a long ways, actually," he said, "We went to Charles together, that's our recruit training base, and then Sergeant MacPruitt taught me hand-to-hand combat on Alexander.

"It's good to see you again, Seth," Ryck said, reaching out to take the former Marine's hand.

"Ma'am, I'd better go check with the team, now. I'll be back to escort you when the meeting is done," MacPruitt said, ignoring Ryck and wheeling about to make his way back to the exit.

The governor laughed and said, "He's a bit prickly at times, but he's capable and extremely loyal. He's not a big fan of you, though, from what he's told me."

"I gather that," Ryck said, feeling foolish and more than a little ticked.

"Well, I'd like to touch base with you after the main meeting, if we can, governor," Ryck said before moving on to his assigned seat in the front row.

"General, good to see you again," Ryck said as he reached his seat next to where his assistant commandant had already claimed his. "The Navy treating you right?"

"As good as can be expected, sir. But it's good to see a few more Marine faces."

"Not too many, though," Ryck said. "Just Bert here, Sergeant Major Phantawisangtong, who I think you know, and Gunnery Sergeant Çağlar. Have you met the gunny before?"

"Not personally, no. But I've heard of him," he said, reaching out to shake Çağlar's hand. "And of course, the sergeant major and I have served a tour together. How are you doing, Hecs?"

"Good to see you again, too, sir," Hecs said.

"So, how many people are here?" Ryck asked. "We've been kept in the dark."

"Everyone has. The loyalists have big ears, and they're not invited. But from what Admiral Attamount told me as we arrived, we're expecting 38 heads of state, all with minimal staffs."

"That's it? Thirty-eight?"

"That's what he said."

Ryck had been hoping for more. Over 100 planetary and national governments, as well as 19 stations, had given their support. Ryck hoped the missing heads of governments was due to logistics and not to lukewarm support or worse, a change of heart.

"Sir, I'll leave you here now," Colonel Edison said. "I'll be in the back coordinating with Captain Douglas, but we've got men stationed throughout the hall. If you need me, just call."

"OK. Looks like the choice of a venue was well-thought out. I don't think your men will be earning their pay today," Ryck said.

"Let's pray that be the case, sir," the FCDC colonel said before leaving the four Marines.

"And foreign representatives?" Ryck asked General Huckmaster, returning to the previous line of discussion.

"The Confederation has four, along with your Major Pohlmeyer. The Brotherhood has one, the Vicar Emmanuel."

Only a vicar? Grubbing hell!

"The Alliance, New Budapest, Outback, Purgatory, the Juliette Group, uh, well, I can give you a full list, but 19 foreign reps are here. Well, you making Corporal Hailstone an observer makes it 20. The vicar is royally pissed, though, that you did that. He says the gladiators have to remain not only above the fray but completely divorced from any inter-governmental conflicts."

Fuck the vicar if he can't take a joke, Ryck thought, bringing to mind an old but trite phrase.

"Greater France?"

"No, sir. Nothing from them."

Shit in a handbasket. We needed them, Ryck thought to himself.

Greater France was the only other major power headquartered on Earth. Ryck had some vague ideas of using Greater France's Earth territory to launch some sort of raid on Brussels. Their lack of response to this invitation was troubling.

"General Lysander, Ryck, it's good to finally meet you," a voice said from behind Ryck.

Ryck turned to see Admiral Chandanasiri approaching arms out for a hug. Ryck was more of a handshake kind of guy, but with holo-cams running, he accepted the admiral's embrace, giving the admiral a good slap on the back.

"Admiral, it's good to see you, too," Ryck said as all eyes turned to the two great men.

"Please, it's Amarin. Or Fred if you want. We're too close for formalities, and we've got a job to do."

But they weren't close. Ryck had only cammed with the admiral a few times, but one thing was evident in person and not on cam. The admiral simply exuded personality. And Ryck couldn't help but notice how he'd positioned himself to show off his medals and catch the gathered holo-cams at a good angle.

The admiral had proven himself in battle. He was no desk-jockey, but a true warrior. But he also had the reputation of being a superb politician, one who'd had his sights set on the Council chairmanship. Ryck had to wonder if the Third Fleet's support had more to do with that ambition than anything else, an effort to cut 15 or 20 years out of the process of rising to the position.

One way or the other, Ryck was glad for the admiral's contribution. Ryck hated the politics, and he was eagerly ceding those duties to the man.

Still, Ryck was beginning to realize that he liked the limelight. He didn't want to perform the smooching and posturing required to be a real politician, but he had to admit he wanted the accolades. Now, standing next to the photogenic admiral, Ryck realized he was puffing up his chest and shifting his position so he would be best recorded. That made him feel somewhat of a hypocrite, but that didn't make him stop preening like a peacock.

"Gentlemen, we're ready to begin," Admiral Attamount said, stepping up to the two.

"Well, then Ryck. Let's take a seat and get this show rolling. We've got a schedule to keep, after all," the admiral said.

Ryck took his assigned seat next to the admiral, right in the middle of the first row as a Navy captain on stage said, "Ladies and gentlemen, would you please take your seats?"

The captain waited a few moments until most of the people were seated before saying, "Ladies and gentlemen, Admiral Amarin

Chandanasiri, the co-chairman of the provisional government of the United Federation."

"That's me," the admiral whispered to Ryck as he got up and walked to the stage to the applause of those in the room.

Ryck was not scheduled to talk, and while part of him was glad of that, given his distaste of public speaking, he had to wonder why. If he was the co-chairman along with the admiral, shouldn't he talk as well? When they had been given the itinerary immediately after emerging from bubble space, Ryck had been both relieved and a little disappointed. Bert had said that the admiral was already maneuvering for the permanent chairmanship, and while Ryck had only a passing interest in it and was willing to support the admiral once all this was over, he wanted that to be his decision, not something forced upon him.

After reaching the podium, the admiral took a long, slow look at the gathered men and women before saying, "Ladies and gentlemen, heads of state, and representatives of our fellow governments in human space, welcome."

"I'm surprised he didn't invite a capy rep," Bert whispered.

"Shh!" Ryck whispered back out of the corner of his mouth, eyes locked on the admiral while he tried not to laugh.

"Back in 2216, Old Reckoning, our founding fathers, sick of the wars that threatened to engulf the planet, sick of the abuse humans were wracking on each other on the homeword, founded the United Federation of Nations. By signing the charter, our founding fathers became marked men and women, traitors to their home countries. But it worked. A reign of peace, prosperity, and expansion resulted. Yes, there've been wars since then. Yes, other governments have chosen to split off, but we've never been in danger of destroying ourselves since then.

"Over the last 40 years, though, the Federation Council has forgotten the ideals in which our beloved Federation was formed. They became the *raison d'etre* for the Federation rather than the servants of it. And their arrogance grew until insanity took over. With their hands in the pockets of big business, they thought they could do anything. What they forgot was that some of us have a moral compass to prevent that.

"When the Council itself, the supposed guardians of the citizens, ordered the murder of 12 billion citizens on Ellison, my co-chairman, General Ryck Lysander, did not stand by hopelessly. He acted and saved those lives."

He looked down with almost a fatherly expression on his face, lowering his right hand to indicate Ryck. Applause grew until it filled the hall.

"Now, I'd like to think I'd have done the same. As I'm sure that all of you would have given the same situation, but it was Ryck, my respected friend, who took that first step. Now it is up to us to take the torch and carry it through.

"The old council is corrupt and rotten to the core. It has to be removed by the will of the people. And that is why we've called you here. You needed to meet us, the Navy and the Marines, to assure yourself and your citizens that we are the true servants of the people. We will rid the Federation of the rot so you, those of you here today, can and will take its place.

"I'm just an old sailor, and Ryck is a Marine. We serve the people. We've declared martial law only until the old council is replaced. After that, the Federation will be given back into the hands of the people. That's you. To that end, and as a transitional council, we welcome five of you to the Civilian Advisory Council, the CAC. This council is your civilian representation to the provisional government, and as soon as we can, Ryck and I will turn over all power to it so they can form a new Federation Council, one free of the corruption now back in Brussels.

"If I can, may I present to you Terrance Gnatson, Lin Hao Bi, Patrick de Misterie, Michiko MacCailín, and Leon Jesus Molina, your Civilian Advisory Council!"

The five stood up to a thunderous round of applause.

The guy is brilliant, Ryck admitted to himself as he stood to clap with the rest.

Any military coup—and no matter how you sliced it, that is what it was—is open to mistrust. By announcing now the formation of the CAC, the provisional government, (that is the admiral and Ryck) was promising that the military control was of a limited duration. He made it sound as if he didn't want to be in charge, something Ryck was sure was a sham. But now, by parading around the CAC, not only was he assuring the planetary and national reps that this was "their" government, he was making a statement to the foreign reps that the largest, most powerful military in human space was not interested in power. And that would be a welcome piece of news to the Brotherhood and the rest who had long had a growing unease at the progressively more aggressive stance emanating out of the Federation.

"We don't have much time here," he continued after the applause died out. "And I don't really enjoy being a public speaker," he added as laughter interrupted him at the tongue-in-cheek lie. "But I want to give Terrance Gnatson a chance to speak, and then we'll open it up to questions before breaking down into groups. I hope this meeting will reap dividends in getting us all on the same page and keeping everything open. Dr. Gnatson, if you will?"

Ryck hadn't been kept in the loop as to the specifics of the meeting. He hadn't even thought at first that the meeting was even necessary, after all, given modern technology and the ability to conduct virtual conferences. But he could feel the excitement in the room. The 38 reps here were probably from the governments most committed, but he knew they were onboard. And once the recordings of the meeting were disseminated, Ryck was pretty sure others would sign on as well.

"Nice job," Ryck whispered to the admiral as he sat back down. "I was wondering where you were going with this."

"Thanks, and sorry I couldn't bring you in on more than this. Only Gnatson, Attamount, and I put this together, and that was all face-to-face. I couldn't risk anything leaking out beforehand, and getting back to the Council."

"Don't mention it," Ryck said.

He did feel a little left out, however. He was the co-chairman, after all, supposedly an equal partner. And if not him, then Huckmaster should have been part of their little planning cell. But he didn't want his ego to get in the way, and what the admiral said was true. The more people brought in on this, the more likelihood of a leak. If the loyalists had any way to reach them, it would be a disaster.

Terrance Gnatson stood at the podium, basking in the applause. He was very well respected and trusted, and his approval ratings were up in the 80th percentile. A grandfatherly figure, he was a good choice to head the CAC.

"Thank you," he said, leaning into the old fashioned mic. "I am honored t—"

The first shot hit him high in the forehead, taking out the back of his head in an explosion of blood, bone, and brain matter.

Ryck was drawing his Ruger, spinning around before his conscious mind registered what had happened. In the back of the hall, FCDC troopers, his troopers, were raising their Reimmasters to take the room under fire. Ryck snapped off two shots, hitting one of the fuckdicks in the face and dropping him before the people realized what had happened. Screams echoed out as people dove to find cover between the rows of seats.

The Reimmasters favored by the FCDC fired a jacketless 120-grain round. It limited the number of rounds when compared to the hypervelocity darts favored by the Marines, but they had a far more visual impact. A dart tended to pass through a body. The Reimmaster round tended to destroy what it hit. Body armor would defeat it, but no one other than the fuckdicks was wearing any.

Marines, as a military service, joined other militaries in using darted weapons as their primary personal arms. A dart would disable or kill an enemy, but the amount of body damage would not be extensive. A KIA could be zombied and have a reasonable chance at resurrection. It may have been a gentlemen's agreement, but resurrecting a soldier took more resources and manpower than burying one, and so there was a strategic advantage to it as well.

Rounds such as the 120-grain expanding bullet destroyed far more tissue. A head shot with one was generally considered non-resurrectable.

A split second after Ryck fired, Çağlar was at his side, trying to get in front of his commandant as he fired his own Ruger.

"Get down!" Ryck shouted, pulling at the bigger Marine's jacket. "And aim those shots!"

The back of Ryck's seat exploded just as Çağlar crouched. Next to him, Ryck heard the admiral grunt, but Ryck couldn't spare the time to look at him. He fired shot after shot, but after that first lucky face shot, his Ruger, designed for short-range self-defense, was not letting him place effective fire on the fuckdicks who were advancing down the aisles, their Reimmasters blazing.

A woman jumped up to flee and was accidently cut down by one of the four Marines. Ryck felt a pang, but he couldn't focus on that at the moment.

Two of the door guards, Navy gunners mates, charged into the room. Their heavier weapons took care of one of the fuckdicks, before the rear-guard troopers shot both men.

Ryck's mind churned, processing information. There were ten troopers, including Edison in the back, who were advancing down to the front row. Two were down, so that meant eleven, along with three Marines, were not in the hall. Ryck didn't know how many security personnel the admiral had, but three, including the OIC, looked to be KIA.

There was a pounding on the back doors, and Ryck suddenly knew this was a suicide mission. The fuckdicks didn't plan on escaping. They'd locked or jammed the doors.

"Push to the right," Ryck told Bert and Hecs. We're too bunched up."

Something large crashed into one of the fuckdicks, sending him flying to bounce horribly into the back of a row of chairs. It was Corporal Hailstone in full gladiator fury. Still moving incredibly fast, he crashed into another.

The fuckdicks might have been ready to die for their cause, but they couldn't have imagined being torn apart by this vision from hell. The fuckdick screamed in terror as Hailstone tore one of his arms off.

Two troopers spun in their tracks to confront the monster Marine, and the nearest one, only 15 meters from Ryck, exposed his neck. He was raising his Reinmaster when Ryck's dart took him at the base of his throat.

The second fuckdick managed to get off several shots as Hailstone closed in on him. The corporal nearly took his head off with one ham-fisted blow before the big man, stopped and looked at the hole in his gut.

Fuck! Ryck thought, though not taking time to stop his firing.

Corporal Peyton Hailstone, UFMC, looked at Ryck with a beseeching expression as he slowly sank to his knees and toppled over.

"Fucking die you traitor scum!" Colonel Edison screamed in rage as he ran down the aisle, rifle ablazing.

He wasn't really aiming, but the rounds were coming so fast that Ryck had to duck behind the chair as shattered pieces of plastic flew into the air. Head down, he caught a glimpse of the admiral, surprisingly alive, if obviously hurting and gasping for air.

Grubbing hell! He's got on armor, Ryck realized.

The rounds stopped for a second, and Ryck risked a glance over the edge of the chairs. A trooper, eschewing the aisle, had jumped up on the back of the chairs and was hopping from one row to the other. He was stepping to the B aisle when Ryck coolly shot the trooper's unarmored foot. With a screech, the man tumbled to bounce off the back of the chair and fall into the next row from Ryck. He heard some thumps of fists on flesh and hoped it was the fuckdick getting pummeled.

"You've got someone on your right!" he yelled out to Bert and Hecs, who just reached the end of the row.

Someone jumped up to grab the fuckdick who was just poking his rifle around the last chair to take the two Marines under fire.

It took a second to realize it was Michiko MacCailín. While a big woman, she was still getting up in years, but she had no problem spinning the trooper around while she lifted at the bottom of his torso armor. Ryck wondered if she was trying to throw him, but when she yelled "Shoot the bastard," he knew she was exposing the man.

It would have been a long shot for his Ruger, but not for Bert, who rolled around the edge of the row and fired two shots up into the man's belly. Both Michiko and the trooper dropped, and Ryck hoped the darts hadn't passed through the fuckdick and into the governor.

There was a sudden silence. The attack had only taken 40 or maybe 50 seconds, but Ryck counted only eight down. There were four more, now taking cover. And while there were five armed Marines, including Huckmaster, the four troopers outgunned them.

There was a scurry of movement at the sides of the hall, but it was only people crawling to get out of the way. Moans sounded from among the chairs, and the smell of blood, piss, and shit overpowered the air cleaners.

"Here he is!" someone shouted a few meters down from Ryck, which was followed by the sound of a shot.

Down the row on the other side of the admiral and his entourage, General Horace Huckmaster rose up to fire five shots down at the trooper. The return fire caught him in the middle of the chest, sending him sprawling.

Ryck immediately vaulted over the backs of the Row A chairs, falling on a cowering woman. As the trooper who had just killed the general poked his head up to see, Ryck fired his remaining darts at the man. One or two of the darts found their way through the man's armor, and he collapsed in a boneless heap.

"Sir! Don't do that!" Çağlar shouted as he vaulted over the row to land beside Ryck but on the legs of the same women who Ryck had landed on.

She grunted and looked at them wild-eyed, but she didn't say a word.

Ryck dropped his Ruger and pulled out his Bianchi. The small gun made a surprisingly big hole when its rounds hit, but it had even a shorter effective range than the Ruger. He checked the load. Eight rounds.

"Give up, General! Your traitor partner is dead. Your civilian puppet is dead. Your revolt is dead!" Edison shouted from a few rows over.

"You, what's your name," he asked someone.

Ryck heard a mumble, then "Louder! So your hero can hear you!"

"Kia, Kia Heinz. Please don't hurt me!" a female voice cried out.

Ryck motioned for the gunny to vault over to the next row.

"I won't hurt you, dear," Edison shouted out, which was followed by a single shot and some muffled cries.

"Oops! I lied. Now even your Kia's dead. And I have more here with me. Are you going to stop me?

"You what's your name?"

"Please don't!" a male voice cried out.

"Your name! The general needs to know who he's killing!"

Ryck knew Edison was doing this to bring Ryck out in the open, to kill him. He knew that as the co-chairman of the provisional government, he couldn't give in. He had bodyguards who needed to sacrifice themselves for the greater good, and without him, the opposition would peter out and fade away. The Council would prevail.

But Ryck, as a man, as a Marine, simply could not back down. It was not in his DNA. Chandanasiri had said the two of them were the servants of the people, and that nameless man facing Edison now, he was one of the people.

"Now," he told Çağlar as he jumped up and started running over the backs of the chairs just as the fuckdick he'd shot in the foot had done. He knew about where Edison was, and he headed for it, trusting himself to keep his footing.

"I've got him!" a voice cried out to Ryck's right as a fuckdick rose up from his ambush to take Ryck in his sights.

Ryck tried to push forward, to make the trooper miss. His target was only two steps away.

Ryck flinched as the fuckdick targeted him, expecting to feel the burn of the round at best, dark nothing at worst. But he'd forgotten Çağlar in his focus. The big Marine crashed into the fuckdick, sending both to the ground and out of sight.

With one more lunge, Ryck launched himself over the last row just as Edison raised his head, probably expecting to see Ryck shot. What he did see what Ryck about to crash into him.

The man was a professional, even if just a fuckdick. He had risen with his weapon at the ready, and he tried to swing it around to engage the diving commandant. It was too late. Ryck fell past the muzzle and onto Edison as the fuckdick commander pulled the trigger. Ryck felt the concussion of the muzzle blast, but not the round itself.

Ryck's knee slammed into the edge of a seat back in the row and the two men fell. Ryck landed on his left shoulder, immediately dislocating it. Pain shot up both his leg and arm, and he almost dropped his Bianchi. He squirmed around as Edison reached up to take Ryck by the throat.

Good God the man is strong! Ryck realized.

He pulled up his right arm with the handgun, and with lightening reflexes, Edison shifted his grip to grab Ryck's arm, stopping it.

Both men came to the realization that the younger colonel was stronger than Ryck, and Edison's face broke out into a smile as he started to force back Ryck's hand.

Grubbing hell! I beat two capys, and I beat a Klethos d'relle. I'm not going to let a fuckdick beat me.

But Edison didn't seem to share that opinion. He started to bend Ryck's hand back, the muzzle of the Bianchi swinging to Ryck's face.

Ryck tried to fight back, but it was a lost cause. But he'd beat the Klethos, even if she was stronger. And he'd done it by being nasty, by being the meanest dog in the fight, just as Seth MacPruitt had pounded into his skull so many years ago.

With his legs tangled beneath him, with his left arm useless and his right in Edison's grip, that left one thing. He pounded forward with his forehead, catching Edison in the nose. Edison screamed but held on until Ryck opened his mouth and bit down with all his might on the man's bruised nose. With a wrench and his jaws locked, Ryck pulled back, a good portion of the fuckdick's nose in his mouth.

One of Edison's hands instinctively reached for his face, and that was all Ryck needed. He wrenched his arm free and rammed the Bianchi under Edison's chin. He pulled the trigger, and the fuckdick's brain rained on crouching people all the way back to Row M.

Ryck let the body slide back, turned his head, and spit out Edison's nose. A man was staring at him, probably the one Edison was going to kill next.

Ryck wrinkled his face and told the man, "Tastes like shit," as he tried to spit out more of the blood that coated his mouth.

"Sir, sir!" Çağlar shouted, his big body having a problem getting to him. He was stepping on people who were still trying to burrow into the flooring.

"There's one more, Hans! Get the hell down!"

"I surrender!" A voice yelled from only one more row over. "Don't shoot!"

At the same time, with a crash, the outer doors opened. Dozens of sailors, Ryck's three Marines, Seth MacPruitt, and 11 fuckdicks burst inside.

Ryck spun to take the troopers under aim as all the men spread out.

"Are you OK, General?" a Navy chief asked. "Where's the admiral?"

"Disarm those troopers," Ryck shouted out.

"What?" Lieutenant Chou, one of the FCDC team leaders and the man in command of the ten fuckdicks who'd just charged in, asked, confused. "What do you mean?"

"Your commander killed Dr. Gnatson and tried to kill the general and the admiral," Çağlar shouted, his anger clearly showing.

"But, no, that's impossible," the lieutenant said, but sounding unsure.

His men wavered, and as the three Marines and the sailors turned on them, meekly gave up their weapons.

"Sir, I don't know anything about this," he protested to Ryck.

"Maybe, but until we do an investigation, you are all under arrest."

Ryck was pretty sure the lieutenant was telling the truth. He and his men had been stationed outside because they weren't part of the plot. But better safe than sorry.

With people streaming out of the hall, the conference was over. The small medical staff, there to treat a slip and fall would be overwhelmed as the wounded were taken out. The dead would be left where they were until later. He needed Hecs to take charge and organize things.

"General Nidischii', where's the sergeant major?" he shouted over to where he could see Bert standing with Governor MacCailín.

Bert looked up, then slowly shook his head.

Ryck's heart fell, and he broke into a run, mindless of his throbbing foot. He stopped just before reaching the two.

Please, don't let it be!

But it was. Sergeant Major Hector Phantawisongtong, UFMC, Ryck's oldest friend, lay on his back in a pool of blood. Most of his head was gone. There was no chance of a resurrection.

Ryck's vision narrowed, and he stumbled, grasping at a seat to keep on his feet.

Hecs!

With a sudden cramping, Ryck bent over and threw up. Part of his vomit splattered on his friend's cooling feet.

Michiko MacCailín stepped forward and knelt, her arm around Ryck's shoulder.

"I know you were close to him. But put it behind you. You can grieve later. We've got dead and wounded here, all thanks to the Council, and the holocams are recording. What you do now will affect our future. Grieve later, but lead now!"

Ryck looked up. The holocams on the back platform were unmanned as the operators had fled, but they were still recording.

She was right. Ryck reached out and took Hecs' hand, giving it a squeeze.

"Semper fi, brother."

He took a deep breath, and then stood up. Trying to keep from limping, he marched to where Admiral Chandanasiri was still sitting surrounded by a doctor and a dozen staff.

"Are you OK?" the admiral asked as Ryck strode up.

"I understand why you had to do this your way. Politics are a fact of life. But now, it's on. I intend to bring it to the Council and their minions. They opened up Pandora's box, and I will make them pay. You've done your thing, now it's time for me to do mine. Are you with me?"

The admiral struggled to sit up straighter. He glanced in the direction of the holocams.

Ryck leaned forward and whispered into the admiral's ear, "Forget the grubbing cams. Forget the politics. You can be chairman when all of this is over for all I care. But right now, I need to know if you are with me, because yes or no, I am going to war!"

As Ryck stood back up, the admiral struggled to get to his feet.

He looked at Ryck, then in a loud voice proclaimed, "Of course I'm with you! We all are with you. The Council showed their true colors, and now we'll make them pay, together!"

Ryck looked at the admiral dispassionately, then spun around to walk off.

"Gunny, get our security detail and recover the assistant commandant, the sergeant major, and Corporal Hailstone. I want to be off-planet in 15 minutes. We've got work to do."

TARAWA

Chapter 18

"The First Brother wants to schedule a conference call," Jorge told Ryck.

With Huckmaster resurrected but in a regen coma, Ryck had elevated Bert to assistant commandant and sent him off just that morning to Admiral Chandanasiri. Jorge then slid into the Chief of Staff billet.

"About Hailstone?" Ryck asked. "How about blaming the Council? They're the ones who sent in Edison."

Corporal Hailstone had been zombied and was undergoing resurrection. The doctors didn't give him much hope, though. As screwed up as his DNA was, the further stress of a resurrection was going to send his stem cells into overdrive. The doctors doubted they could keep ahead of the Brick long enough for Hailstone to wake up.

The problem was that Corporal Hailstone was not a Marine Corps asset, to put it crudely. He was an asset to humankind, one who had defeated a Klethos queen after the imposition of the new rules of combat. And the Brotherhood, along with others, was livid, to say the least. Even though their own vicar had been killed in the assassination attempt, their ire was aimed solely at Ryck.

Ryck knew he'd been wrong in allowing Corporal Hailstone to attend the conference, but he hadn't pulled the trigger. It had been Edison and his men, at the behest of the Council.

And it was the Council. The lone survivor, the trooper who had decided at the last moment a suicide mission was not in his best interests, had confirmed that they had been ordered to join the evolutionaries for just such a mission.

Ryck had been tempted to pawn the issue off on Governor MacCailín, who had taken over as the new chairman of the CAC, but the decision had been his, and he needed to face the music. But he really, really hated dealing with the politics. He had a war to conduct, not play make-nice with foreign heads-of-state. And that war, at least their first offensive action, was to kick off in three days.

But there was something else that Ryck was going to do despite the planning going on. And despite the pleas from his new chief of security. But he wouldn't miss it for the world.

"OK, I'll be back here at 1600. Schedule it for his early morning, whenever that is. Maybe his mind will be still half asleep," Ryck told Jorge.

"Roger, that, sir."

"And, I've got to get out of here. Is the Stork ready? Storks, I mean?" he asked.

"Inbound now."

"Then I'm done here. I assume Çağlar's in the outer office?"

"Yes, sir, as nervous as a cat in a rocking chair factory, but he's there. He thinks this is a bad idea."

"Along with Colonel Browne and about everyone else. What about you? You haven't said anything."

"Well sir, I didn't see any reason to express my opinion. I know you're going no matter what, so why waste my energy?"

"Smart man, Jorge. And that's why you're going to make a great chief of staff."

The two Marines left the inner office and into the outer where Çağlar jumped to his feet.

"This way, sir," he said, opening the hatch to the passageway.

"Vivian, I don't care who calls, I don't want to be bothered."

"Yes, sir."

"Well, I mean, it depends," Ryck said, altering his first statement.

"I've got it, General. If God calls, I'll push him through. Anyone else will have to wait until you come back," she said.

"Sir, the birds are almost here," Çağlar reminded him.

Ryck let himself be escorted out of the office. Two Marines in street clothes and armed with both M77's and riot guns fell in on either side of him.

Armed guards inside the headquarters, Ryck thought with scorn. *What have we come to?*

Ryck could hear the three Storks land as he reached the front entrance. Not one to take him, but three, so anyone wanting to shoot him down would have to choose which bird he was in. And with a flight of Wasps overhead providing cover, Ryck didn't think anyone could get close to him. But Dunderdunk Browne had been insistent, and he was backed by Bert and probably the entire general staff.

Ryck felt guilty at the expenditure of manpower for this, but there was no way Ryck would miss this ceremony.

Ryck got into the third Stork. All three lifted off and started weaving some crazy pattern. The trip, which should have taken ten minutes, stretched out to over fifteen. As the Stork flared into a landing at Camp Charles' LZ, Ryck let out a small sigh of relief. All the commotion concerning his security had gotten to him, to his embarrassment. He was a combat vet, and a little trip like this got to him? He was getting soft.

Sams, Dunderdunk, and Colonel Joab Ling, the training command CO—and at least a dozen bodyguards—were waiting at the edge of the LZ with a small golf cart.

All that fuss, and a golf cart? Ryck thought as he tried not to laugh. *And not even an armored cart?*

Ryck shook Colonel Ling's hand. "Good to see you, Joab. How're you holding out?"

"Busy, but we're managing. With the surge ops, well, no rest for the wicked, sir."

Ryck had full confidence in Ling. Ryck had first met PFC Ling back when Ryck was a sergeant, and he'd thought Ling a useless dirtball at the time. But the man had proven himself in combat time and time again, as indicated by the Federation Nova on his chest. Not all warriors made good managers, but Joab Ling was both—he was on the potential fast-track to take Ryck's job someday.

"Well, lead on, commander," Ryck said. "I don't want to keep everyone waiting."

Together with his bodyguards, a newsie ran alongside the golf cart recording Ryck's short jaunt to the parade deck. Ryck didn't know how to look professional and worthy while sitting in an E-Z-Go, so he just wished the man would stop. Mercifully, the trip was only two minutes, and Ryck got out, shook a few hands of the worthies, and took his place in the Guest of Honor's seat in the bleachers.

"Glad you could make it, sir," Sergeant Major Ito said, taking a seat next to him.

"I'm sorry to have thrown all of this at you, but we needed to get this up and running and you were the most experienced Marine available," Ryck said. "If you think it's ready, then I'd like to get you back to Headquarters where you can get back to your duties."

"I'd be honored, sir. And I'm sorry about Hector. He was a good man."

"Yes, he was," Ryck said, turning away quickly to watch the start of the march-on.

Four series of recruits—almost Marines—marched onto the parade deck. Ryck's heart gave a little jump as he saw the guidon bearer for Series 67-11. A feeling of pride washed over him as Recruit Benjamin Hope-of-Life marched ramrod straight, ready to start his career as a Marine.

"He earned it, right?" Ryck asked the sergeant major.

"Every bit of it, sir. You have my oath on that. Colonel Ling knows who he is, and I think one or two others, but to his DIs, he was just one more broke-dick recruit. Only he wasn't so broke-dick after all. He's going to make a fine Marine, sir, a fine Marine, and you should be proud of him."

Ryck didn't know if the sergeant major was just kissing his ass or not, but Ryck was proud. Ben, more than Esther and more than Noah, was his pride and joy. He saw himself in his youngest son, and while he would never admit it, Ben was his favorite. And now he was about to become a Marine.

The class was oversized because of the surge, and 689 young men stood proudly in the afternoon sun, sweating in their blues,

Ryck knew, but overjoyed to have succeeded. It was only yesterday, it seemed, when Ryck himself was standing out there, in another era, but in the same place spiritually.

The drill instructors marched the recruits into formation before turning them over to the officers. The colors were marched on to the music of the band. Colonel Ling gave a short speech, but Ryck's eyes were glued on Ben, everything else going over his head.

"And now," Joab Ling said, "I have the honor to present to you our guest of honor, a man I would follow to the gates of Hell themselves, a two-time awardee of the Federation Nova, the Commandant of the Marine Corps, and the Co-Chairman of the Federation provisional government, General Ryck Lysander!"

The recruits seemed to stand taller, and the guests applauded Ryck as he stepped up to stand beside Colonel Ling. He tapped the little sound bud on his collar, making sure it was picking him up.

He swept his gaze out over the recruits, trying not to linger on Ben. Montero had prepared a policy speech for him to give, but this was not his day, it was not a time for politics. In front of him stood 689 men who were about to become Marines. This was their day. Ryck was very aware of the horde of holocams recording the event, but he tuned them out. What he had to say was for the recruits.

"Recruits! Today is the day you become United Federation Marines. Today you begin the rest of your lives. Some of you will serve a tour, then go back to your previous lives. Some of you will fall in battle. And some of you will make a career of the Corps. But no one can change history. Today you will be Marines, and that will never leave you. That will define who you are, *what* you are.

"All of you enlisted during the current crises. And all of you could be thrust into battle soon, fighting fellow Federation citizens, maybe even fighting friends and family. But let me make one thing perfectly clear. Those who choose to fight for the old regime are not our enemies. They may be misguided, they may be foolish, but we are fighting for that factory worker in India on Earth just as we are fighting for the shopkeeper here in Tarawa. We are fighting for all citizens, to make the Federation their protector instead of their oppressor.

"So when you are out there in a week, in a month, in a year, and you have to bring arms against others, remember that. Fight like the devil dogs you are, close in with and kill those on the other side, but after this is over, when they have surrendered their arms, it will be your job to protect them. Our enemies are those who pervert and corrupt power for their own ends, not those enslaved to them.

"We were formed from 48 different marine corps. Each infantry battalion has a patron unit, one of those 48 corps, and we honor those units and the battles they fought, from Belle Isle to Iwo Jima to Isla Clarión to Mount Derby. Now it's your turn to create new honors and keep the tradition alive."

Ryck turned to look at the bleachers. Not many family members had come to witness the graduation, but given the situation, that was to be expected.

"Parents, brothers, and sisters. Friends and girlfriends. Wives. I want you to look out over these recruits, these men, and feel the same pride I feel when I look at them. These men are putting themselves on the line for those less able to defend themselves, and that should fill you so full of pride that your heart is about to burst. You gave us boys, and we are giving you back men."

He turned back and faced Joab.

"Colonel, I believe these recruits are waiting for something?"

Joab stepped forward and faced the formation.

"Class, atten-HUT!" he called out.

With four series commanders in a combined class, it was a little awkward, so Joab had decided that he would administer the oath to them en masse. Each recruit had given the oath upon enlistment, but it had been a tradition over the last ten years or so to re-administer the oath during the graduation, marking the transition from recruit to Marine.

The orders went down the line as the recruits came to attention and then raised their right hands in unison.

Colonel Ling shouted out the oath, repeated by each recruit:

I, state your name, *do solemnly swear, to support and defend the Articles of Council of the United Federation of Nations, against all enemies, foreign and domestic; that I will bear true faith and allegiance to the same and above all others; and that I will obey the orders of the Chairman of the United Federation and the orders of the officers appointed over me, according to the Uniform Code of Military Justice. So help me God.*

There had been some concern about the wording of the oath, but the SJA, backed by Ryck, insisted that the oath remain the same. Anything else could invalidate their claim to be the true and legal government of the Federation.

"Congratulations, Marines!" Joab said.

There were no cheers or breaking of the ranks as might be expected. The Marines stood tall and silent.

The lieutenant pressed into duties as the parade adjutant stepped forward and shouted out, "Personnel to be promoted, front and center . . . MARCH!"

The senior drill instruction for each series turned to take the series guidons, and the four new privates executed a right face and marched to the edge of the formation before conducting two column lefts, coming to a stop in front of Ryck and Joab.

The adjutant called out:

To all you shall see these presents, greeting:

Know ye that reposing special trust and confidence in the abilities of Giovanni Listman Caster, Ivan Stevanivitch, Benjamin Hope-of-Life, and Quincy Stapleton Lee, I do appoint them a Private First Class, meritoriously, in the United Federation Marine Corps, to rank as such from the fourteenth day of August, three-hundred sixty-seven.

This appointee will therefore well and diligently discharge the duties of the grade to which appointed by doing and performing all manner of things thereunto pertaining. And I do strictly charge and require all personnel of lesser grades to render obedience to appropriate orders. And this appointee is to observe and follow such orders and directions as may be given from time to time by seniors acting according to the rules and articles governing the discipline of the Armed Forces of the United Federation.

Given under my hand this fourteenth day of August, three hundred sixty-seven.

Ryck Lysander, General, Commandant of the Marine Corps.

As the adjutant finished with Ryck's name, the depot sergeant major, Joab, and Ryck stepped forward to the first honor graduate.

"Private First Class Caster, congratulations," Ryck said as he took the stripe from the sergeant major and pinned to the Marine's left arm as Joab pinned the other to his right.

It was a very temporary fix, good enough for the Marine to march off, but not permanent. But with dress blues, it was about as good as they could get.

"Where are you from?"

"Daxby, sir!"

"Daxby? Good people there. I know they're proud of you. I'm proud."

Ryck thought PFC Caster was going to bust right out of his blues he was puffing up his chest so much as Ryck shook his hand.

The three senior Marines did a right face and moved to the next Marine.

"Private First Class Stevanivitch is the Class honor grad with a score of 99.2," Joab said as Ryck faced the Marine.

Hell, I never came close to that!

"That's simply outstanding, Marine. Really outstanding," Ryck told the beaming Marine. "Your promotion is well deserved. How did you manage to do so well, if I can ask?"

"Just never gave up, sir. A Marine never quits!"

Ryck shook Stevanivitch's hand and stepped off to stand in front of Ben.

"And's what's your name, Marine? Ryck asked, his voice almost catching.

"Private First Class Benjamin Hope-of-Life, General!"

Ryck nodded as he took the chevrons and attached them to Ben's arm.

Some bicep he's got building there, he noted.

"And, uh. . ."

Ryck had rehearsed something say, to let Ben know how proud he was, how much he loved him, but his thoughts were jumbled. He wished Hannah was there to share the moment, and that choked him up.

"How did you find Mount Motherfucker?" he spit out.

What the hell am I saying?

Ben seemed to think about the same thing as he wrinkled up his brow and said, "Uh, it was tough, General. But as Recruit Stevan . . . I mean Private First Class Stevanivitch said, a Marine never gives up. My father taught me that."

"Your father must be a remarkable man," Joab said from beside Ryck.

"Yes, sir, the best!" Ben almost shouted.

Ryck couldn't say anything. Nothing would come out. He shook his son's hand, then stepped off to the last Marine to be promoted.

He didn't quite remember what he said to PFC Lee, but he hoped it was memorable for the Marine's sake. He didn't quite remember getting back in front of the formation as the four marched back to their positions. He didn't quite remember Joab Ling ordering the series commanders to dismiss their Marines.

What he did remember, and always would, was the cheer that erupted from the throats of 689 Marines, and the look of unadulterated joy on his son's face as he flung his cover high into the air.

Chapter 19

Two days later, Ryck was in the MCCC, following Operation First Strike. First Battalion, Tenth Marines, under Lieutenant Colonel Case Twelvetrees, landed on Wrym, the terraformed moon of Demeter VII.

The moon had little strategic value. It had been an experiment some 200 years earlier as the first attempt to terraform a moon of a gas giant. Titan in the home system had been colonized and mined, but no gas giant's moon had been completely terraformed to allow for humans to live unprotected on its surface. The attempt on Wyrm was a success—in theory. Demeter VII exerted such a huge gravitational pull on the moon that building there was problematic, however, so while the moon had an atmosphere and a somewhat diverse biology, any attempt to develop the moon was abandoned within a couple of decades. Now, the moon was both a scientific waystation and the closest outpost of the FCDC to the void.

Invading and taking Wrym was more of a statement than anything else. It shouted out to the rest of humanity that the provisional government was ready to assume its duties to defend humanity from the unknown, and it was a message to the Council that the provisional government was coming.

The FCDC garrison numbered more than 1,000, but with some 2,500 Marines landed and now advancing on their main post, it was only a matter of time before they fell. They were putting up somewhat a fight, though, which surprised Ryck, but was in line with Jorge's predictions.

"Another WIA," Sergeant Major Ito said as the display counter clicked up one.

The Marines had landed over five hours ago, and the supply depot had been secured at the cost of two Marines KIA and one WIA. As with most PICS operations, killed in action outnumbered the wounded. Now, two more Marines had joined the WIA count and two to the KIA. These were small numbers compared to the scope of the operation, but each one hit Ryck in the gut.

Ryck knew that he was a good warrior, able to think on his feet and improvise. He knew he had a knack for outmaneuvering his foe. But he'd never learned to slough off casualties, something the great leaders had to be able to do. Leaders had to fight with big arrows on the battleplans, not down to the individual Marines.

Twelvetrees was moving his battalion methodically, too slow for Ryck's mind. He kept looking at his comms, set up with a direct link to both Twelvetrees as well as Colonel Warner, the overall operational commander. But he restrained himself. Too many cooks spoiled the soup, and too many commanders just got people killed.

"Top? Do you have anything to drink?" Ryck asked Marten Ekema, his throat dry.

"Right here, sir," the top said, handing Ryck some frothy, citrusy concoction.

Ryck didn't know what it was, but it cut through the dryness of this throat while calming him down.

"This is so much harder than leading men into battle," he remarked quietly to Jorge.

"True, but don't worry. Twelvetrees and Warner have this in hand. It's only a matter of time. And this is just the first salvo, the slapping of the glove across the Council's face. They'll probably be a lot more fights, and we don't need you tied up in knots during each engagement. Look, they've breached the outer walls of the fort."

Ryck had been facing Jorge, and now he swung around to the command display. Marines in PICS were pouring into the fort to minimal resistance. Within two minutes, the FCDC commander surrendered.

"*Acta est fibula, plaudit,*" Jorge said.

Ryck just looked at his chief of staff expectantly, waiting for the translation.

"The drama has been acted out. Applaud."

As is on cue, the MCCC broke into applause. Marines and sailors stood up and congratulated each other.

It wasn't us, Ryck thought. *It was them out there.*

But he accepted Admiral Mendez' congratulations.

This was just a dress rehearsal, though, against an overwhelmed FCDC force. When they faced fellow Marines, as Ryck was sure would happen, it wouldn't be such a cakewalk.

Chapter 20

"Look, I don't care if you have to shit them, just take care of it," Ryck almost snarled at Lieutenant General Marv Oppenheimer, his chief of logistics.

God I'm beginning to hate him, Ryck thought as the general wearily sat back down in his seat.

He wasn't being fair, he knew. The general was working 20 hours a day trying to make sure Marines had what they needed when they needed. And with Ryck's plan of light engagements, the Marines were very dispersed. Ryck's wasn't too concerned about any ground forces, but he didn't want to be concentrated enough to tempt the loyalist Navy into a strike against him.

Besides, the issue with the PICS coldpacks was not Marv's fault. The manufacturer and the main depot for the coldpacks, which were vital to the operation of a PICS, were on First Step, which was firmly in loyalist control. And when General Nottingham had led the defectors to Alexander, he'd managed to raid several of the remaining depots, right under the Marines' noses, of a number of vital components, the coldpacks being one of them. Now, Marv had just informed him that they had only enough of them for six days of total combat. It pissed Ryck off to no end that his mighty force of PICS Marines could be sidelined for want of a 128 credit part. What hit doubly hard was that the theft was done under his watch. He'd already been sworn in as commandant.

Ryck had already canceled one operation by Fourth Division, and he'd delayed another because of the shortage. That galled him bitterly. But better to use the PICS where and when they could do the most good.

Ryck was fed up to his neck with the seemingly innocuous problems that seemed to be able to bring the government to a halt. Ryck wanted to focus on the fight, to bring others to his cause, and crush the old regime. But he couldn't. Life went on. Couples were getting married. Babies were being born. Kids were going to school.

People were aging and dying. Nothing stopped just because a full-out war was waiting to break out. And all those people, all those babies, all those in ill health demanded attention. Ryck tried to push as much of that off to the CAC, but some things just had to be done by him, it seemed. This morning, before his staff brief, he'd spent almost 45 minutes with two different heads of state who demanded Ryck's attention. It just never ended.

"What's next," he sourly asked Jorge.

"This one," his chief of staff said, punching up an Immediate Action Issue on everyone's PA. "Weyerhaeuser is demanding that they receive transport for their wheat crop."

"But Weyerhaeuser declared for the loyalists," Ryck protested.

"That was their headquarters in Seattle. This is Weyerhaeuser 4, and their wheat is needed by our own people."

"So Weyerhaeuser 4 is with us?" Ryck asked.

"And more than a few others," Sams said. "It sort of depends on where they're located. Can't rightly up and move their superfarms."

"And why can't they ship their own crops?"

"Because WSC, the Weyerhaeuser shipping company, is with the loyalists," Jorge said.

"So let me get this straight. Our Weyerhaeuser, the good guys, their headquarters are with the bad guys, but the company's ships, which go where they want, can't take their grain because they're with the bad guys."

"Yes, that's about right, sir," Jorge said.

Ryck shook his head and simply looked up at the ceiling.

Un-grubbing believable. I've got Marines about to go into battle in five hours, and I have to deal with this?

"Admiral Mendez," he said as he sat back up. "Does the Navy have that kind of lift?"

"Well, technically, yes, but the CNO[11] won't release them for that. It would tie them up."

[11] CNO: Chief of Naval Operations

Ryck as tempted to call up the admiral and make a demand, but he knew his liaison was right. They couldn't tie up warships because some company's wheat would spoil. Let them stick it in stasis until the war was over, and screw the cost.

"General Simone, I want you to get a hold of Major Pohlmeyer when we're done here. Offer him licensing concessions, whatever, but convince him that some this would be a windfall for some Confed shipping firm. See if he'll bite."

"Roger that, sir," Jorge said.

"Look, gentlemen, I've got to get to an operational brief, so let's wrap up this mundane garbage in record time. What's next?"

God save us from ourselves, he thought, his eyes glazing over as Jorge brought up the next issue.

Chapter 21

"Fourteen ships lost," Vice Admiral Jeremy Mendez said, his voice low and in shock.

The two men were alone in Ryck's office as his Navy liaison broke the news.

"My old ship, the *Marseilles*, was one of them," the admiral continued.

The Marines were on a clean sweep. Five operations with unqualified success. The Navy had not been so fortunate. First, there was their lack of ability to protect the GT-3 hub. Now, fourteen ships had been lost in a devastating ambush.

This is one fucked up war, Ryck thought, putting a hand on the admiral's shoulder.

With the UAM, spearheaded by the Brotherhood, demanding that neither Navy use weapons of mass destruction on any planet, the loyalist and evolutionary navies were somewhat hamstrung. With all their massive power, they couldn't do much, and that had relegated this "war" to a handful of small Marine raids that while successful, did nothing to swing the tides between the two governments. The Navy was left more in a protective mode.

Navies are led by fighting men, though, men who don't shirk from battle and even seek it out. And when a 20-ship task force from Third Fleet started aggressively patrolling near the Corinthia, a loyalist planet in an otherwise evolutionary sector of space, the task force was ambushed, losing 14 ships. The loyalists lost five ships in one of the fiercest naval battles in recent years. Twenty-five thousand men lost. All for what was simple posturing.

Ryck wasn't sure how a naval force of equal capabilities could ambush another in open space, but now wasn't the time to ask. Mendez was not in any shape to answer.

The newsies would be all over this, Ryck knew, and that could be devastating. There were still planets and nations that had not declared, and others could be swayed from one side to the other as the tides of war turned. This was more than a naval victory for the loyalists; it was a political one.

Ryck knew he had to act before the damage became entrenched.

"Vivian, get me my staff, and ask General Yarrow to come over with his Three. Tell them it's going to be a long one.

Twelve hours later, he looked out over the cluttered conference table to where his and the division staff and looked back expectantly at him.

"So are you men up to it, Javontee?" he asked his First Division commanding general.

"Yes, sir. Just give us the mission," Major General Yarrow said eagerly.

They all want to hit back, he realized. *But are we acting or reacting?*

Ryck walked back to his comms station.

"Get me Admiral Chandanasiri," he said.

"But sir, it's 3:20 in the morning on *Prometheus Station,*" the voice on the other side said uncertainly.

"I didn't ask you the time. I simply gave you an order."

"Uh, yes, sir. Right away sir."

Less than 20 seconds later, a sleepy-sounding voice picked up the other side, the visuals off, "Yes?"

"Admiral, we're hitting First Step. We're going to pay those bastards back."

Cheers erupted in the conference room, perhaps none louder than that of Vice Admiral Jeremy Mendez'.

Chapter 22

"You keep telling me that your government is supporting us," Ryck told Major Pohlmeyer. "But I don't see much in the way of that."

"We have ships in your sector," the major said, sitting in the chair across from Ryck in the inner office. "And we moved your grain for you, sir."

"One of your companies did, and at rather exorbitant rates, I might add."

"That's the risk factor of doing business in a war zone," the major replied easily. "And don't forget we backed the Brotherhood in getting the ship-to-shore decree through the Universal Assembly. That was to your advantage. The Council is much better armed in that regard. Your advantage is in the Corps, and the decree protects you more than it protects their ground forces."

"They have five times our number in FCDC troops," Ryck said.

"Really, General? You are comparing Marines with glorified policemen?"

"Those 'policemen' were dedicated enough for a suicide mission to take out our leadership."

"I'm not denigrating their bravery, General. But they have neither the training nor equipment, despite what General Filmont is attempting, to conduct advanced military ops," the major said.

Which is true, Ryck acknowledged to himself.

Not that he was going to give into the major.

"FCDC or not, there are Marines facing us for the op. And our Navy will be outgunned," Ryck said.

"And just where is the target?" the major asked for the third or fourth time since the meeting began.

"Commit some ships, and I'll tell you."

"And as I told you, while we do support you, we think it would be a strategic mistake to reveal our hand too soon, especially as you are requesting naval support only as an augmentation. I hardly think Admiral Chandanasiri would approve any mission if his ships will be significantly out-gunned."

"The admiral is supporting me on this. This is our mission, not the Navy's," Ryck said with more than a bit of an edge in his voice.

"Of course, sir. I understand. I'll pass back your request again to New Mumbai. That's all I can do."

"And your recommendation will be?" Ryck asked, knowing full well that the major's opinion carried significant weight.

Ryck still didn't know exactly what position Titus held, but it was not a simple major in the Confed security branch.

"I will see what I can say about it," the major said.

Which means you will not support it, Ryck thought as he was beginning to understand diplomatic-speak.

"Please do," Ryck said. "And thank you for coming by."

"I'm at your beck and call," Major Pohlmeyer said, standing up. "I will revert back to you with the response."

With friends like these. . . Ryck thought as the major turned to make his exit.

"Well?' Tomtom Copperwait asked as he, Jorge, and General Yarrow came into the office after the major left.

"No go. They don't think it's a *'strategic'* move at this time. Sorry about that, Javontee, but you're going to have to count on only those ships that Third Fleet is cutting loose for this.

"Well, you said this would happen, sir. So now we just do more with less," the division commanding general said.

"Which is what we do, gentlemen. We are Marines, after all.

"So let's get cracking. Operation Winter Snatch will be a success, and I will accept nothing less."

Chapter 23

Ryck reached into the closet and slowly took out the chartreuse angora sweater hanging there. He pulled it into his nose, closed his eyes, and inhaled deeply.

Hannah!

He could still smell her on the sweater. He'd never liked it, but it was real animal fiber, and Hannah had loved it. Now if he could only have her back, he'd buy her a dozen of them.

"General, your son is here," Lieutenant Chou said, poking his head in the door.

Ryck guiltily thrust the sweater back into the closet before turning around to face the FCDC officer. He wasn't sure what he felt about keeping the FCDC around. It had been Colonel Edison and his fellow fuckdicks who'd been planted agents and who'd killed Hecs. But the lieutenant and his team had been assigned the outer corridor by Edison because they were loyal to the evolutionary cause, and some pretty pointed interrogation had confirmed that. The lieutenant had volunteered to undergo a Propoxinal interrogation to clear his men—which of course would have ruined the young officer for any use as the drug fried his brain and that which made him who he was.

Jorge pointed out that men anxious to prove their loyalty were the most trusted of men, and Ryck had relented. Marines guarded the outer perimeter, but the ten FCDC troopers made up half of Ryck's inner security force.

And Ryck's insistence on going home had made things tougher on them. Ryck had moved into the Commandant's quarters, more for ease of security and proximity to the headquarters building than simply because it was the home that came with the billet. But for tonight, he wanted to be in his home at Star City in the Bonnyman Annex, where he'd lived with his family since picking up his first star. It was hard being there without Hannah and the twins, but he felt it was right.

"Thank you, Lieutenant. I'll be right down."

He took a quick look in the mirror. He was in a tattered T-shirt and an old pair of chef's pants. This was not a Marine Corps function but a family one, and he wanted to make that clear. His uniform might have been OK when Ben was a civilian, but now with him a Marine, Ryck just felt better being in old civvies.

Led by Chou, Ryck walked down the stairs to where Ben was standing by the sofa. Ben was in a nice pair of khaki slacks and a button-down oxford shirt (the seemingly civilian "uniform de rigueur" of all Marines throughout the ages), and as Ryck came into view, his son came to a position of attention.

"Relax, son. You're not at boot camp anymore. This is your home."

Ben gave a rueful smile and tried to relax his posture with only a modicum of success.

Ryck gave Ben a hug, and only while looking over his son's shoulder noticed Top Ekema standing in the doorway with one of the FCDC guards who was going through what looked to be carry-out containers.

"What's this? I was going to cook," Ryck asked.

Top rolled his eyes to look up at the ceiling, but Ben was not so circumspect.

"Look, Dad, I know you and mom had this thing going where you cooked us meals from scratch, and you both thought you were pretty good at it, but really, and I say this with love, you both kinda suck at it. And if I'm shipping out in a few hours, I sorta wanted something good."

"What? But our food is good!" Ryck protested.

"Not really, Dad. Now if Noah were cooking, that would be different, but he's not he. . ." he started before stopping as he realized what he was saying.

"I, uh, sorry, Dad," he stammered out.

"No reason to be sorry. I miss him, too. And Esther. And your mom.

"Hey, Top, why don't you plop that down on the table so we can see what you've prepared," Ryck said too loudly, anxious to change the subject.

"Sure thing, sir," Top Ekema said, taking his bag from the guard who'd evidently decided that the top was not trying to poison Ryck.

I'm just surprised he didn't taste it first, Ryck thought.

Both Lysanders followed the top to the dining room table. Top took out the first container and handed it to Ryck.

"Oh, geez, Dad. That garbage again?" Ben said as he saw what was in the box.

"Top, with all due respect, you promised me a good meal. If I'd known you were going to bring bacon with raspberry sauce, I'd have gone to The New Shanghai and gotten carry-out."

"You don't know what you're missing, son," Ryck said, grabbing a piece slathered in sauce and popping it in his mouth.

"And with all due respect to you, too, Sir Commandant, I do know what I'm missing. I've lived 17 years in this family, and we all know your weakness."

"It's sort of a tradition, Ben. . .uh, PFC," Top said, suddenly wondering how to address the young man. Top Ekema had been a friend of the family and had spent quite a bit of time mentoring Noah with his cooking, which of course had brought him into contact with Ben ever since he was about ten. "Your dad likes it, and it's sort of a treat. But I think you'll be pleased with what else I've brought."

The top opened the vac seal of the second container, and the rich smell of boeuf bourguignon wafted out to fill the room. Ryck put down his bacon and leaned forward, his mouth watering.

"Wow, Top! My favorite!" Ben shouted excitedly.

"As if I didn't know that," the top said. "You're the one going into combat, not your dad. So you get your favorite."

The top took out some buttered noodles and then what looked to be organic green beans. Fabricated green beans had a variety of shapes and sizes programmed into the extrusion process, but these varied too much. Knowing Top, he'd ordered them on his own, and Ryck reminded himself to pay the Marine for them.

"Well, sir—and you too, boot—I think I'll get out of your hair so you can enjoy some family time," Top said, taking the empty containers as he left.

"Uh, Lieutenant, can you give us some privacy?" Ryck asked Chou when the trooper made no move to leave.

Chou looked concerned, but he nodded and left, carefully closing the door. Ryck knew he wouldn't stray more than a few centimeters from it until Ryck was back on base.

"So what time do you have to report back?" Ryck asked as he spooned some of the beef onto Ben's plate.

"We've got muster at 0100, so I'm thinking midnight. I'm almost ready to go."

"So we have some time. Let's just sit back and enjoy the meal," Ryck told him.

And that's what they did for the next hour, talking about sports, the latest season of *No, You Won't*, and other inconsequential things. Ryck enjoyed being divorced from the Marine Corps for an hour in the company of Ben. Not general and PFC, but father and son. The upcoming mission was always looming in the background, however, its presence ignored but felt.

After they were done, Ryck cleared the table, picking up a small box he'd previously staged in the kitchen. As he came back out with two coffees, he placed the box down alongside Ben's cup.

"What's this?" Ben asked.

"Well, I'd imagine you could figure that out if you opened the grubbing thing."

Ben rolled his eyes, and then picked up the box, turning it around and examining the outside.

"Geez, just open it already," Ryck told him.

Ben flipped up the lid and stared at the combat knife inside.

"Is this. . .?" he asked hesitantly as he turned the knife over in his hand to catch the light.

"Yes. It's my Hwa Win."

"Dad, I can't take this," Ben protested.

"I know you like that big Kyocera pigsticker of yours, but humor me," Ryck said.

"That's not it. I mean, this has been with you for years!"

"And I'm going into combat again when?" Ryck asked. "I want you to have it. Think of it as a good luck charm. It's brought me back safe and sound each time—well, not always sound, I grant you—and I want you back here when the mission is over."

"I . . . I'd be honored to, Dad. Honored."

Ben put the knife back in the box and lunged at Ryck, hugging him tight with a strength that surprised him. In many ways, Ben was still the little boy in his mini-utilities, hanging around base, loving all things Marine. But now he was a man, ready to face combat for the first time.

His face still buried in Ryck's shoulder, he asked, "But what if I fuck up? What if I don't do my job and someone else gets hurt? What if I'm scared?"

Ryck pushed Ben back so he could look into his son's face. "Of course you're going to be scared. Any sane man would be. But what matters is how you react to it. And I know you, Ben. You are not going to run away and hide. There is a will about you that your mom and I have seen since you were a toddler.

"Don't worry, son. You're going to do fine."

"But—"

"But nothing. Soldiers throughout history have had to face their first battle, and every one of them has wondered the same thing. I had to. Soldiers, straight from training, hitting the beach in Normandy had to. Roman legionnaires facing the Visigoths—and Visigoths facing the legionnaires—had to. And most of them found the strength to do what was necessary.

"You are a fine man, Ben, and I am so proud of you. I know you will do your duty, and do it well."

Ben didn't seem convinced, but he gave a rueful smile and said, "I'm sorry, Dad. I'm just, it's just that I don't want to let anyone down. We're not even in the main assault, you know, so I might not see any action."

"Just be prepared for anything, follow your NCOs and let your training guide you. You'll do fine."

But now Ryck was feeling a little apprehension. Operation Winter Snatch had been in planning for the last two weeks. It was a relatively small operation, but due to the importance, Ryck and his staff had been heavily involved. To Ryck, it had been all big arrows and big units. But as with all battles, the fight was made at the individual rifleman level. It was the Marine or soldier who carried the field of battle or lost it, not the generals back at headquarters.

Ryck had to divorce himself from that individual Marine if he was to be effective. Sometimes individuals had to be sacrificed for the greater good, as he'd discovered, to his dismay, with his brother-in-law Joshua.

But in this case, one of those riflemen was his son. To the general in him, Ben was an asset, a cog in the greater battle, and Ryck had to ignore the potential risk to individuals. This was inhuman of him, but it had to be that way. But Ben was his son, and as a father, he was nervous. As Ben had said, his battalion was in a support position, but the enemy was not known to play along with plans often, and this time, the Marines would be facing not only FCDC troops but Marines who had chosen the loyalist side.

Ryck didn't want to let Ben see his apprehension, so he slapped his son on the shoulder and said, "You up for a game of lightening before you leave? I'd dearly love to crush you once more."

"Crush me?" Ben protested, Ryck's attempt to shift the mood a success. "You've beat me, what, twice in your entire life? Bring it on, old man. Let me teach you a lesson in humility."

For the next two hours, the two Marines played, Ryck winning two hands, but mostly getting stomped by his son. He didn't care. He was happy.

He wasn't as happy when he asked Lieutenant Chou to get the driver to take Ben to his battalion. He waved as the hover left the lot, a smile on his face, though, trying to exude confidence.

"Can I take you back now, sir?" Chou asked anxiously as Ben's hover pulled out of sight.

He obviously wanted to get Ryck back to the safer confines of the base proper.

"Sure, Lieutenant. Let's get on back."

Chou locked the quarters, the click a trigger reminding Ryck that there was still work to do. Ryck forced himself out of dad mode and back to commandant mode. He had a battle to fight. Or rather he had a battle to monitor and give whatever support he could.

Chapter 24

Ryck sat in the MCCC, ready to watch the battle unfold. He chewed on his fingernails nervously.

Throughout his career, Ryck had been personally involved with each of his fights, there on the ground and in harm's way. This was the first time, however, he'd sent a significant number of Marines into a major battle and had to watch from afar.

He hated it.

The battle was out of his hands. He'd done all he could to create the scenario where his Marines could accomplish the mission, but now the operation was up to others. Colonel Richard Gruber was the brigade expeditionary force commander, and it was his battle to fight.

The first salvos of the battle had already been fired. Three Navy monitors and a destroyer had been in-system when the task force arrived. The destroyer had been a known quantity, but the monitors had been stood down and shielded and were a surprise. If it hadn't taken them a few minutes to power up, things could have been hot for the task force's ships. Because of the delay, though, the monitors had been knocked out and the destroyer driven off, and with only minor damage to two task force ships.

The entire brigade made it to the planet's surface unscathed, which was a huge relief to Ryck. Given the UAM's expanded restrictions placed on space-to-ground weapons, restrictions to which both forces were still adhering, the Marines were most vulnerable while shipborne. Once on the ground, only other ground forces could stop them. The Marines would still have to get off the planet and back into Evolution space, but for now, they were relatively secure. Facing the 4,000 Marines were some 18,000 FCDC troops and around 1,000 loyalist Marines, but a planet is a big place, and fewer than 1,500 fuckdicks and all the loyalist Marines were in the objective's AO. Ryck was confident that the brigade would prevail, but they had to get it done before the rest of the fuckdicks could mobilize and form a counterattack, and they had to get back shipboard and in bubble space before the loyalist Navy could get on scene. Ryck's biggest nightmare would be to have the loyalist Navy drive off the Third Fleet task force, stranding the Marines on the planet's surface and allowing the FCDC commander to marshal his forces and attack the brigade when he felt ready.

During the War of the Far Reaches, Colonel Derek Asherton had conducted a successful raid against a Fordham forward installation on an unnamed asteroid in the Pellas system, but after his naval support had fled the system, the Fordites had mounted a large-scale counterattack. Out of ammo and with 75% casualties, he'd surrendered the remainder of his force to the inevitable. Despite the tactical realities of the situation, the Federation executed Colonel Asherton after the war for surrendering. Ryck had no intention of executing anyone if that scenario was repeated on First Step, but he also had no intention of defeat.

"Watch 2/4," Tomtom said needlessly. "Their lead elements are about to enter the complex. Resistance is minimal so far. This is going to work!"

"Where are the Marines?" Jorge asked. "They landed at New Hartford, and that's fewer than 45 klicks from the factory."

The MCCC was packed to overflowing with over 90 techs, analysts, and First Marine Division and Ryck's staff, but most men were keeping their thoughts to themselves, with the top brass doing most of the speaking. Ryck knew that having so much brass in one spot could be daunting, but he trusted his techs to speak up if something turned up at their station that could be important.

"They're there, sir. I can feel it," Sams said.

"I agree with Top Samuelson," Sergeant Major Ito said, one outnumbered SNCO sticking up for another amidst all the stars and eagles.

Ryck said nothing, but he had to agree. If the Council had placed Marines on First Step, they would keep them near the industrial heartland. And with the brigade landing, the more mobile loyalist Marines should have had time to close in on the brigade.

Unless they can't be risked fighting a superior force and have been ordered to withdraw, Ryck thought hopefully.

"Any sign of loyalist ships?" Ryck called out, only 20 minutes since the last time he's asked.

"No, sir," the Navy lieutenant commander monitoring his five ratings manning their comms said. "Nothing."

"He'll tell us if anything changes," Sams whispered to him. "This isn't the Telchines."

Ryck knew a rebuke when it came, no matter how it was worded. And he knew it was warranted. As a captain, Ryck and his battalion had been temporarily abandoned by the Navy in the action against the Confederation in the Telchines. He knew that had affected him deeply—he'd lost his good friend Donte Ward there. And now dredging up thoughts of Colonel Asherton was adding to his anxiousness. But he had to project an attitude of calm confidence. He had to gather himself.

It's just so much harder sitting here with my finger up my ass! Let me do something!

"Roger that, Sams," Ryck whispered back as he took a couple of deep breaths and settled back into his seat.

Ryck just observed the fight, feeling anxious as he watched the display AI that moved the little lights around the battlespace map, but trying to quell any sign of his nerves. He attempted, but failed, to think of those lights as only some war game electrons. No matter how hard he tried, he knew those lights represented living, breathing Marines.

One of those lights represented Second Squad, Third Platoon, Echo Company, Second Battalion, Third Marines, the "Fuzos." Ryck had commanded the Fuzos, so there was that personal connection, but more pertinent to him now, that squad had one PFC Benjamin Hope-of-Life as rifleman. He couldn't tell just which light represented the squad, and no matter how much he wanted to, he resisted the impulse to have the AI identify it, or worse, ask it to identify individual Marines. Still, Ryck kept glancing over to where the Fuzos had established their blocking position instead of where 2/4 was approaching the main objective.

Two-four was advancing quickly. Four minutes after breaching the industrial estate, the lead elements were entering the objective. The cam-relay gave a first-shooter view as the loading dock door was blasted off its track and the lead squad entered the warehouse. The first Marine was cut down by a waiting fuckdick, and the cam-view immediately shifted to another Marine as return fire dropped the small FCDC element.

Several Marines and sailors within the MCCC high-fived and fist-bumped each other as the tide of 2/4 Marines poured into the building, but there was no cheering. Too much could still go wrong, and the longer it took, the more the likelihood was that something would go wrong.

And as 2/4 Marines swarmed Stasis Chamber 5, the loyalist plan started to reveal itself.

"We've got contact at Feed 8," a station tech shouted out moments before the AI brought the feed to Prime.

What had before been a quiet sector of residential buildings five klicks to the east erupted as avatars representing PICS seemed to appear out of nowhere.

"Give me a visual," Brigadier General Jun Kim, the MCCC flag watch officer shouted out.

Moments later, a drone shot confirmed that loyalist Marines in PICS were emerging from three buildings and moving forward to meet the Marine forces. The buildings had to be heavily shielded, but as the loyalists emerged, they were picked up.

"Get me numbers and who they are!" Kim shouted.

Numbers would be helpful, but Ryck knew who they were. Their unit was meaningless at the moment. They were loyalists, bent on stopping the brigade.

Ryck listened in as Colonel Gruber gave orders to orient 2/3 and 3/3 to meet the threat. The loyalists had emerged a little less than two klicks from 3/3's lines, and depending on how long it would take them to get moving, they could be on the Marines within five minutes.

The number of PICS loyalists seemed to quit at 146, which was bad, but better than Ryck could have hoped. Marines on foot followed, as well as several Armadillos.

Ryck knew that the loyalists were vulnerable as they emerged and formed up for movement, but he couldn't access ship-to-ground fire support. The same proscriptions that seemed to favor the Marines overall were a hindrance here.

Almost immediately, mortars from 2/3 and 3/3 opened up, but Ryck knew their effectiveness would be limited against the PICS forces even if more so against dismounted infantry. And as the brigade was a raid force where speed was of an essence, no heavier artillery had been landed.

The brigade was heavy in Storks, and if Colonel Gruber ordered them to hit the loyalists, Ryck would have understood. But those Storks were configured as troop and cargo carriers, and their efficacy against PICS was not as good as a Wasp would be. The brigade's only two Wasps, however, had been shot down by ground anti-air while the two fighters had destroyed the local airfield.

"Who are they? Which units?" General Kim asked the harried station tech.

"I'm getting nothing, sir."

All Marines had biochips that identified them and carried a wealth of information. The Marine sensors should have been able to read those chips, but evidently, the loyalists had either removed them or changed their security access in some way that Ryck's AI's couldn't penetrate yet.

"Wait, sir, I do have one reading. I'm sending it to the big board now," the tech said.

"Son of a bitch!" Sams said as the information was displayed.

The only chip that their sensors could read belonged to Brigadier General Sandy Haunish Peltier-Aswad, United Federation Marine Corps.

"They knew we were coming," Ryck said, more to himself than to anyone else.

"How do you know that?" Sams asked.

"Because the only chip we can pick up is Peltier-Aswad's," Jorge answered, immediately understanding what Ryck had meant. "They want us to know he's there leading the defense."

"But why does that mean they knew we were hitting First Step?"

"Do you think this is a coincidence, Sams?" Ryck asked. "They've got close to 100,000 Marines on their side, and they just happen to pick the commander on their side who knows me the best to lead only 1,000 men there?"

"Well, maybe so, sir. But, what can he do? I mean, he's good, but not that good, especially 'cause we've got them outgunned. And they let us get into the objective facing only fuckdicks. What kind of tactics are those?"

The station techs and officers focused on their jobs. Who was leading the assault had little import to them. But the senior officers around the conference table watched the commandant, waiting to hear his response to Sams' question.

"They don't need to stop us from reaching the objective. They only need to keep us from leaving. And by waiting, we're now as dispersed as we will ever be. This is what a smaller force needs, to be able to concentrate their numbers against a more dispersed force. Numbers as a whole don't matter; it's numbers in a specific area, numbers actually in contact with each other," Ryck said.

"And as far as Colonel, well, Brigadier General Peltier-Aswad, they think that could throw a wrench into things. They think it could affect how we react. They are wrong."

Ryck's heart had jumped when he had seen Sandy's name, and it was still beating hard. Sandy had chosen sides, though, and Ryck would not let personal matters change anything in the conduct of the operation. The fact that the loyalists knew the Marines were coming was far more bothersome, and that meant the loyalist Navy could be much closer than they had thought.

With the entire battle being played out on the display, Ryck glanced back at 2/4's assault. The resistance had either been neutralized or had retreated. Cognizant that a trap could have been laid, Lieutenant Colonel Polizzi, the battalion CO, sent in only one company inside the warehouse, leaving the other companies outside for security. It looked like that one company would be sufficient, and already, the attached Navy Seabee drivers were appropriating the warehouse forklifts and moving material. Ryck listened in as the Navy lieutenant reported that they could start loading in five minutes, and they should be finished in twenty.

Second Battalion, Fourth Marines might have been the point of main effort, but it looked like 2/3 and 3/3 were going to face the brunt of the loyalist counterattack. Colonel Gruber couldn't shift 1/1 to help meet the loyalists as that would leave a security gap covering 2/4 as they loaded up the crates. For the two battalions facing the approaching loyalists, this was one of those times when tricky maneuvers were not the answer. This time, it was who were more determined to win out and who were the meanest sons-of-bitches on the field of battle. This had always been the Federation Marines in Ryck's career, but this time, those were Marines facing the brigade, too.

Unless Sandy had some ace up his sleeve, the brigade should be able to handle his 1,000 Marines. But while the assault on the objective was relatively bloodless, with only eight KIAs and double that number of WIAs, the loyalists counterattack could end up being be a slugfest with large numbers of casualties. Ryck just hoped most of those would be on the loyalist side.

Maybe we should have just used more of the H71's for lift and kept a few Storks as gunships, Ryck thought, second-guessing the plan.

The H71 shuttles had a much better personnel capacity than the tactical Storks, but they were also much slower. Having a few Storks kept as gunships would disrupt the loyalists, but it would increase the time the Marines were on the planet, and if the loyalist Navy was out there somewhere about to pounce, time was of an essence. Ryck didn't want to hold First Step; he wanted to get in and get out in the absolute minimum amount of time.

No, the loyalists had to be met with the two battalions facing them. Ryck had to let the battalion commanders fight the fight.

That didn't keep him from watching the avatars maneuver on the tactical display. The loyalist PICS closed in on 3/3's hasty defense. Facing them was a full company of PICS Marines and two companies of straight-leg infantry, which should be more than enough to turn back the counter-attack.

Ryck glanced up at Jorge, who was concentrating on the display.

Good job on pushing for a company of PICS, he thought.

With lift being a major concern, the brigade had originally planned on only a platoon of PICS per battalion given what they knew about the opposing forces. Jorge had disagreed, and he'd convinced Ryck to step in and overturn the decision, ordering a company of PICS Marines per battalion. Ryck had hated to interfere with the brigade's planning, especially as it bypassed division, but now he was glad he had. Jorge had been right.

A 3/3 M249 opened up, scoring a direct hit on a loyalist PICS, and the battle was joined. Within moments, the battalion and the loyalists were fully engaged.

"First time in Federation history that Marines have fought Marines, and the first time that PICS had fought PICS," Jorge remarked.

Marines in PICS had fought armored infantry before. Ryck had engaged Greater France and Confederation armored infantry himself. But Jorge was correct. This was the first engagement of PICS versus PICS. The history books would note it, and the fight would be examined and re-examined by analysts and historians. That it should come to this, though, was a sad state of affairs.

As the Seabees started loading the first shuttle at the main objective, 3/3 seemed to be holding. But that brought up a secondary concern. The Seabees would be done in another ten minutes or so. The brigade needed to get off the planet immediately, and if 3/3 were still in contact, that would be problematic. Ten minutes was no time at all in a fight of this magnitude.

"General Yarrow, I think you need to go to Contingency 4," Ryck said.

"Roger that, sir. Colonel Peterson and I were just discussing that," the division commander told him.

Contingency Plan 4 was one of many plans that had been formed to take into account enemy actions. The current plan was that as the last of the two cargo shuttles lifted off, 2/4 would be loading the rest of the H71s. 1/1, 2/3, and 3/3 were to start collapsing on the center, loading the Storks to get off the planet. 1/1 and most of 2/3 could still do that, but 3/3 was engaged. In order to break contact and get off the planet, 3/3 would now have to assault the enemy, taking away their momentum and forcing them back on their heels. This would give the bulk of the brigade more breathing room to load the Storks and shuttles.

"Time is beyond discussing it," Ryck said. "We start retrograding in a little over nine minutes."

"Done, sir. 2/4 is already beginning to embark."

With the other three battalions providing security, that was probably a safe bet, but Ryck still would have waited until both cargo shuttles had taken off.

Looking back as the display statistics, Ryck was surprised at the lack of a decisive engagement. 3/3 had only lost two PICS and five infantry Marines, while 2/3, barely engaged, had one KIA. The loyalists seemed content to engage at range instead of closing in. They were seemingly only trying to fix 3/3 in place, which made sense if the loyalist Navy was inbound.

Unless Sandy has something else up his sleeve.

Moments later, Ryck found out what that was.

The display AI's calm voice noted that the three Armadillos had split and were speeding up into contact. Ryck heard Colonel Peterson warn the brigade, but he watched the Armadillos' tracks to determine just what they were doing.

The Armadillos were not much of an asset, Ryck thought. They were too lightly armed, for one thing, even if their 25mm chain gun was an impressive piece of hardware. The engines and suspension had been upgraded since Ryck's days with them, so they were very fast, but their lack of protection was still their Achilles' heel. Given only a slight bit of luck, even a straight-leg infantry Marine could stop one with an M-77 Bunker Buster or M-219 grenade launcher with the anti-armor.

Two of the Armadillos emerged from behind a line of shops fewer than 500 meters out and lurched into their top speed to rush 3/3's lines. Incredibly quick, they closed the distance as the Marines opened up.

"It's a suicide charge," someone said.

Something wasn't right about that to Ryck. First, it was not in Marine culture to blow oneself up to attack and enemy. Second, against ground troops, a trac could use its bulk as a weapon, true. But it was a personnel carrier, not an armored attack vehicle despite its chain gun. To use its gun, it had the capability to stand off at two klicks to engage the Marines. Now the two Armadillos were charging with their chain guns silent.

Ryck's mind was putting together the pieces when at 300 meters out, one of the tracs exploded with such force that the display hiccupped while the AI compensated for the release of energy.

"They're full of explosives!" several people, including Ryck, shouted out in various permutations.

The second Armadillo continued forward despite the intense fire being levied on it.

"The enemy Armadillo has a tungsten-ceramic front plate attached," the AI calmly noted.

"Mother fuck!" Tomtom said in amazement.

The AI had been able to analyze the small signatures being picked up by the surveillance sensors as Marine rounds hit the Armadillo. With some sort of plate attached, the Armadillos would be far more impervious to the incoming fire. Such a plate would be impractical in a maneuver battlefield, but it would give better protection for a frontal assault where all the trac had to do was speed forward.

Which can also be done by remote control, Ryck realized.

Within five seconds, the second Armadillo had just reached 3/3's front lines when it went up, probably hit by someone who had an oblique angle and could hit it in the sides. Once again, the blast was so massive as to cause the display to flicker.

And immediately, the AI registered the carnage. Thirty-five Marines, including ten in PICS, were KIA. Another 62 were WIA.

The third Armadillo, the one that had broken away from the other two, had just come up from a stream bed and turned into 2/3, only 220 meters away. It would be within the battalion's lines within seconds.

Ryck stood up as he watched the display track the Armadillo, willing the battalion to destroy it. He felt a surge of joy, then, when 90 meters out, the trac exploded. Two Marines were immediately listed as KIA, but no one else was even touched.

"Son of a bitch," Sams muttered while Ryck just stared at the data stream.

Ryck was just about to step in when he realized that a multitude of orders was being given to both 3/3 and 2/3. The AIs did not have access to individual loyalists (except for Sandy, who was well back from the fight), but there was more than enough surveillance to plot the main body of them. With the three blasts, their commanders evidently thought the Marines would be in disarray, and they were moving forward.

That was a foolish assumption.

Both battalions were not only ready, but they were also taking the fight to the loyalists. They were charging them—and wreaking havoc. The loyalist assault slowed, then stalled.

"The second cargo shuttle has departed the planet's surface," the display AI passed to the room.

In the lower right corner of the display (from Ryck's perspective) a real-time view of the shuttle lifting off appeared. The shuttle would take a full 35 minutes to reach its ship. By the time it docked, Ryck wanted all the Marines off the planet. That was the plan, at least. But two battalions were in full contact. At some point, they'd have to break off.

But it was the loyalist Marines who broke off first. En masse, the loyalists turned away from the Marines. The uniformity was indicative that they were breaking off under orders and not just running. Ryck thought that meant either the loyalist Navy was about to arrive on scene or that they realized it was too late and wanted to husband their remaining Marines. He hoped it was the latter explanation.

Colonel Gruber ordered the two PICS companies to keep up the pressure while the straight infantry pulled back to their designated or alternate LZs for pick-up. It was a sound decision that made sure the loyalist retreat was not just a feint that could result in Marines being caught as they loaded the Storks.

The two PICS companies did more than put on the pressure. They drove through the loyalists all the way back to the cluster of buildings that had initially shielded them. At one point, Sandy's avatar grayed out. Ryck didn't know how he felt about that, and he wouldn't dwell on it until later.

All of 2/4 and most of 1/1 were loaded and on the way to the ships before the colonel ordered the two companies to stop. They were ordered back to their LZs at top speed. Once again, the colonel had good instincts. The only loyalists who could match that speed were the remaining PICS loyalists, which the AIs put at an estimated 63.

The loyalists didn't give chase, though. They seemed to be done with the fight.

At 42 minutes after the second cargo shuttle lifted off, the last Stork left the planet's surface. Marines in the MCCC seemed to let out a collective breath of relief, but Ryck was very well aware that the fight was not over. The loyalist Navy was out there somewhere, and with more than enough strength to defeat the Third Fleet forces in the system.

The Storks only required about 20 minutes to reach their ships, and Ryck watched the delicate ballet on the display that decried the chaos that had to be occurring among the ships. More than a few LSOs had to be about ready to suffer heart attacks as the Storks came in hot and fast into the hangar bays. Finally, even before the Storks were secured, the last ship was moving out of orbit.

Ten minutes later, it was in bubble space, and only then could Ryck begin to relax.

They had done it!

Ryck stood up and the MCC went quiet. "Gentlemen, great job today. The fight today may not have seemed too important in the grand scheme of things, but it could change the course of the conflict. I want to congratulate all of you. Those Marines conducted the fight, but they could never have been there in the first place without you.

"We've all put in a lot of hours. And we're going to go over this again, but not now. Go home, see your family, have a beer. I'm going to want to see all headquarters staff back here at zero-eight, no make it ten-hundred, tomorrow.

"General Kim, the MCCC is yours again. Everyone else, get out of here."

The MCCC burst out into applause. It had been a dicey mission, and it had gone off better than could have been expected. A success or not, still there were 42 Marine KIAs with a yet unknown number of them who could be resurrected. And while Ryck would have gladly accepted that number prior to the operation, to the families of those men, the devastation would be just as powerful as had the brigade suffered far more during the fight.

"Sams, get me the casualty list," Ryck said.

He'd personally add a letter of condolence to each Marine and sailor's family.

"Well, that went about as well as we could have hoped for," Ryck remarked to Jorge as Marines began to gather their belongings and leave the MCCC.

"Yes, I'll agree with you there."

"No small part in thanks to you," Ryck added.

"I'm not so sure about that. It was Colonel Gruber's plan, his and division's."

"Codswallop, Jorge, and you know it. You need to learn to take credit when it's due. Your fingerprints were all over the plan, not the least was to have a full company of PICS in each battalion."

Jorge gave a small, non-committal grunt and shrugged his shoulders. Over his shoulder, Ryck could see Sams returning, a physical printout of the casualty list in his hand. His expression was something Ryck hadn't seen before, sort of shocky, sort of frightened.

"What is it, Sams?" Ryck asked, wondering what could have affected his stalwart friend.

Without a word, Sams handed over the printout.

Ryck glanced down at it. Forty-two KIAs as he had thought. Seventy-one WIAs, which was a few more than he'd thought, but still quite reasonable. He looked at some of the names. There wasn't anyone he'd known in 2/4, but he'd find out about them before he'd write the letters.

Three-three's list was more extensive, and Ryck personally knew four of the Marines. One of them was Gunny Nunci, someone he knew Sams knew as well.

"Gunny Nunci?" Ryck asked.

Sams shook his head and pointed at the list.

Ryck looked at the final unit, 2/3, the Fuzos. Corporal Yale Haerter and . . .

Ryck dropped the sheet, the world closing in on him.

"I'm so sorry, sir," he vaguely heard Sams say just before everything went blank.

The final name on the list was that of Private First Class Benjamin Hope-of-Life.

Chapter 25

"I'm sorry, sir. I can't let you pass," the nervous lance corporal said, twitching as he blocked Ryck's way, M99 at the ready.

"Do you know who I am, son?"

"Yes, sir, I do, sir. You're the commandant."

"And you still won't let me pass?"

"No, sir. I can't. The gunny, he said don't let anyone except him or the lieutenant pass, and he said not even the Commandant of the Marine Corps, and that's you, so I can't let you pass."

Part of Ryck wanted to blow up, to take out his anger on the young kid. And another time and place, he might see the humor in it. But right now, there was a pretty miserable looking lance corporal standing in his way, and he couldn't take it out on him.

"I tell you what. How about you get your gunny on your comms and ask him to come over here," Ryck said calmly.

"Uh, right sir. I mean aye-aye, sir," the young Marine said. "Uh, Gunny, this is Lance Corporal Davis. I'm on post, and the commandant is here and wants to enter the C-hut,[12] and you said that even if he comes, he isn't supposed to come in. I think you need to get over here."

Within 45 seconds, not only the gunny, but a lieutenant and a major came pelting over the tarmac at a dead run.

"Sir!" the major shouted as he slid to a stop. "I'm so sorry about this! Lance Corporal Davis is over-reacting!"

"Did you tell Lance Corporal Davis that 'even the Commandant of the Marine Corps' wasn't to get past him, Gunny?" Ryck asked the gunnery sergeant.

"Well, yes, sir. But I was exaggerating. I didn't mean to say you don't have access, sir!"

"Well, then, I guess Lance Corporal Davis was just doing his job now, wasn't he? And I'd advise you to be a little more accurate

[12] C-Hut: A temporary building that can be erected within 30 minutes.

when giving orders in the future. Now, if you would like to adjust your orders so I can pass, I would appreciate it."

"Certainly, sir! Davis, let the commandant pass," the gunny managed to get out.

Lance Corporal Davis stepped aside in obvious relief, bringing his M99 to present arms. The major jumped forward to hold open the door as Ryck stepped inside the C-hut.

C-huts were expeditionary shelters, and no matter the configuration, they always had that expeditionary feel to Ryck. This one was no different despite the stacks of pallets that filled it.

This one did not have its own flooring—Ryck stood on the tarmac plasti-crete. By tomorrow, Ryck knew, the pallets would be gone, distributed to the divisions. The C-hut would be disassembled, and there would be no sign of the *raison d'etre* for the mission. Before that happened, Ryck had to see the pallets, to stand among them.

Forty-one Marines and a sailor had died to obtain the pallets. An amazing 28 of them were in the process of being resurrected with very good prognoses.

Ben was not among those 28.

Ryck had watched the recording more than a dozen times. He hated watching it, but something drove him to do it.

Ben and Corporal Yale Haerter had been sent forward 150 meters to emplace mines in front of 2/3's lines when the first two Armadillos hit 3/3. The two Marines were informed that the third Armadillo was heading their way and to take cover. They did not obey that order.

As the remote-controlled Armadillo launched itself out of the depression it had used as an axis of advance and oriented on the battalion, it would be able to reach the lines within eight seconds. The two Marines, without looking at each other, chose to stand and engage the Armadillo. The impacts of their first four grenades were clearly visible as they hit the armored plate bolted to the front. Several larger impacts were also visible from the battalion's heavier weapons, but they had no better luck in stopping the trac.

Other men, seeing the behemoth bearing down on them and knowing that they were having little effect on it, would have dove out of the way and let it past. Neither Yale nor Ben was one of those kind of men. Not only did they stand their ground, they leaned *into* the trac, pouring fire into it. And as the Armadillo churned toward them, mud flinging from the tracks, its front armor still protected it. But the extra armor was not on the side, and from less than 20 meters away as the trac passed them, both Marines fired their grenades. Corporal Haerter's grenade hit the trac a split second before Ben's, and that was enough. The heavily-ladened trac exploded in an immense fireball, momentarily whitening out the surveillance. As the AIs adjusted, parts of what used to be an Armadillo fell back to the muddy ground.

As for Ben and Yale, they had simply disappeared.

Even had the two Marines been in PICS, they would almost certainly have been killed as a result of the blast. In their skins and bones, there was not much left for the rest of the Marines to find to bring home.

Ryck looked at the Hwa Win combat knife he'd carried into the C-hut. It had been recovered from the field and given to Ryck earlier in the day. The sturdy blade was warped, and the heat had turned the tungsten-carbide blade hues of blue and gold. Other than a fused M219, the knife was the largest piece of Ben, or at least Ben's gear, that had been recovered.

Ryck looked back up and surveyed the pallets. They had come at a cost—not too high, all things told, to General Ryck Lysander, Commandant of the Marines Corps. But it was unbearably high for Ryck Lysander, father.

The Hwa Win was warped, but it didn't have a problem with the strapping of the nearest pallet. With a snap, the strapping fell away. Ryck pulled down the top bundle and cut it open. Inside the bundle were eight PICS cold packs.

He picked one up and turned it around, just looking at it. All that pain for two kg of a fairly old-tech piece of gear. They weren't much, and cost only 128 credits each, but without them the multimillion-credit PICS would be dead in the water within ten minutes. Ryck's operation had bought the Marines time. Each PICS in the inventory now had a month's worth of operating potential.

He carefully placed the coldpack back into its position.

I'm so sorry, Hannah!

The tears were not there, though. He was numb, he was angry, but he was not grieving. That bothered him to no end. He felt the presence of the grief, it seemed to him, deep down inside of him, down where he was pushing it. He didn't think he should be able to do that, and that made him wonder if he was normal, or if he was just an automaton formed by years in the Corps. For the sake of his humanity, he wanted to let it out, to let it consume him. But he was the commandant now, and he couldn't afford the time. He hoped that if—when—the grief did strike, it would be at a time when it wouldn't get in the way of his mission.

He looked down one more time at the Hwa Win in his hand for a moment, before he suddenly whirled and sunk the warped knife to the hilt in one of the cold-packs. Without a word, he turned and strode out of the C-hut.

The war was not over yet.

Chapter 26

For the next two months, Ryck never left Headquarters. He had a bed put in his office, he ate in the cafeteria when Top Ekema could not entice him with favorites, and he hit the weight room and bikes late at night when he could be alone. Jorge, Sams, and Çağlar tried to draw him out, but they'd given up, instead just hovering around to be there if needed.

Without his family, Ryck told them, there was no reason to use his quarters. The more time he spent at his job, the sooner he'd be reunited with Hannah and the twins.

And despite a direct link to any specific causation, things were going well from a military standpoint. While the Navy battled essentially to a draw in three skirmishes since the ambush off Corinthia, the Marines had won a flurry of limited battles, taking two stations, and destroying facilities on three planets and a loyalist country.

Others were taking notes. Two planets declared for the evolutionaries, and emissaries from all over human space were making contact. With the prohibition against massive naval strikes on planets, the situation favored the provisional government and the Marines, and Ryck was not about to let up. Admiral Chandanasiri had asked Ryck to slow down the tempo—it was his ships and chartered civilian vessels that had to transport the Marines overall—but Ryck said they had to fight while momentum was on their side.

And now, Ryck was going over the after action report of the capture of Geilgud. Intel (provided by the Confederation) had revealed that this stalwart loyalist planet, close to the home system, was not as loyalist as they had been led to believe. With First Marine Division, in whose AO Geilgud lay, in the process of taking the huge PTA Mining fields in the Stravonskiya Belt, Fourth Marines, en masse, "snuck" in behind the loyalist major defenses and quickly took down the capital, defeating a much larger FCDC and local militia force. There were not enough Marines in the

Corps, probably, much less in Fourth Division, to hold the planet, but the Confeds had been right. The citizens were not hard-and-fast loyalists. Far from it. They welcomed the Marines, in fact, and within two days, the Fourth Division was leaving a planet that was being organized as the newest member of the "legal" Federation.

Ryck was proud of how quickly Major General Hank Uttley, the Fourth Marine Division commanding general, had reacted. Between Hank, Jorge, and Ryck, they were the only flag officers from their NOTC class.

What with Geilgud and the other planets declaring for them, there was now close to a parity between those who supported the loyalists and those who supported the evolutionaries. And with the navies somewhat hobbled, the balance was shifting away from the loyalists.

Yes, things were looking up, and for once, Ryck had a true hope that they would prevail.

He was glad for that, and he felt a sense of justified pride. But as he settled into his cot in the back of his office to try and get some sleep, he was not a happy man.

Chapter 27

"Shit happens, sir, in war. That's the way it's always been," Zeke Montero said.

"That 'shit' was 11,000 civilians," Ryck said coldly.

"Loyalists," Montero said.

"They were civilians, and we don't fight civilians," Ryck said, rising to his feet.

I hate this guy!

Jorge interrupted before Ryck could explode. "Zeke, those people did not deserve to die. We targeted the complex, and we leveled it before we realized who was in it. Yes, 'shit happens' in war, but we need to rise above the level of barbarians. We're the good guys, right?"

"Of course," the public affairs liaison said as if brushing it off. "But issuing an apology won't do anyone any good, and it will stop the momentum we've been experiencing. We can't just say we fucked up. Maybe later, after we're in power, we can run an investigation, and you can slaughter a sacrificial lamb, but not now."

I'd really like to slaughter you, Ryck thought, hoping the man had ESP and could catch that.

"No, for now, the loyalists cowardly used civilians as human shields. We reacted accordingly, and once we realized that civilians were being sacrificed by the militia, we stopped our assault."

Jorge jumped in again, cutting off Ryck and technically taking responsibility for the decision. "OK, run with it. But I want a comment that we will conduct a thorough investigation."

"I can live with that, as long as there isn't one until after we're emplaced in power," Montero said happily.

"Does he realize that those were people there, people we killed?" Ryck asked as Montero left the office.

"Of course he does," Jorge said. "He just doesn't care. This is all a game for him. He'd be happy with us or back on Earth with the loyalists, just as long as he got to play in the sandbox."

"I caught what you did. You gave the order. Are you trying to protect me in case this all goes rotten?" Ryck asked.

"Not really, sir."

"Bullshit, Jorge. You really need to learn to lie. Remind me never to put you in front of the holocams to explain this."

Jorge shrugged, then looked at his PA to see what was next. Ryck reached out and pushed the PA back to the table's surface.

"Should we have authorized the thermobarics?"[13] Ryck asked.

Ryck knew that one of his weaknesses was second guessing himself after the fact, but he really wanted to know what Jorge thought.

"No, we shouldn't have, but that was hindsight. Given what we knew, it was the right decision. I hate that maggot Montero, but he was right. Shit happens."

"But 11,000 people!"

"And you saved 12 billion on Ellison? Look, sir, I grieve for them, and I swear I'll get to the bottom of what happened now and not later. But we chose thermobarics to destroy the complex before the militia division could launch a counterattack. OK, it was bad intel, but our decision, based on what we knew, was sound. And we prevailed in the mission.

"And now, sir, with all due respect, we've still got the list from the CAC, all 62 items that need yours and the admiral's OK. We've got the conference with the admiral at 1100, so we need to put Watershed behind us and get about the job of governing."

[13] Thermobarics: a type of explosive that utilizes oxygen from the surrounding air to generate an intense, high-temperature explosion.

Chapter 28

Slowly, but surely, the noose was tightening around the loyalists. Goods and material were flowing into the evolutionary side, most through supposed independent ship owners, but in reality, Confederation contractors. The Confederation paid the bills, too, for the imports. At least, they lent the money for the bills. Ryck knew they were incurring a huge debt to the Confeds, and he didn't like that one bit, but it was better than slowly being strangled by the loyalists.

The loyalists had instituted a draft for their Marines, something that hadn't been done since the Federation was formed, while Ryck's Marines had more volunteers than the ability to train them up. Camp Charles was bursting at the seams.

Ryck dispatched Sergeant Major Ito once more to the camp to make sure that standards were still maintained and to do an initial evaluation of how women were being integrated into the process. It would do no good to have more Marines, but Marines who could not perform as Marines should.

On the ground, the Marines had racked up one victory after the other. Watershed had the huge number of civilian casualties, but from a military standpoint, the Marines had swept aside a full five divisions of militia, so even their lone setback was not much of one from a tactical standpoint. Yes, the Tenth Marine Brigade was stuck on Killdeer, trapped by five loyalist ships, but they had succeeded in destroying DelPat's largest munitions plant first. The loyalist ships couldn't do anything about the Marines on the ground, but they could keep them there, so Ryck and the admiral decided just to leave them on Killdeer for the time being. That kept two cruisers, a frigate, and two destroyers tied up and out of the fight, and the Marines in the brigade were able to train unmolested for their next mission, whenever that might be.

Ryck knew it must be killing the Council members. The Navy could sit off and devastate the Marines on the ground, but their hands were tied.

Ryck and Jorge had discussed at great length the probability that the loyalists would continue to hold their hand. They still had the advantage in ships, but as more forces and governments defected to the evolutionaries, even that could shift. Ryck was fairly certain that the Council would not let that happen, the rest of humanity be damned. Jorge felt that they might try something else, but he doubted that they would resort to planetary bombardment.

Jorge was right, as it turned out.

"Vice-Bishop Hadad is here to see you," Vivian said over the intercom as Ryck was eating a quick tuna sandwich at his desk.

"Did I miss something? Did we have an appointment?"

"No, sir. He just showed up at security. He says it's vital that he sees you."

The vice-bishop was one of two Brotherhood representatives to the provisional government. "Observer" was the term they used. The Brotherhood was officially neutral, so it would not appoint an ambassador, but the fact that the previous ambassador on Earth had not been recalled spoke volumes to Ryck. And that pissed Ryck off to no end.

According to the provisional government's own Intel, the proscription against space to ground weapons was instigated by the Brotherhood in an effort to protect Mother Earth. They hadn't realized until after it had been rammed through the Universal Assembly that the proscription would heavily play into the evolutionaries' hands. By then, and with the Confederation's full support (who realized the tactical advantage that gave the evolutionaries, according to Pohlmeyer), it was too late for them to back down.

Ryck wanted to tell the vice-bishop to make an appointment, but he knew he couldn't. Even if the Brotherhood favored the loyalists, Ryck could not afford to piss them off.

"OK, tell security to let him through," Ryck said.

He wolfed down the rest of the sandwich, licking his fingers clean. It might have been just tuna, but Top Ekema, in his indubitable fashion, had somehow made it into something special, and Ryck had just treated it like the ghost shit they ate while in their PICS.

Ryck started to get up to wash his hands, expecting he'd have to shake the vice-bishop's hand, but on second thought, he sat back down. If he had a little spit on his fingers, what of it?

It took the vice-bishop a few minutes to be escorted in to see Ryck, not that Ryck got anything done in the interim. He wondered what the man had to say that was so important, getting the feeling that it would just be one more headache. He looked at the clocks above the door—the one on *Prometheus*-time showed 21:52.

At least its working hours here, he thought, guessing that the vice-bishop's counterpart with the Third Fleet was showing up to see the admiral at the exact same time.

"Vice-Bishop, what can I do for you?" Ryck asked as Vivian escorted the man inside the inner office.

Ryck offered his licked-clean hand to shake, but the vice-bishop didn't take it, merely handing over a recording stylus instead.

Damn! Didn't get him with that, Ryck thought as he took the stylus.

"A physical message, Vice-Bishop?" Ryck asked. "Isn't that rather cloak-and-dagger?"

"General, I'd appreciate it if you could read it," was all the vice-bishop said.

Curiouser and curiouser.

Ryck stared at the envoy for a moment, then shrugged and started to touch it to his PA jack, stopping just short of actually making the transfer. Instead, he opened his drawer and took out a stand-alone PA, making the data transfer onto it.

It wasn't that he didn't exactly trust Hadad, and his security would have scanned the stylus, but still, there was no use taking any chances.

The screen flickered, and to Ryck's surprise, the smiling face of Hopkins Garrison, the loyalist First Minister and Ryck's former boss, appeared. Ryck stopped the recording and looked at the vice-bishop.

"Have you seen this?" Ryck asked.

"Yes, I have. It was sent via a Level 12 encryption to our liaison office. I was ordered to personally make a physical copy under a CAD, so only I have seen it. I was told that my superiors have not seen it, yet.

A Copy And Delete was a high-level transfer that moved a file from one system to another, deleting the file from the first host.

"And this is a CAD-1?" Ryck asked.

"CAD-2T," the vice-bishop said.

Well, no shit, Ryck. Come on. Think before opening your mouth!

It had to be sent to the vice admiral first, so a CAD-1 wouldn't work. It had to be at least a CAD-2, allowing for one more transfer, which Ryck had just done. And it being a CAD-2T, or terminal, then it could be viewed only once.

"I think I need to get some other people in here," Ryck said.

The vice-admiral held up the stylus cap.

"I've been instructed that if you attempt to do that, or if you try and remove me from your office, I'm to delete the file," the vice-bishop said.

Ryck stared at the man.

Is he bluffing? Security should have caught a remote trigger, but it's certainly possible. Grubbing hell, I'll just watch the damned thing. It's not as if I need witnesses when I relay what it says.

His mind made up, he turned back on the recording.

"Major General Lysander—or, General, if you want—I'm not sure you'll be too surprised to hear from me. You've done pretty well, I grant you, in out-playing that idiot Fred Nottingham, so maybe you've been expecting this.

"As long as I'm mentioning General Nottingham, I've got to ask you, is he still working with you? He might as well be," the first minister said with a laugh.

What the grubbing hell? The first minister's playing comedian? What is all of this?

"Eh, not that it matters. He's out the door one way or the other. And when I say 'out the door,' I think you know what I mean."

Yeah, I know. The Federation does not suffer losers lightly. A quick trip out to the Cube[14] *and an equally quick execution.*

"Well, if you haven't figured it out already, the chairman is not too happy with you, and he's not pleased with the way things have progressed. I might add that he's not happy with me, either, considering you worked for me, but no hard feelings, huh?"

The first minister's flippant attitude was beginning to piss Ryck off, and he wished the man would get to the point.

"And lately, your little band of oathbreakers. . ."

That stung Ryck. No matter the justification, he had broken his oath.

". . .has managed some surprising gains. Do you know that on Varius, the oddsmakers have raised you from 23% to 54% to succeed? The chairman was livid when he heard."

54%? That's up from 43% yesterday. What changed in the last 24 hours? Ryck wondered.

None of the gambling meccas in the Federation—either one—had issued odds, but humanity is vast, and gambling is part of the human DNA. The two biggest gambling planets were the "twin V's," Vegas and Varius, and Varius was in the Confederation, so it was not surprising that they had been keeping the odds and taking bets. They knew how to extract wagers on just about anything.

"So, as you can imagine, he's ordered a game-changer, and that's what I'm here to convey to you."

Ryck's heart skipped a beat. He looked up at the vice-bishop, but the man was giving away nothing.

The recording switched from the first minister, sitting behind his desk, to a barren room with three people in it. It was not the best quality recording, and it took Ryck a moment to recognize the three.

"Hannah!" Ryck said, jumping to his feet, unable to contain himself.

Hannah and the twins were sitting at a table, the only furniture in the room. The twins were on one side, Hannah on the other. Hannah and Esther were holding hands across the table.

---

[14] The Cube: an orbital prison located beyond the moon's orbit

After about five seconds, the recording switched back to the first minister.

"Well, Ryck, it's like this. We're pressing charges against your family. Treason, of course. The trial will be quick, the trip to the Cube quicker. All completely legal, of course, I might add. Oh, your Confed friends might scream and shout, but the law is the law."

The blood rushed from Ryck's head. He'd been worried about his family, despite the assurances from intermediaries that they were fine. And this was why. He knew that the Council wouldn't hesitate to use them against him. He'd been hoping that his family would be kept out of the fray, but that had been naiveté and wishful thinking.

There was no doubt in his mind that the first minister was telling the truth. It would be a quick trial, and then his Hannah, his Esther, and his Noah, would be taken up to the execution chamber in the Cube. Hell, they'd just take them behind the courthouse and shoot them like dogs if capital punishment was still allowed on Mother Earth itself, and that rule was one they'd never broken in the 290-odd years since the Tripoli Accords which ceded most of the control of the planet to the Federation to administer.

"Did you know this?" Ryck shouted at the vice-bishop, needing to let loose at someone, anyone.

"Yes, I'm sorry to say. We do not condone this, of course."

"But you're willing to let it happen!"

"It is not in our control," the vice-bishop said quietly.

". . .sign of a traitor ship, and we might not wait to take them to the Cube. Accidents do happen, you know," the first minister was continuing.

Ryck pushed the vice-bishop out of his mind. He had to listen. He'd missed the first part of what the first minister had just said, and he couldn't afford to miss anything else.

"I hate to be the bearer of bad news—no, the hell with it. I don't hate it. I'm rather enjoying it. We had such high hopes for you, and now you've screwed me and stabbed me in the back. I'm not that far from the Cube myself, so to be honest, I'm happy I was the one chosen to give you the message.

"So it almost pains me to tell you there is a way out."

A way out? How? Ryck wondered, hope springing to life.

"The thing is, we need a trial, and a public trial is best. And who better to stand accused than the great oathbreaker himself? The one who ordered his men to slaughter 11,000—or maybe that was 50,000—civilians on Watershed?

"Oh, before you get your panties in a twist, that might not be quite what happened, but the truth is written by the victors, don't you know?

"But you know what I'm getting at. You for them. An even swap. You come in, and we release them, as simple as that."

Ryck's subconscious probably knew that was coming, and hearing it was almost a relief. There was a way out for his family. Ben might be gone, but Hannah and the twins could live.

"Now I can say you've lived a good life, that you've survived battles, the Brick, and all that, but let's not get bogged down with sentimentalities. Let's keep it pure and simple. You for them.

"You've got 24 hours to decide. You know my secured line. I haven't changed it. Dial me up and say 'Pantry Elephant.' That will clear you to me. Don't call me, and your family dies. Forget the access code, they die. Call me to tell me to fuck off, they die, and the next time you see them will be a holo of them being executed.

"Twenty-four hours, Ryck. Let me know."

The recording cut off as Ryck sank back in his chair, his emotions a whirlwind of despair and hope.

"General, I—"

"Get out," Ryck said with a surprisingly calm voice.

He had some thinking to do.

Chapter 29

"Bert, I need you to get back here ASAP," Ryck told the assistant commandant.

Bert's sleep-filled eyes looked back from *Prometheus Station* where Ryck had just woken him up. Bert rubbed his eyes, yawned, then seemed to focus on what Ryck was saying.

"Sure thing, but what's up?" he asked, stifling a yawn.

"I don't want to pass it over comms," Ryck told him. "I'll leave you a message on a stylus. It'll be in the top left drawer of my desk."

"You'll be gone?" Bert asked as he swung his feet out of the bed and sat up at the edge. "Where will you be?"

"It will all be on the message."

Bert wrinkled his brow as he listened before saying, "Roger that, sir. I think we have a courier run at 1300 our time. I'll be on it."

"No, I want you to leave now. Do what you have to, but get back here."

"I . . . sure, I can get a ride. But—"

"No buts, Bert. I'll explain it all on the stylus."

"Aye-aye, sir," Bert responded, clearly brimming with questions he wanted to ask.

"I've got to go. Just. . .just take care, OK?" Ryck said, quickly closing the connection.

He stared at his blank PA screen for a full moment before he recorded the message to Bert, which appointed him as the new Commandant of the Marine Corps. This recording would be seen by others, so other than a "Good luck," he didn't explain much.

That wasn't fair to his friend, he knew, so after transferring the recording to a stylus, he decided to record a more personal message. He explained the situation with Hannah and the twins and why he was giving himself up to the loyalists.

It's still a shitty way to say goodbye, Ryck acknowledged to himself as he transferred the recording to a second stylus, affixing a "Personal for General Nidischii'" label on it.

Ryck had intended to consider long and hard on his course of action, weighing the lives of his wife and kids against the future of the Federation. Intellectually, he knew their lives were almost meaningless in the grand scheme of things. But their lives were not meaningless to him. And while he knew he was important to the cause, he was not really necessary. He knew he was a warrior, but he also knew for this fight, he was a symbol more than anything else, despite his positions as a co-chairman and the commandant. And as a symbol, he didn't have to be alive. In fact, it might be better if he were dead, not only so he wouldn't have any more Watersheds that could tarnish his image, but humans tended to idolize their fallen leaders more than when they'd been alive.

Ryck also knew that his absence would not handicap the Corps. Bert was a better manager than he was, and he had his fighting chops as well. Far from hurting the Corps, having Bert in the position would be a benefit. That was his rationalization, at least.

Within five minutes, which was all he could manage in a vain attempt to make a reasonable decision, he had decided on the course of action, the one he knew he'd make from the minute he'd watched the recording.

A concerned Gunnery Sergeant Çağlar came into the office and handed Ryck a flight plan. Ryck barely glanced at it before punching in the number on his PA. Various whistles and chirps sounded before Ryck heard a single, long beep.

"Pantry Elephant," he said slowly and clearly.

Within a few seconds, the first minister was on the other line. "That was quick. I saw you had viewed my little message to you just 35 minutes ago. So?"

"I'm coming in. I'll be on the sloop *FS While Away*, registry number FS8739-4464. Gunnery Sergeant Hans Çağlar will be on board with me. The—"

"No, you need to come alone," the first minister interrupted.

"And who will take back my family? Gunnery Sergeant Çağlar is coming. The ship's transponder will be broadcasting. We'll land at McHale—"

"No, Earth, at the Cairo FCDC port. Not Luna."

"I'm not negotiating with you. I'm telling you how this is going down. I need to make sure my family is released, and I don't trust any one of you."

"I may be an opportunistic asshole, Ryck, but have I ever lied to you?"

"No, not to the best of my knowledge, you haven't. But you don't have control over the situation, and the chairman could be playing you, knowing I'd believe you."

"Touché, mon général," the first minister said with a wry smile. "You do have a point. So what are your conditions?"

"I want you to clear Hangar D. You, and you alone, will escort my family into the hangar. We'll bring the sloop into the hangar and lower the ramp. I'll get out and you will release my family. I'll say goodbye, they'll go to the ship, and as soon as they pierce the gate, I'm yours."

"And what's to stop you from bolting for the ship as well?"

"Nothing, except for the ships and fuckdicks you'll have lurking around."

"OK, I think I can arrange all of that."

"Oh, and I guess I should tell you that I'll be packing explosives."

A sudden look of concern replaced the first minister's almost condescending attitude.

"And why is that?" he asked, his voice cracking ever-so-slightly.

"Because if you do anything to harm my wife or kids, or if you try to intercept them, I will detonate the charges."

"Killing yourself? You're going to have a date with the Cube's executioner for a dangle[15] anyway, so why should that be a deterrent?"

[15] Dangle: slang for hanging

"Because I'll have deprived you of your show trial, of your need to show your blind followers that you caught the big bad rebel leader," Ryck answered, hoping that he'd guessed right. "You need me alive."

"You're not thinking of trying to take both of us out there, are you?" the first minister asked.

"No."

He seemed taken aback by Ryck's abrupt response.

"And how do I know that?"

"I'll come back with your own response to me. Have you ever known me to lie?"

The first minister smiled and seemed to relax. "Once again, touché. OK, we'll play this out your way. It won't make any difference in the end.

"When can I expect you?"

"We'll file a flight plan as soon as the ship's AI calculates it all. Just be sure my family is there waiting," Ryck answered.

The two men stared at each other for a moment before Ryck said, "I guess that's it. I'll be seeing you."

He cut the connection, and only then looked up at the gunny. Çağlar looked miserable as he stood there, wringing his hands.

"Thanks, Hans. I couldn't do this without you."

"I shouldn't be helping you, sir. Its treason! I'm helping you kill yourself."

"No, it's not treason. You are one friend helping another. And there's no one else I would trust to get my wife and kids back to safety.

Çağlar did not look convinced, but Ryck knew he'd obey. The man was the very definition of loyalty, and he'd march into hell and back if Ryck asked him to.

"Security?" Ryck asked.

"You're cleared. I told Sergeant Pickers that you have a secret meeting with the CAC, and his team is going to escort us out one of the service tunnels, and then get us to the port."

"And the ship?"

"Fueled and waiting. I showed the authorization you gave me to the director and told him only that a VIP would be going to an undisclosed destination."

With the tight security, Ryck had wondered how he'd be able to sneak off Tarawa. He knew that if anyone got wind of his plans, he'd be stopped, and he wasn't going to let that happen. With Çağlar's help, though, he thought his plan should work.

For the next six long, almost unbearable hours, Ryck carried on his routine. He'd been sure Jorge would have noticed his state of mind during the 2000 meeting with his principle staff, but his friend hadn't acted any differently.

After that meeting, Sams and Jorge had shared the Bourbon BBQ ribs and potato salad that Top Ekema had brought in. Ryck usually loved the ribs, but this time, they were tasteless. And as much as he loved Sams, his old friend's drawn-out story about a liberty adventure in New Davao had been more annoying than anything else, and Ryck had finally pleaded a headache and the need to get to sleep early. This would be the last time he'd see the two Marines, and here he was cutting them off.

Some friend I am, he thought as he lay on the rack in the back office feigning sleep. He'd have to lay there in the dark for another two hours before Çağlar came to collect him. Only he wasn't feigning. Somehow, he really had fallen asleep, which was a godsend. Anything was better than being alone with his thoughts.

"Sir, it's time," Çağlar said quietly, his hand on Ryck's shoulder, shaking him awake.

Ryck woke up with a start, then bolted to his feet.

"I'm ready," he said almost guiltily.

He gathered his wits, and then picked up his small travel kit. It was pretty light, not that he'd have much need for anything in it. Following Çağlar, he left his office without a backward glance.

Two guards were waiting for them in the outer office, and they led Ryck and Çağlar down the darkened hallway. The headquarters never shut down, of course, but the "Prime Passage" was pretty empty. General Boniface had the duty, but he'd be down in the MCCC at this hour.

The two guards led Ryck and Çağlar into a service corridor, and with more than a few twists and turns, they reached a hatch that opened into the night air. A golf cart was waiting that whisked them to the small HQ spaceport some 15 minutes away. Normally used for shuttles and Storks, it was big enough for a sloop, one of the few classes of ships that both landed on planets and entered bubble space.

The port director was a retired Navy master chief, and he seemed surprised that no one was accompanying the two Marines. He offered to drum up a pilot to fly them, which Ryck refused. Sloops were popular among the extremely wealthy, and they were pretty much self-flying. Once the destination was entered, the ship's AI did the rest.

Ryck thanked the port director, then shooed the well-meaning man off. Five minutes later, with Gunnery Sergeant Çağlar by his side, the *FS While Away* took off. Ryck nervously awaited any attempt to turn him back, sure that the director had smelled something fishy and had contacted someone. A sloop was pretty much hands-free, but that meant it was easily controlled by port AIs. It wasn't until an hour later when the ship entered bubble space that he could relax.

He was on his way to rescue Hannah and the twins.

LUNA

Chapter 30

The *While Away* looked like a civilian vessel, but it was military, and its guidance system kicked in as it approached McHale Base. Hovering above the lunar surface, it followed the tractor assists to Hangar D. The tarmac was deserted, an oddity, but Ryck knew there were eyes on the sloop as they edged in.

Ryck was both excited and in anguish at the same time. He'd finally see Hannah and the twins, but the sight would be too brief. And it would be the last time he'd see them, he knew. This was it, and that was something with which he'd come to grips. But the closer he got to his family, the less he wanted to accept it. Various schemes popped into his head of how he could rescue his family, then get away with them himself, but that only happened in Hollybolly flicks. That was not real life. Anything he tried would not only fail, but his family would pay the price. He forced those fantasies from his mind.

Most sloops had actual windows of crystallized carbon-4, a concession to their civilian use. Ryck was standing in front of the *While Away's* front windows, anxiously trying to spot Hannah. As the ship eased its way through the hangar gate lights flared up, blocking his view. Once the tail end of the ship cleared the gate, though, the lights ceased, and standing at the far end, only 150 meters away, were Hannah, Esther, and Noah.

He gave the suicide belt he wore one more op check. The slowly flashing green light confirmed that it was armed.

"Stay in the ship," Ryck told the gunny as he bolted for the hatch.

"Shouldn't I be with you?"

"No, and I need you to get the hell out of here the second they get onboard."

"Sir, are you sure?" Çağlar asked plaintively. "There's still time to change your mind."

Ryck took a moment to look back as he hit the hatch release. Hans Çağlar had been with him a long time, and it must have taken a tremendous effort for him to actively assist Ryck. Ryck wanted nothing more than to run to Hannah, but instead, he took a step to the gunny and put his arms around the big man.

"It's OK, Hans. I've lived longer than I ever should have, and I'm at peace with myself. Thank you for everything."

He felt Çağlar shudder as a sob escaped the gunny. Ryck held the hug a few moments, then slowly let go.

"Take care of them, Hans," he said as he stepped out the hatch.

"Dad!" Esther screamed, her voice a dagger into his heart—and a bolt of joy at the same time.

Ryck wanted to run, but he felt they were all still in deadly danger, the first minister's promises notwithstanding, and a mindless run in enemy territory could have drastic consequences. Ryck slowly marched forward, his senses on alert.

"Send them over!" he shouted at the first minister when he'd reached the halfway point between them.

Ryck's eyes were locked on Hannah's, and he could see the despair threatening to take over her. The first minister said something that Ryck couldn't hear, then nudged her forward. That nudge was all Esther needed, and she broke into a run to Ryck.

Ryck wanted to tell her to stop, fearful that she could invoke some reaction from unseen loyalist troops, but part of him wanted her to run faster. She crossed the intervening 75 meters in seconds, slamming into Ryck and almost knocking him flat.

"Daddy!" she sobbed into his shoulder while Ryck squeezed her tight.

"It's all right, snugglebunny," he said, "You're safe now."

Over Esther's shoulder, his eyes were still locked on Hannah's as she and Noah made their way to him, Noah with one arm around his mother's shoulders.

"But you're not safe. The first minister, he said what they're going to do to you!"

Bastard! Couldn't you at least let them get away first before they found out?

"I'll be fine, Esther. I always am," he said as he tried to sooth her.

And then Hannah reached him. Her eyes were red and puffy, and she looked about ready to collapse. That killed him, his strong, capable wife, reduced to having her son help her across the hangar deck.

"Ryck," she said.

"I know," he replied, bringing her into the hug.

Noah joined, and the four stood there for a moment, a family again.

"I'm so sorry, Hannah. And Ben. . ."

"We know. They told us."

"I. . .it's my fault, I let him enlist, and now, I've dragged you into this."

"That's about all the time you have!" the first minister shouted from the where he still stood. "Let's go!"

"Why did you agree to this?" Hannah asked.

"Do you really have to ask? Because I love you, all of you."

"But the rebellion—"

"Will do fine without me. And you mean more to me than anything else."

"That's time, Ryck!" the first minister shouted out again.

"Look, you've got to go. Hans is waiting for you in the ship."

"No, daddy!" Esther shouted, hugging him tighter.

Ryck had to reach down and peel her arms from around him.

"Noah, take your sister to the ship."

Noah tried to say something, but only a strangled grunt came out. He nodded, then put his arm around the sobbing Esther and started to the *While Away*.

"I love you, Hannah, with all my heart. You've made me the luckiest man in the world."

"Why, Ryck? Now I have to live with this, to live alone without you. I'd rather stay here."

He embraced his wife and kissed her gently on her forehead. "Go, Hannah. Take care of the kids."

His heart was breaking as he pushed her hands down and gave her a gentle shove towards the ship. Without hesitating, he turned back and started walking to the first minister. He knew if he hesitated any longer, he'd lose his nerve.

"Daddy, I love you!" Esther's voice cried out.

"You can stop there," the first minister said as Ryck approached. He pointed at the body armor he wore and added, "No use for me taking any chances now, right?"

Ryck nodded and stopped, then slowly turned around. Esther was already in the ship and Noah was climbing aboard. Hannah reached it, and one hand on the ladder, turned to face Ryck. She blew him a kiss, and then disappeared inside the ship.

Within seconds, the hatch closed, and the *While Away* rose up on the tractors and backed out of the hangar. The gate flared as it passed, and then it was through. Two seconds later, it was out of sight, and Ryck was alone to face his fate.

EARTH

Chapter 31

Two armed loyalist Marines instead of FCDC guards stood silently over Ryck and the first minister. The insult was not subtle. Ryck was in prison oranges, his hand and legs shackled. They were deep within the bowels of the Federation Court in Brussels.

What am I going to do? Make a break for it? he wondered, refusing to meet the eyes of the guards.

The first minister, who was currently engrossed in something on his PA, had accompanied him from the moon to Brussels, had watched the body cavity search, and had stayed with him as he was hustled to the court building and down into the high-security courtrooms. A holocam crew had recorded the entire process, but for the moment, they were not in the holding room.

No matter, Ryck thought, looking up at the security cams. *They're making sure all of this is captured.*

Ryck had only been on the planet for an hour-and-a-half, but already, his "trial" and execution were in process. He thought he should be more stressed, more nervous, but he was surprisingly calm. He figured it was probably simple resignation to the inevitable.

He was thirsty, and he wanted a drink, but he was damned if he was going to ask the two Marines for some water. He considered ordering them to get him something. The first minister had told him that he was still a major general on the loyalist roles of Marines given that there hadn't been a court martial yet, so the two guards should obey him. But they probably wouldn't, and Ryck didn't want to be put in the position of being refused.

The first minister laughed at something, then turned off his PA. "That *Bradley's House*, that's some funny stuff. You ever watch it?"

"I've seen it," Ryck said.

"Well, you should see the latest episode. Hortense comes over to ask about the tree again, but this time, Malik is gone on a fishing trip, and Hortense—you know she likes Bradley, right? Well, she asks him to look at the tree overhang, and she 'accidently' falls into the pool," the first minister continued, finger-quoting "accidently." "And, well, it gets complicated, but it's real funny. You should watch it. Well, if you had more time, I mean. I guess that's the problem for you, right?"

Ryck said nothing, ignoring the man's baiting.

"You're doing well, I have to admit," the first minister said after a few moments with the tiniest bit of grudging respect in his voice. "Cool and calm, despite everything. I guess I should have expected nothing less from the great Ryck Lysander.

"You know, it really is such a shame it had to come to this."

The first minister seemed to consider something for a moment, then reached into his pocket. He pulled out his privacy generator, something most high-level officials carried. He turned it on, and the sphere formed around the two men. The two guards didn't seem surprised nor worried. They could still see the two of them, but they wouldn't be able to hear anything.

"You were being groomed, you know?" the first minister asked after his control light turned green.

Despite himself, Ryck turned to look at his former boss.

"I thought that might surprise you. But think of it. Why were you assigned to me? It was so we could guide you for the future."

"What, for commandant?" Ryck asked.

"You think too small, Ryck."

Ryck didn't know what to make of that, so he said nothing.

"There you go again, keeping your cards close to the table. I know you want to know what I meant, but you won't ask. But I'll tell you anyway. Yes, you getting the commandant's position was inevitable, but it was only to be a stepping stone. We had bigger things in mind for you."

"The Council? Marines don't serve on the Council," Ryck said.

"Only one has, but there's no reason why another one couldn't. And who better than the hero Ryck Lysander? Not even the Navy could object. And from a seat on the Council, who knows?"

Things suddenly clicked into place. The first minister was in charge of the military, but he'd never served. And the Navy had most of the Council positions and the chairmanship locked up. They were the real power, which might rub the civilians the wrong way.

"You want to diminish the hold of the Navy!"

Ryck glanced up at the security cameras. The privacy sphere might block sound, but the cams were still recording, and lips could be read.

"Don't worry about the cams," the first minister said after seeing Ryck look up. "We control them for now."

"And who is 'we?'"

"Oh, you'll never find out now. Just suffice it to say that with the Navy's increasing influence and power, there are those of us who'd like to see it sent back down to a manageable level. You were to be the first step, a wedge in the door, and one with which the Navy couldn't complain."

Ryck thought about it for a moment. "And I was going to be indebted to you?"

The first minister nodded.

"And appoint more of you, whoever 'you' are, to positions of authority?"

Another slight smile from the first minister.

"But business as usual. As on Ellison?"

The flippant look on the first minister's face clouded over for a moment. "No, not like that. That was the chairman's idea, and that's exactly why we needed to make a change. The Federation is sliding into a shit-hole, and we need to stop that trip to eventual destruction."

"Then why fight me?"

"Because you were too brash, too moralistic for your own good. You always were, Ryck. It was too soon."

"Too soon for the 12 billion on Ellison?" Ryck asked scornfully.

"Taking the long view, yes. They would have been a sacrifice for a better future, when we could prevail. But for now, you couldn't win, and we'd be exposing our hand."

"But we are winning."

The flippant look came back as the first minister said, "Well, there is that. If we'd known Chandanasiri would flip, maybe we would have made our move and avoided all of this. But we didn't, and now it's too late."

"It's never too late. If you're serious about a better Federation, you can still effect that change," Ryck said, the tiniest glimmer of hope creeping into his voice.

"No, Ryck. We played our hand. Can't take it back now."

"And if we win?"

"You won't. But if somehow you did, I'd actually welcome that, my own personal goals be damned," the first minister said.

Something in his voice convinced Ryck that the man was telling the truth.

"And I like you, Ryck. Oh, I'm madder than hell that you forced this on us. And I wasn't shitting you when I told you I might be following you to the Cube next. You're brash and too moralistic, and that's a deadly combination for politics. But I respect you and your service. Part of me wants to pull the lever myself on the gallows for putting me, for putting us in this position, but part of me will mourn you. You could have been such a great tool for the Federation."

Right then, the inner door opened and the court clerk looked in.

The first minster quickly turned off the sphere in time for them to hear ". . .eral Lysander, you are ordered to appear before the court.

"Time to face your judgment, *General*," the first minister said, his flippant side back on display.

Ryck stood up, and with the two guards behind him, shuffled the best he could into the courtroom. It was a closed court, Ryck saw, with just the judge, the bailiff standing at his side, and the clerk making it up. The first minister took a seat in the back of the court, and the two guards stood at the door. The holocam team had already set up their recording gear.

Ryck took the position indicated by the clerk. He was tempted to just plop on the chair in silent defiance, but he was aware of the camcrew, and he didn't want to give the loyalist propaganda teams any more ammunition than possible. He stood silently, waiting for the clerk to scan his retina and swear him in. The retina scan was quick and confirmed for the record that Ryck was Ryck.

"Do you, Ryck Lysander, solemnly swear to tell the truth, the whole truth, and nothing but the truth?" the clerk asked.

"I do."

That formality finished, the judge sat up straighter and looked across the six or seven meters to where Ryck stood.

"Major General Ryck Lysander, FP8785678, you have been brought before me under a series of charges. Do you understand that?"

"Yes, I do."

"You have been charged with twenty-three counts of crimes against the Federation, four counts of crimes against humanity, and one count of violating a Universal Assembly of Man treaty."

What? OK, the humanity is going to be the First Step massacre. But treaty? Maybe Corporal Hailstone?

"To ensure each of these is addressed correctly, I will read each charge, and you will plead to that charge and that charge alone. Do you understand that?"

"Yes."

The judge waited for a moment as if expecting Ryck to say something else.

When Ryck was silent, the judge cleared his throat and said, "General Lysander, you are charged with Penal Code 1001, Treason against the state. How do you plead?"

"I don't plead."

The judge looked up from his court PA. "Excuse me?"

"I don't plead."

"It's pretty easy, General. You are either guilty or not. How do you plead?"

"I don't plead. I do not recognize your authority over me, so I cannot plead to any of your so-called charges."

The judge rolled his eyes, then said, "OK, General, let me play your game for a moment. You are a major general in the United Federation Marine Corps, correct?"

"I am a general in the United Federation Marines Corps, true."

"A major general, but even so, as a superior court judge in the Federation, you feel I don't have jurisdiction over you?"

"The group you represent has been legally deposed for crimes against the charter and against humanity. So no, you have no legal basis to decide on any charges leveled against me. Additionally, as the co-chairman of the legal United Federation, I am a head of state. Therefore, as a citizen, and only as a general citizen, you may file charges against me for any perceived crime, but they must be heard by the Universal Court."

Ryck was completely under the loyalists' control, and he didn't have any real expectations of getting out of his situation. And he knew the judge would reject his claim that the loyalist government was the illegal one. But his internet sleuthing on the trip over had uncovered the rules concerning heads of state. It could be enough to give them pause. Doubtful, but possible.

The judge just stared at him for a moment before saying, "I'm going to enter a plea of not guilty for you."

"And I object. Bring me up to the Universal Court, and I will cooperate. But I do not accept your plea for me."

"As to Penal Code 1009, Inciting an Armed Rebellion—"

"And once again, I object!" Ryck shouted out, cutting off the judge. "You cannot enter a plea for a defendant until there has been a full psychological exam. That's paragraph 4.34.56 of the penal code," he said, hoping he'd memorized it correctly.

The judge was getting angry now, and he positively glowered at Ryck. This was supposed to be a cut-and-dry proceeding justifying Ryck's execution. And Ryck was not cooperating, surprise, surprise.

A slight smile suddenly came over the judge's face as he said, "Are you familiar with paragraph 3.44.21, General?"

"No, I'm not," Ryck said, his heart sinking.

"Well, to put it in terms you might understand, it gives any superior court judge, of which I am one, the authority to reach a judgment in a Class 1 Felony case whether the defendant is there to plead or not."

Ryck didn't know the paragraph, of course, but he did know that the law gave the right so that defendants could be tried in absentia or after they were dead.

"But I am here!" he shouted out.

"Oh, so you are here, in front of a court that has jurisdiction over you?"

"No! I mean, I am here, but you have no right to judge me."

"You can't have it both ways, General. You are either here under my jurisdiction, and I can enter a plea—after we take a short recess for your psychological evaluation, of course—or you are not here submitting to my judgment."

Ryck's mind was churning. There was something wrong with what the judge was saying, but he couldn't quite unravel it. Not that it made any difference. There was no doubt in Ryck's mind that the execution had already been ordered. Now it was just a matter of crossing the t's and dotting the i's. He'd hoped to throw a wrench into things and leave the loyalist PR guys with less to work with, but he wasn't gaining much traction there.

"I refuse to plead as you have no jurisdiction over me," he simply said.

"So noted. In that case, I am able to render judgment without a plea. I have read the reports and examined the evidence. I have enough to render judgment without calling in witnesses."

Witnesses who could say things the chairman doesn't want said.

"For violation of Penal Code, 1001, Treason: I find the defendant guilty.

"For violation of Penal Code 1009, Inciting an Armed Rebellion Against the State: I find the defendant guilty."

And so the judge went down the list, one after the other. Ryck was found guilty of each charge, no surprise.

Ryck looked up as the judge read off 26 guilties before reaching the treaty violation. As expected, it had to do with bringing Corporal Hailstone to the meeting. Ryck wanted to protest the finding of guilty for that one, too, as that should have been a matter for the Universal Court, and it was the loyalists who actually killed the Marine, but he held his tongue.

"Major General Lysander, considering the seriousness of the crimes you have committed, I sentence you to a reduction to the rank of private, full forfeiture of all pay and allowances, and to be given a dishonorable discharge from the Marine Corps. I also order you transferred to the Thielsen Federal Correction Facility where you will be put to death before 24:00, GMT, tomorrow, June 19, 368. Bailiff, escort the prisoner to the holding cell where he will await judicial review and transport."

Ryck was numb as the bailiff took him by the arm and led him to the door. The first minister raised one eyebrow as Ryck passed but said nothing. With the two guards in tow, the four men marched out of the courtroom and down to the line of holding cells.

Ryck had expected the outcome, but to hear it was somehow different. He quietly sat down on the hard bench, refusing the bailiff's offer of water.

The judge's finding would be forwarded where the third minister would rubber stamp it. Sometime within the next dozen hours, he'd be taken from the cell and loaded into a ship for transport to the cube. Then as early as 0001 tomorrow, and as late as 2359 GMT, he'd be hung. It was a simple as that.

Chapter 32

"So, it is true. That's your final meal?" the first minister said through the front intercom.

Ryck looked up from his bacon with raspberry sauce. Ever efficient, whoever was in charge of the prisoners had decided to give him his final meal on Earth rather than delay things upon his arrival at the Cube.

How considerate of him, Ryck had thought at the time.

He could have chosen anything, he knew. A fabricator was a fabricator, and duck a l'orange was as easy to program as a cup of tea, but somehow, bacon with raspberry sauce seemed more appropriate. He'd dawdled over it, trying to sense every taste bud as the salty bacon and the tart raspberry sauce hit them. This would be the last time he'd experience taste, and he wanted to savor it.

"You coming to witness it?" Ryck asked, picking up another piece of bacon.

"Me? Hell no. I plan on staying as far away as possible from that place. No, you'll have another witness. I just wanted to come by to, well, to say goodbye, I guess. And to say I'm sorry it all worked out this way."

The first minister seemed sincere for the first time since Ryck had surrendered himself.

"You messed up and let your sense of simplistic morality derail you, but you're a good man."

"I'm sure you're crying about it."

"I'm angry that you gummed up the works, and I'm angry that you put me personally in danger, but, yes, I regret this. You could really have gone far, you know."

"So you told me," Ryck said, licking his finger clean of sauce.

"Well, I just wanted to say that. Your execution order is signed, and they'll be coming for you pretty soon, so you might want to prepare yourself."

"Thanks for your concern. I'm touched," Ryck said with mock sincerity.

The first minister was peering at Ryck through the small window, and as Ryck looked up to catch his eye, he thought the first minister would say something else. But the man suddenly turned away and stepped out of sight.

Ryck quickly ate the rest of his meal, not willing to leave anything on the plate. Which pissed Ryck off because it was more than 45 minutes later that the jailer looked in, told Ryck to stand at the back of the cell, and opened the door.

The second man to enter caught Ryck by surprise. Brigadier General Sandy Peltier-Aswad stood in the doorway.

"I'm surprised to see you here. I thought you were dead," Ryck said.

"Almost, but I'm harder to kill than most people think," Sandy said.

"So you are the witness. You're going to watch me hang?"

"Yes, sir, I am."

"Sir? Come on, Sandy. Didn't you hear? I'm supposedly a private now," Ryck said bitterly.

Ryck had expected the death sentence, but not the reduction and dishonorable discharge. For some reason, that really bothered him.

Sandy merely shrugged as the jailer came forward with the shackles.

"Is this really necessary?" Ryck asked.

Sandy looked back where four guards waited.

"Are you going to go along quietly?" he asked.

"What you expect me to take out all of your guards, make my way to a spaceport, and escape? I'm good, Sandy, but not that good."

Sandy shrugged, then told the jailer, "Leave them off."

"But regulations!" the jailer protested.

"Duly noted. I will take responsibility," he said before turning back to Ryck. "If you would, General?"

Ryck preceded Sandy out of the cell where four guards, FCDC guards this time, surrounded him. The hallways were empty as the little group made its way to the elevators and up to the back transfer station. An armored ground car was waiting for them there, and Ryck was loaded inside.

For five minutes, they rode in silence, Sandy sitting across from him, their knees almost touching.

Finally, Sandy broke the silence with "Why, sir? Why did you do it?"

"To save the lives of 12 billion people."

"But after that? Why start a revolution?"

"Why does anyone start a revolution? To make things better, I suppose."

"But you broke your oath. I thought you had honor."

Ryck knew he'd done the right thing, but the accusation of being an oathbreaker hit him hard. But he was an oathbreaker, even for the best of reasons. And Ryck was raised to believe a man was only as good as his word.

"And now you are serving this corrupt, murderous regime?"

Two of the guards were listening in, but they said nothing.

"Because I swore an oath. And I believe I can do more good for change from the inside than from out."

"Careful there, Sandy. Those words could be taken against you, should any of our guards here choose to repeat them."

Sandy said nothing more, and they rode to the spaceport in silence.

Ryck almost fell asleep when the car came to a lurching halt, and the back door was opened. Four armed jimmylegs[16] were waiting for them. Due to the convoluted agreements the Federation, Greater France, and the scattered independent nations of Earth had signed, at the insistence of the UAM, capital punishment could not be carried out on Earth soil, and some legal analysts felt that meant condemned prisoners could not be transported on government shipping to be executed. Others disagreed, but both the Federation and Fiji, the only two governments located on Earth that still carried the death penalty, simply hired a civilian security firm, Sunray Global, a subsidiary of Razor Security, to take their prisoners to the

[16] Jimmylegs: military slang for civilian security guards

Cube. Razor Security Holdings administered the Cube under contract to six different governments, but each of the governments ran their own prison wing, and both the Federation and Fiji had their own execution chamber. The Federation used the ancient method of hanging while Fiji used a neuro-scrambler.

Ryck didn't have a choice, but if he did, he'd preferred to get scrambled than dangled. The Federation conducted a large number of executions throughout Federation space at any given time, but those at the Cube were for federal and for a few local Earth-jurisdiction cases.

The head jimmylegs asked for the transfer documents, which one of the guards gave him. Ryck was escorted out of the truck for the retinal scan. Both his FCDC guards and the jimmylegs seemed to tense up, which almost made Ryck laugh.

Yeah, I'm going to make a break for it running across the tarmac.

The scan light went green, and the jimmylegs chief accepted custody.

"This way, sir," he said to Sandy, who was there as a witness, but who did not actually have custody of Ryck.

The six men walked over to the waiting ramp. The packet was a small ship, about the size of a sloop. It could carry about 15 men comfortably, 20 in a pinch. Although it had bubble space capability, it was generally used within systems. Packets weren't comfortable, not that Ryck would care, but what they were was heavily armored. Pirates knew they weren't worth the effort to try and take them.

And criminal gangs know that trying to take one to rescue a prisoner was probably going to fail.

Once in a packet, a prisoner—or items of great wealth that had to go from one place to another—was safe from being taken by others. A packet was like a space-going armored car.

Ryck couldn't help but look up as he was led to the ramp. If there were any kind of rescue in the works, it would have to be now.

But other than Çağlar, he'd never told anyone where he was going. Bert would know now, of course, as the new commandant. But there wouldn't have been time to launch anything.

Still, Ryck was a little disappointed as he stepped into the ship. He'd be delivered to the Cube in another hour or three, depending on traffic control, and it would already be June 19th by then. He could conceivably be taken straight to the gallows.

The jimmyleg guards escorted Sandy and Ryck to the main passenger chamber just under the bridge. Limited by the need to be able to travel in atmosphere and gravity as well as space, it was not laid out as well as a space-only ship, but it would do. It was better than what awaited him at the end of the short journey.

"Where's Mr. Capulto?" Sandy asked.

"Mr. Capulto? He had to, uh, he had to go home for a family emergency," one of the jimmylegs said.

"I just talked to him a half an hour ago," Sandy said. "What about Mr. Jones?"

"He took Mr. Caputo. But no problem. We've got it," the jimmylegs said.

Sandy pulled out his Ruger and shot the jimmylegs in the face.

Sandy's saving me! Ryck thought with a sudden surge of hope.

Ryck quickly stepped in back of Sandy, wondering what the plan was.

"There isn't any Mr. Jones," Sandy said, his handgun covering the eight remaining men in the ship.

"Steady there, sir. We're here to take you to the Cube."

"Bullshit! I don't know how you did it, but you've taken over the ship, and I'm not going let that happen. The general is going to his execution."

What? What's going on?

"General, if you'd just join those men there?" Sandy said, motioning with his Ruger as he pulled out his PA.

Grubbing hell! Ryck thought. *I've fucked up!*

Ryck let himself deflate as he stepped forward to join the others. And just as Sandy spoke into the PA, saying, "We've got a situation here," Ryck sprang into action.

Sandy was a brilliant mind and a sound tactician. He could lead troops into battle, and his bravery was unquestioned. But he was not a dirty street fighter, a warrior who let nothing get in his way.

Ryck was.

Ryck dropped down to the ground as the startled Sandy fired off a string of shots over his head. From down at Sandy's feet, he sprang back up, knocking the gun hand up and out of the way. His shoulder smashed into Sandy's chin, sending both men back into the bulkhead. Ryck brought up a knee into Sandy's gut, rained two vicious elbows into his face, and as Sandy started to fall, Ryck took Sandy's throat in his hands, and using it as a handle, smashed Sandy's head with all the force he could muster against the corner of one of the control chairs.

On the third blow, the back of Sandy's head broke open like a ripe watermelon. Ryck thought he saw the surprise and well, the hurt in Sandy's eyes as the life fled from his old friend. Or maybe it was relief Ryck saw. He hoped it was.

"Sir, we've got activity!" a voice cried out from behind Ryck and he lay Sandy flat on the deck.

"Take her up now!" another voice shouted out. "And get Bertrand ziplocked!"

"Roger!"

A hand grabbed Ryck on the shoulder.

"Sir, if you can get into one of the acceleration seats, it might be getting a little hairy here."

"What? Oh, sure. What about him?" Ryck asked, pointing back at Sandy's body.

"We'll put him in with the rest later, but we've got to get in the seats."

As if on cue, Ryck felt the ship shudder as the engines lit up.

Ryck hurried and sat down, strapping in. Artificial gravity worked fine for most ships, but if the packet was going to be using evasive maneuvers, it was better to be secured while all that was going on.

"Thanks for taking out the brigadier," one of the men said, sitting down beside Ryck.

"Uh, sure. But I think I'm more in debt to you. Who are you?"

"Lieutenant Colonel Regent Wispon-Franks, Confederation of Free States Army, Exploratores, at your service. I believe you know my boss, Major Titus Pohlmeyer?"

"Yes, I do, Colonel. Yes, I do. I've known the good *major*, who has been a so-called major, I might add, for the last 18 years at least. And he's your boss, *Colonel*?"

"Ah, you know how it is, sir, with the spooks," the lieutenant colonel said with a smile.

Just then, the ship lurched into the air, overcoming the artificial gravity for a moment. Ryck had to gulp.

Sandy's body flopped over in the disruption, his arm flinging out so the hand landed palm up just half-a-meter from Ryck's foot.

As the ship juked and jived out of Earth's atmosphere, Sandy's body was flung back and forth. Ryck stared emotionlessly at the shell of what had once been his friend. Ben's godfather.

It wasn't until the little packet broke through into bubble space that the ride smoothed out and Ryck and the rest were able to leave their seats.

"Good job, Jensen," Lieutenant Colonel Wispon-Franks said. "For a squid, I mean."

"Someone's got to watch you ground-pounders, sir," the sailor said, fist-bumping one of the other men.

"Someone take the Fed general to the aft hold with the others," the Exploratores team leader ordered a couple of the men.

"I'll get Sandy," Ryck told him.

"Do you know him?"

"He was my friend."

"Oh, sorry about that. Do you want him ziplocked to try for a resurrection?"

Ryck looked down at Sandy's lifeless body for a full 20 seconds before replying, "No."

With one of the soldiers showing him the way, Ryck dragged Sandy to a small storeroom where six other bodies were stored.

The previous crew, I presume?

Four of the bodies were ziplocked. Two were pretty obviously too far gone for any chance of resurrection.

Ryck dropped Sandy's body on top of a man whose head and part of his chest were gone.

"Sorry, Sandy, but it was your choice. I tried to teach you over and over that to survive, you had to be the meanest son-of-a-bitch in a fight, and you never were that. Now you're dead, and I'm alive."

Then it hit him.

I'm alive! I'm mother grubbing, sure as shit alive!

TARAWA

Chapter 33

The shuttle landed at the small Headquarters LZ, and Ryck was off before the engines wound down. Various Marines were waiting, but Ryck ignored them, scanning the group until he saw a certain slightly overweight, somewhat aging woman who was the most beautiful sight in the world. He rushed past Bert and the rest to sweep Hannah up in his arms. A moment later, Esther rammed into them like a rugger, clinging tightly.

"I can't believe it, Ryck," Hannah kept saying, running one hand up alongside his face. "I can't believe it."

A hand reached across his shoulder as his normally unresponsive son joined the family huddle.

He'd been waiting for this for too long. Upon their escape from Earth and entering bubble space, the Confederation Special Ops team had fled not towards Evolutionary space, not towards Confederation space, but to the Outer Reaches and the Alliance. They'd married up with a New Budapest-flagged freighter in the Void, transferred to that ship, and set the packet on self-destruct. From there, the dead and ziplocked were left in an unmarked lifeboat and sent towards Brotherhood space with the rescue beacon blaring.

With plenty of time to kill as they made their roundabout way to Tarawa, Lieutenant Colonel Wispon-Franks had explained the rescue. His team had been a sleeper cell emplaced within the Federation over seven years prior, on call, so-to-speak, for any needed operation. Four of the team members had jobs at the spaceport as cargo handlers, and the others, including the team leader, worked within the local food service industry. When Major

Pohlmeyer activated them, they had swung into action, creating a pretty, well, simple plan. With the packet sitting on the apron, it didn't take a genius to figure out that it would be the vessel taking Ryck to the Cube. And as the Federation had not yet publicized Ryck's arrest, no extra security measures had been taken.

The port cargo handlers had been able to insert a worm program that sabotaged the coffee-maker on the packet—which had only the basic anti-virus protection, unlike the nav or power systems—figuring the crew wouldn't want to sit for who knew how long without the coffee. They were right. An immediate call went out for a tech to fix it, which the team intercepted, and three members of the team had come in under the guise of being repairmen. Once inside, it had been quick work to take out the crew, and then for the others to join them. Then all they had to do was wait for the notice from the court that "the package" was on the way and play the part of the real crew.

The plan was too simple to work—except that it had, something for which Ryck would be eternally grateful. And he planned to sit down with the good Major Pohlmeyer, find out how he'd known to swing his team into action, and more importantly, find out exactly what position he had within the Confederation.

And looking over Hannah's shoulder at the gathered men waiting for him, he'd meet with all of them and get caught up. But that would come later. Right now, he had to reconnect with his family, to celebrate their reunion and grieve Ben's death.

"Come on, Hannah, let's go home."

Chapter 34

"Our target is Hartford," Ryck told his principal staff.

"Shit, nothing like grabbing for the brass ring!" Sams said.

"Do you have a problem with that, Master Gunnery Sergeant Samuelson?" Ryck snapped, his eyes blazing.

"Oh, no, sir! It's just that, well Hartford is, well Hartford. That's their second most important holding, and it's pretty well defended."

"So you think it should be hands off? Do any of the rest of you think the same?" Ryck asked, looking around the table.

Only a few Marines met his eyes, and most looked uncomfortable.

"I'm sick and tired of this pattycake we're playing with them. And the longer we wait, the more the disparity between our relative economic strength. If we are at war, then we need to take it to them, pure and simple. Earth as a target? Well, our allies or pseudo-allies are not going to be too supportive of that. So what's next? Hartford, that's what."

"I didn't mean to disagree, sir," Sams said. "It's just that it'll be a tough nut to crack."

"Anything worthwhile is. And that's why I'm tasking you, General Copperwait, to develop the plan that will crack that nut. You've got two weeks and all the assets of the Corps, and I mean all of them."

"Two weeks?" Tomtom asked. "That's not much time."

"Well, then, I wouldn't be wasting any of that time, General."

"What about lift?" Jorge asked.

"General Nidischii' is on his way back to the Doughnut as we speak. He's been tasked with getting us all the lift we need as well as the capital ships needed to hold off the loyalists. For the sake of planning, assume you'll get the lift.

For the next 45 minutes, various proposals were thrown back and forth. And while Ryck had tasked Tomtom Copperwait with developing the plan, Ryck wanted to make sure his commander's intent was understood. Ryck and Bert had spent the previous night working out a general operation outline that Ryck thought had a good chance of success, and Ryck didn't want to stray too far from that concept.

Sams had been right, though, when he said Hartford would be a tough nut to crack. The planet was well defended with ground to air systems, an 800,000-man militia, and according to the latest intel, a brigade of loyalist Marines. Ryck knew that his Marines could take on and defeat the dispersed militia, but they had to get on the planet's surface first, all without space-to-ground weapons. The proscription didn't apply to atmospheric craft, though, according to his staff judge advocate, and Ryck was going to rely on that loophole. If they could get enough Wasps, Ospreys, and Experions into the planets' atmosphere, they should be able to neutralize enough of the defenses so that most of the landing craft could get through.

Ryck knew that Marines would die—probably in huge numbers. But even if taking Hartford was not a knock-out blow, it should turn the tide of the war. It would be a statement to the rest of humanity, and it would seriously degrade if not cripple the loyalists' war effort.

Ryck would mourn each and every Marine death later, but that was the price of waging war.

Chapter 35

The Klethos *d'relle* swung her mace at the Brotherhood gladiator. The gladiator ducked, bringing up his sword to block, but the force of the queen's swing neutralized the block, dealing a blow to the gladiator's shoulder.

Ryck grimaced. The mace was a new weapon the Klethos had started to bring to the fights, and in Ryck's mind, a more effective one. Even if the human gladiator reacted correctly to block it, the power generated by it was just too much.

"His shoulder is shot," Jorge noted. "This one is over."

Ryck had to agree, and he was tempted to turn off the feed, but he felt he had to give moral support to the gladiator. He'd never met the Brotherhood fighter, but he'd followed him somewhat over the course of his preparation, as he'd followed all gladiators. It was hard not to with all the press detailing every meal, every training session, every moment of downtime. Ryck was frankly amazed that the public didn't get detailed reports as to the size and consistency of their shits.

Ishmael Franzoni fought on, but Jorge was right. The fight was over. Within 30 seconds, the queen brought down a tremendous blow that crushed the gladiator's head. The queen stepped on the prone body, then lifted her head in her victory screech.

"Grubbing hell," Ryck said succinctly, wondering if Corporal Hailstone might have won the fight.

This was the 25th duel between Klethos and humans since the humans had switched to genmodded gladiators. Humans had won sixteen of them, the Klethos nine. But the Klethos had won four of the last five, and until the humans adjusted their genmods, it looked like they would be winning more.

What made this duel more significant, at least to the talking heads who covered the fights, was that it was for the Brotherhood planet of Belinda II—one of the two planets settled by the

Trinoculars after the Klethos had driven them out of their original holdings. A human gladiator had tried to defend them but failed, and now they'd have to evacuate again and find another home.

"Well, back to the real world," Ryck said, switching off the holo. "What's next? Copperwait?"

"No, Tomtom is going through a simulation right now. He'll be done at 2200 if you want to review the results."

"He's been busting his balls, huh? I wasn't 100% sure about him, but I think he'll be fine as the force commander."

Ryck knew that Jorge had wanted to lead the expeditionary force, which would be made up of almost 75% of the total corps strength, but as much as Ryck admired Jorge's capabilities, he hadn't much combat experience, and he would be more valuable back at headquarters making sure that all the support ran smoothly.

"Yes, it's going well, better than I expected," Jorge said. "But now, we've got Sergeant Major Ito, Joab Ling, and your good buddy Montero."

"All three? What is Montero bitching about now?"

"It has to do with the women in recruit training now."

It had taken Ryck a little longer to put in place the full suffrage he had promised Michiko MacCailín. The Navy had been quicker to get women through recruit training, but with the Marines, the physicality of boot camp had to be examined and adjusted where practical. Which given the "no weaker standards" directive Ryck had issued, meant not much was changed in the long run. The uniform sizes had to be expanded to take into account a greater percentage of smaller recruits, and ergonomic testing of weapons conducted, but in the end, for the first recruit class with women, there were only a very few minor adjustments made.

"OK, let's get this over with. I want to make a call to Bert to see where we are on the lift."

Admiral Chandanasiri had been against the plan to attack Hartford from the beginning, but he'd finally relented. He still was dragging his feet, though, with providing the ship-support the Marines needed, and while Bert was doing a bang-up job, Ryck wanted to lend his weight if needed.

Ryck shook hands with the sergeant major and Joab Ling eagerly, and then Montero's a little less enthusiastically.

"So, everything at Camp Charles going well?" he asked.

"Yes, sir," Joab said. "We just graduated a class of 958 with a retention rate of 84%. I'll be sending you the full report later tonight."

"Eighty-four percent?" Ryck asked incredulously. "With no lowering of the standards?"

"No, sir. Not a bit. As you know, the volunteer rate is skyrocketing. Everyone wants to join, so Manpower can be more selective of who is accepted."

"Eighty-four percent? That's amazing. But General Simone here told me you wanted to see me about the women in training?"

"Well, actually, sir, Mr. Montero wanted to see you. The sergeant major and I had a meeting with General Della Cotta, and since this concerns recruit training, we tagged along, if that's OK."

Della Cotta was Ryck's Deputy Chief of Staff for Manpower, one of the two generals with direct control over Joab and recruit training.

"OK, Mr. Montero, since you requested this, what do you want?" Ryck asked.

"If I may?" the public affairs liaison asked, synching his PA to the display.

A moment later, the image of a talking head sitting behind a desk appeared. Ryck recognized him as one of the GBC News commentators.

"Another sign of the desperation in the criminal faction is the fact that they are forcing women into their military. Women!"

A scene, obviously recorded at Camp Charles, showed a young woman running up to the wall climb on the obstacle course. She tried to jump up and grab the top, but she missed. Stepping back a few meters, she ran up again, jumped, and managed to get one hand on the top. She hung on for less than two seconds before she fell to the ground. A DI came into the recording field and told her to go around the wall. The woman stood up, brushed a loose strand of hair back around her ear, and slowly jogged around the wall and out of view.

"As you can see, this is hardly a force to be feared," the commentator said with an obvious smirk on his face. "The traitors are merely tyrannical bullies who force women to fight where men are too frightened. I don't think our professional military men are too concerned.

"On other news—" he started before Montero cut the recording.

"I thought you told me standards were not lowered," Ryck said, his anger beginning to rise.

"They weren't. That recording was made during our ergonomic testing. That woman was one of our DI's wives who volunteered to help out the evaluation."

"She was not a recruit?"

"No, sir. We were testing all aspects of training for women of various sizes and shapes as well as uniform and armor fit. I can assure you that the actual recruits are performing to the same standard as the men."

Ryck let that sink in for a moment, glad for the reassurance.

"So, Mr. Montero, what do we do about this?" he asked.

"Embrace it, sir."

"What? That made us look like idiots, incompetent idiots."

"Oh, we let it be known that Ms. Reynolds is a middle-aged mother of four who was just trying to experience what her husband goes through—you know, a family day. Then we show video of actual recruits.

"I can't believe those bozos actually opened themselves up to this. The latest surveys show that 68% of the population approve of women serving," he continued, unable to hide his glee.

"Sixty-eight percent of our side, not the loyalists," Jorge corrected.

"No, the loyalist side. For us, we're over 74%."

"How do you know about the loyalist side?" Jorge asked.

"Please, sir! We've got connections everywhere. We just asked someone on that side to do the research."

That slightly turned Ryck's stomach, even though it didn't surprise him. He knew he needed Montero, but if he had such easy access to the loyalist planets, what else did he know? And what might he be providing them?

"Did you take this up with General Della Cotta?" Ryck asked Joab.

"Not yet," Montero answered for the colonel.

"He's your boss. Brief him, and he'll coordinate," Ryck said, addressing Joab again and ignoring Montero.

"Aye-aye, sir."

"General? I think you need to look at this?" Jorge said interrupting, his voice low and barely audible.

His chief of staff was looking at his command PA. Ryck's PA was back at his desk, and he didn't want to get up, so he reached over for Jorge's. Jorge handed it over, his face white.

What the. . .?

Ryck felt the blood rush from his head as he read the message. It was from the naval command center on *Prometheus Station.* Four-hundred-and-fifty-two ships had emerged from bubble space within a million klicks of the station.

"Get to the MCCC. All hands! And put us on Class A alert!" he shouted at Jorge as he bolted from the office.

By the time Ryck reached the MCCC, the battle was in full tilt. The loyalist ships were swarming the few Third Fleet ships on picket duty. A few loyalist ships were taken out, but the picket ships were outnumbered and knocked off, one-by-one. The station defenses opened up, taking out more of the attackers as ships docked at the station started to pull away to get into the fight.

Ryck and the rest of the Marines, and joined by Admiral Mendez, watched in horror as one Third Fleet ship after another fell.

"I've got him, sir!" one of the comm techs shouted, holding up a phone.

Ryck grabbed it and said, "Bert! What's happening?"

"It looks bad, sir. Our shields are failing, and we can't get our ships out and into the defense."

"Can you evacuate the station?"

"I don't think so, sir. I'll—"

Bert was cut off as the display showed the station in full fight mode one moment, then as an exploding sphere of light the next before everything went black.

"What the fuck?" a voice shouted out clearly among the gasps and murmuring.

An image started to show up as AIs routed to surviving sensors. It wasn't as clear, but it was clear enough to show that *Prometheus Station* was gone, along with most of the ships of the fleet.

"What the grubbing hell happened?" Ryck yelled out.

"They used a planet buster, sir! A planet buster!" one of the station techs answered.

"The agreement!" another voice shouted out. "It was proscribed!"

Proscribed or not, the loyalists had just murdered 30,000 civilians and wiped out the Third Fleet. And General Bert Nidischii'.

The war had just taken a horrible turn for the worse.

Chapter 36

"But they used a planet buster," Ryck protested. "Over 30,000 civilians killed and 25,000 sailors. How can your government accept that?"

"Sir, they don't accept it. But as I said, it wasn't against a planet, and that is the loophole. The New Budapest ambassador to the UAM will register a protest, and we applaud that, but they did not contravene the actual proscription. I'm sorry about that," Major Titus Pohlmeyer said.

"But with half of our fleet destroyed, we need your help. We need your lift."

"I have brought that to the attention of our Forum, and while we are committed to a presence off Tarawa and the other listed planets, we cannot join an offensive operation at the moment."

Ryck was frustrated to no end. He had four full Marine divisions ready to move on Hartford, but he had no way to get them there, nor did he have a way to protect a task force in transit. He didn't even have what was left of the Third Fleet at the moment. Vice Admiral Mendez was the new commander of the decimated Third Fleet, and he was busy just trying to take stock of what he had left and what to do next.

Over 200 Third Fleet Ships had been destroyed or damaged. The loyalists had lost almost 100, many in the same blast that had destroyed the station. But they had started with 40% more ships under their banner before the attack, and now they owned the space lanes.

Ryck needed the Confederation navy, and it didn't look like that was forthcoming. And the longer it took, the more likely something would leak out to the loyalists, who had to know by the training tempo that an operation was brewing.

"So there is no way you are going to budge, Titus?" Ryck said, beginning to accept the inevitable.

"I wish there was. I truly do. But now, even if they're crippled, we can't risk a shooting war with the loyalists. It was hard enough to authorize the ships we've deployed as a deterrent."

Without the Confed navy, the operation on Hartford had to be put on hold. There just wasn't a way to make things work. Ryck knew he would have to come up with something else in the meantime until he could gather the naval forces necessary to take Hartford.

Ryck looked across his desk at the major before asking, "When you gave me that phone, what, 17 years ago, did you think things would work out this way?"

"Eighteen percent," the major said after only a moment's hesitation.

"What? What do you mean?"

"I mean we calculated that there would be an 18% chance that this would happen. Not *Prometheus Station*, not the exact way it would work out, but that you personally would be involved in a revolt against the government. That was the second highest projection for anyone we analyzed."

The revelation floored Ryck. "You had me analyzed? And it said there was an 18% chance I'd turn on my government?" he asked, completely astounded.

"Those were the figures."

"How the hell can you calculate that?" Ryck asked, still not believing it.

"We've got some pretty accurate psychoanalysts, and then our AIs are second to none in crunching the numbers. Those same AIs had the appearance of the Klethos, or some other aggressive race, at 82%."

If what the major was saying was true, then the Confeds were far more advanced than the Federation in this field, at least as far as Ryck knew. Given the missteps by the Federation, he doubted the Council had a crystal ball anywhere as accurate.

"Eighteen percent? And someone else was higher? Who?"

"A Navy officer was at 23%. He was killed in the Trinocular War, though. We've been following close to 100 other Federation citizens from all walks of life, too. You know one: Michiko MacCailín."

"Hmph," Ryck snorted for lack of anything better to say. "And Admiral Chandanasiri?"

"He wasn't on our radar, no," the major admitted.

"Well, Major, this has been an eye-opener, I have to admit. I'd never have guessed you guys were that, well, that you looked so far into the future. And I thank you for coming in. But now I've got to come up with a plan. Without the full Third Fleet, my options are rather limited."

Major Pohlmeyer stood up and said, "Certainly, sir. I'll get out of your hair. I'll coordinate with your new Navy liaison about our ships arriving."

He started to walk out, but halfway to the door, turned and said, "If it means anything, sir, I not only admire you, but I respect you. It would have been great for the Free States had you been born there, but I still think you have destiny written all over you. You'll pull it out, and I personally put that at 100%."

Ryck stared after the major a good minute after the door closed behind him. He wished he had the same confidence in himself as the major had in him, but frankly, at the moment, he didn't have a clue as to what he could do.

Chapter 37

Ryck sat in the dark of the cavernous library, an open but still full Corona in his hand getting warm. He stared into the empty fireplace, his mind blank. Soft footsteps sounded behind him, but he didn't move as Hannah's arms wrapped around him from behind.

"Be you coming to bed? It's 2:00 in the morning," she said, a question, not a demand.

"I'll be there soon, honey," he answered.

Hannah sighed, then started to leave.

"Wait," Ryck said suddenly, reaching around the back of the chair to take her arm and leading her around and into his lap. "I'm sorry. Since you've been back, I really haven't been here for you."

"There be bigger things for you right now. I understand."

"But you are the biggest thing for me. You and Esther and Noah."

His thoughts went to Ben, and he wished he could just let go and grieve for his son. He hadn't done it yet, and he knew he had to. But he was afraid that if he let go, he might never gain control again. He could lose his ability to make decisions. He could lose his ability to order more men into harm's way.

"We know, Ryck. Don't worry about us."

"I'm just sorry for everything. This isn't what you signed up for when you agreed to marry me."

"This be exactly what I signed up for, Ryck Lysander. I knew the minute you walked into our home with Joshua that you were a man of destiny, and I was to be by your side. This be the man I fell in love with."

Ryck felt her snuggle her chin into the crook of his shoulder and neck.

"You knew the first time you met me? Why did you make me work so hard to get you to marry me then?"

"Because I was afraid. I was afraid that you would consume me in your rise. For all their brilliance, shooting stars burn in their wake, after all," she said quietly. "And I wanted you to appreciate me more," she added as she snuggled deeper into him, a hint of the irreverent girl he loved showing through.

"Ah, but rest assured, my lady, I do appreciate you."

His hand dropped to cup her breast through her nightgown. They hadn't made love since they'd been reunited. Stress, Ben, and everything else had gotten in the way, and Ryck hadn't shifted his hand with that in mind. He just wanted to share the closeness with her.

But when his hand touched her breast, he felt her stiffen. Thinking it was too soon for her, he started to pull away, but she grabbed his hand and kept it there, pressing it into her harder. She leaned back so he could bend down to kiss her. A sudden need filled him. He had to feel human. He had to feel normal. And in his need, he devoured her, and she devoured him. On the overstuffed chair in the 300-year-old commandants' quarters, with armed guards standing 20 meters away outside the curtained windows, Ryck Lysander and Hannah Hope-of-Life Lysander made love as husband and wife.

Chapter 38

The next morning, Hannah was all smiles as Ryck came downstairs.

"Did you sleep well, Ryck?" she asked innocently.

"Best sleep in months," he said, realizing it was true as he spoke the words.

From everything facing him, he'd been able to escape for a short time. In a few minutes, he'd make his way to the headquarters, and it would be back to the war. But for the moment, at least, he felt refreshed.

"I made you buckwheat waffles," she said, putting a plate down in front of him.

"Made" was a generous term, given that she had simply dialed the fabricator, but it was the thought that counted. He patted her butt as he sat down.

"Mr. Lysander," she said with mock anger. "Manners!"

"You weren't saying 'Mr. Lysander' last night," he retorted, letting the melting butter and maple syrup start to flow down the stack before cutting a corner off and putting it in his mouth.

"No, I wasn't," she said with a laugh. "That was, well, special, Ryck. One to go into my diary."

"You note when we make love in a diary? Scandalous, my lady!"

"Only the special times."

"Really, like when?"

"Well, last night. The time at the beach on Papilotte. Oh, the time in the duck egg, of course."

Ryck broke out in a laugh. Their attempt at an intimate liaison in the Inert Atmospheric Insertion Capsule, or "duck egg," had been a physical disaster and a rather risky escapade, but it had been extremely fun. As a lieutenant in recon, Ryck had mentioned "69'ing" Sams in the duck egg during the insert onto GenAg 13. After explaining the relevance of the term to Hannah, she had insisted that they try it for real. More than a little intrigued, Ryck had agreed, and he'd snuck Hannah into the maintenance shop where an egg was being worked on one Sunday morning, and the two of them had attempted to perform the actual feat in a duck egg. But the duck egg in the shop was under normal gravity, not space's Zero G, and after a smashed nose, a black eye, and a bruised area that shouldn't be bruised, the giggling couple had abandoned the attempt.

As an erotic adventure, it was pretty much a zero, but as a bonding experience and a fond memory, it ranked right up there with the best.

"Well, my love, you are a much better duck egg partner than Sams," he said. "That Marine is not the smallest guy around."

"I think you had your chance. We're getting a little old for those kinds of acrobatics. No, I think neither one of us will get in one of those again," she said with a laugh.

"Ah, I'm still fit," Ryck said, slapping his chest. "I could get in one today for a 30-hour insert."

He flexed one arm to show off a bicep—and stopped dead.

"Ryck? Are you OK?" Hannah asked.

Ryck shook his head, jumped up, and kissed Hannah on the forehead.

"You're a genius, Hannah, and I love you!"

He bolted for the front door, startling the guard there as he ran out and on to headquarters.

Chapter 39

"I can't tell you how important this is," Ryck said to Lieutenant General Maldonado. "Everything could ride on it."

"I know, sir, and I'm taking it as my solemn duty. All of us are."

Lieutenant General Pasqual Jesus Maldonado, "Buck," was the Outer Forces commanding general. The four divisions under his command had been the least engaged in the limited operations against the loyalists so far, and the Third Fleet ships in his AOR had not been hit by the attack on *Prometheus Station*.

It had still taken more than a little effort to convince Admiral Mendez to release the ships for the operation. The man was understandably hesitant to send a large portion of his remaining ships straight into the heart of loyalist space, and Ryck at one point had been tempted just to order the admiral to obey. But it was never a good idea to issue an order that would be disobeyed, so he'd taken the time to bring Mendez onboard.

"Buck, this could go terribly wrong. . ." Ryck began.

"And it could go right," Buck said with a smile. "And it's about time we out in the Outer Forces get to play. It's always the Inner Forces that get all the glory."

Ryck had to smile at the general's faux jealousy.

"Well, Buck, now you can show up Liam and the Inner Forces. I've got it on good authority that he doesn't mind. I'll let you go now. Go with God, and fair winds and following seas."

As the connection was cut, Ryck started his habit of second-guessing himself. Buck's mission could end in total disaster, and for what? Was the risk worth it?

If loyalist spies hadn't determined by now that Hartford had been Ryck's target, a few planted hints should have now confirmed it. A couple of seemingly drunken comments about "taking it to" the Hartford militia in bars out in town. An increase in web searches on "Hartford." A few messages from Marines who had family on

Hartford telling them to leave. Nothing overboard, but enough that the loyalist analysts should have picked them up.

Add that to the embark of Marines from four different bases that would commence in two hours, led by a three-star commander, Ryck was reasonably confident that the loyalists would react. After the attack on *Prometheus Station*, they would have to consider this a chance to deal a final fatal blow to the evolutionaries and end the rebellion.

The thing was, it could end the revolution. Ryck could be playing into their hands. But the plan was the only one he could envision that could result in victory.

The wet-water Navy hero John Paul Jones said, “He who will not risk cannot win.”

Well, Ryck had the risk part down, at least.

Chapter 40

Hannah straightened out Ryck's skins and brushed off some imaginary lint. With her hand still on his shoulders, she looked at him, worry in her eyes.

"I'll expect to be seeing you before you know it," she said, her voice only slightly catching.

Esther and Noah stood silently, but when Ryck opened his arms, both came into them for a hug.

"You take care of your mother," he said, giving them both an extra squeeze.

He gave Hannah a kiss, picked up his assault pack, and with his family in tow, left the inner office and entered the outer office where Jorge, Sams, Joab, Tomtom, Vivian, and Liam Hanata waited.

He held up a hand to forestall any talking, turned around, and stuck a note on his inner office door.

"Gone to Florida to fight the Indians. Will be back when the war is over," Sams said as he read the note, obviously puzzled.

"Read your history, Sams," Jorge said. "Colonel Archibald Henderson, the fifth commandant of the US Marines."

"But where's Florida?" Sams asked quietly as Ryck started shaking hands of those waiting.

This was a small group to send someone off to fight, but it was fine with Ryck. He wished Hecs and Bert were there, though. And Ben, of course. He shook off the melancholy that threatened to overtake his thoughts and forced a smile on his face.

All wished him well, and Sams turned his handshake into a hug.

When he got to Liam, he said, "If something happens, well, you've got it. Do what you think is right for the Corps."

Lieutenant General Liam Hanata was the commanding general for the Inner Forces, and as Bert had not been replaced yet, he was the senior three-star Marine. If Ryck fell, he'd be next in line for the position of commandant.

"I don't expect to have to. You'll be back once this is over," Liam said, pointing at the note. "History demands it."

"Well, all of you, thanks for the send-off. Keep the fires burning and the lights on."

With one more kiss to Hannah's cheek, the 92nd Commandant of the United Federation Marine Corps stepped out of the office to meet his fate.

NB DANUBE DREAM

Chapter 41

Thirty minutes later, a heavily guarded Ryck was escorted into a waiting shuttle and lifted off Tarawa to one of three waiting Navy ships. A relieved-looking Gunnery Sergeant Hans Çağlar met him at the airlock and escorted him to the bridge where he shook hands with the ship's captain and took a seat out of the way of the crew.

If someone noted that close to a thousand Marines on three ships was a large number just to provide security, well that could be reasonable given recent events. Ryck was not only the commandant but now the sole chairman of the provisional government.

"Welcome, Toad, sir," a voice said from behind him as Ryck sat down.

"Killer Angel, as I live and breathe," Ryck said, standing up to shake Colonel Kyle Granger's hand. "It's good to see you."

Ryck and Kyle had served together in recon and had fought the capys on GenAg 13. Now, Kyle was the CO of the recon regiment and the commander of troops for the operation. While Ryck had seen Kyle on the cam conferences, this was the first time he'd seen his old recon-mate face-to-face for at least five years. With the regimental headquarters on Gobi, their paths hadn't crossed often.

Çağlar looked mortified at the colonel's familiarity, but the nicknames prevalent in recon were sometimes a hard habit to break, even if one of the Marines was the commandant. The "sir" Kyle had added after "Toad" was the one concession to Ryck's vaulted position.

"Is everything on track?" Ryck asked.

"Yes, sir. As you know, it was somewhat round-about to gather the teams, but we're here, 982 hard-charging Marines and corpsmen at your beck and call."

"Do you think we're ready?" Ryck asked.

"I think so, sir. Yes, I wish we'd been able to do a real rehearsal. But they're good Marines, and they're ready."

There had been no time, given the three-week window in which the operation had to be planned, and with opsec an issue, the coming mission had never been fully rehearsed. The Marine involved had gone through linked RCT[17] run-throughs, but with the Marines in no less than six locations, and given the limited size of each RCT, the rehearsal value had been less than optimal.

"As soon as we enter bubble space, I want to meet with all the team leaders aboard this ship. I want Major Danneys to go over some minor modification to the initial insert."

"We'll be there," Kyle said.

Ryck could have started the meeting immediately. It wasn't as if he'd have any input to the ship, but he wanted to make sure they entered bubble space OK, and he just felt better watching that from the bridge.

He needn't have worried. The ship entered bubble space cleanly, on a track that buttressed the impression that the three ships were going to join up with Liam Hanata's task force. In reality, though, the entry was slightly different, and the three ships emerged from bubble space several parsecs away where they linked up with a New Budapest freighter, the *NB Danube Dream*. In a very closely coordinated procedure, all the Marines and their gear were transferred to the *Danube Dream*, and the three Navy ships reentered bubble space on their way to join up with the task force.

As the Marines were being settled into their cramped quarters, Ryck, Kyle, and Sergeant Major Howard Brasie, the recon regimental sergeant major, and followed by Çağlar, immediately went to the cargo hold where 500 duck eggs, the entire number available to the Marines, were still in the process of being cradled.

"Captain Plummer," Ryck called out to the man in commercial overalls who seemed to be in charge of putting the launchers together.

The man turned and smiled, walking over to greet them.

---

[17] RCT: Realistic Combat Trainer: a large computerized simulation in which Marines can maneuver and react to electronic combat situations.

"Sorry, I didn't meet you. We're way behind on these things. Nothing is standardized," the captain said.

"You look good in red," Ryck said, nodding at the smudged and well-worn overalls.

The Navy captain wiped a hand on his legs before offering his hand. "Well, you know how it is. Deniability for our friends on New Budapest. They've got the paperwork to show this tub was leased by Propitious Interstellar. It does feel pretty weird, though, not being in uniform."

"I'm glad you're taking us, though. Kyle, this is Brian Plummer. We were on the *Kravitch* together when all this started. Brian, Kyle is the commander of troops for this. And Howard here's the sergeant major," Ryck said, introducing the group. "And this hulking Marine is Gunnery Sergeant Hans Çağlar. We go back a long ways.

"Can you give me a quick brief on where we're at now?"

The "quick brief" took over 50 minutes. The duck eggs themselves had arrived in seven loads, and the transfer had been relatively painless. A crew was op-checking them all now. The issue was with the launchers. They needed eight launchers in order to get the full complement of eggs launched within the window, and Federation launchers did not seem to mesh well with the New Budapest ship's cargo hold. In today's day and age, Ryck would have thought that things like this would have been standardized, but he'd have been wrong in that.

Captain Plummer promised that his crew would get the launchers up in time, and Ryck had to trust the man on that. There was no Plan B if they couldn't launch.

EARTH

Chapter 42

Ryck stood outwardly at ease waiting to load their duck egg. Inside, though, his nerves were afire. He'd had more than his fair share of combat before, but with the possible exception of his fight with the Klethos queen, this upcoming battle might have the most ramifications. He couldn't screw up.

His position in the assault had been a huge bone of contention. To a man, his staff had told him not to go on the assault, and they'd enlisted the CAC to join in the discussion, even if they hadn't revealed the objective to the civilian leaders. Jorge had almost insisted that he lead the mission, but Jorge had never conducted an egg drop before. Not many senior officers had, and there were not only psych evals to be done first, but there was training necessary in order to make the drop. It wasn't as if someone just hopped in a duck egg and emerged on the ground some time later.

More than the practical issues, though, Ryck knew he had to be on the mission itself. He couldn't follow it down later. Only he had the position within the provisional government to act immediately to cement the situation were they successful. A delay in his arriving could throw away any chance for a strategic victory.

As they emerged from bubble space, several far orbital relays brought them up to speed. It looked as if the loyalists had taken the bait. Most of the loyalist First Fleet had left the quadrant, as had what had to be almost all of the loyalist Marines. The evolutionary task force had been engaged as it emerged from bubble space outside Hartford, and it had been engaged in a running battle ever since, with 14 ships lost—two of them being two of the three ships that had supposedly brought Ryck to observe the battle. With the

Danube Dream emerging outside the Sol System, the evolutionary task force was now breaking contact and scattering.

Ryck deeply mourned the loss of those 14 ships in what was just a show of force, a feint, and he hoped no more would be lost as they made their escape.

He also hoped their sacrifice would not be in vain. In another 30 minutes, the duck eggs would launch, and it would be too late for those loyalist ships out near Hartford to get back in time to have any effect on the outcome of the coming battle.

"Sir, you're up," the Navy petty officer said.

Ryck and Çağlar had 69'ed before, and the big Marine was hardly an ideal partner for an insert. The Marine just took up too much space. But they were used to one another, and Ryck knew Çağlar simply wouldn't allow anyone else to be his egg-mate.

"Don't do anything we wouldn't do, sir," Shart, Master Sergeant Clarence Gutierrez called out as he waited to load his own egg.

The jibe was probably as old as duck eggs were, and it was a tradition that someone had to say it. Shart had served with Ryck twice, and he was almost as irreverent as Sams was, so it fell to him to send the commandant on his way with the traditional admonition.

Ryck raised a middle finger in retort as he climbed into position. A moment later, Çağlar was sliding in.

"Closing," the sailor said. "God's speed."

As always, this was the worst part of the process. The ship needed to keep artificial gravity in order to expedite the loading, but with Ryck now upside down, the blood poured into his head. If it weren't for the drugs now coursing through his system, he doubted that he could take it for long.

Ryck felt the duck egg jolt around as it joined up with three others. Together, the four would hurtle through space towards the insert point, when the outer layer would ablate away, sending each individual egg on its own route down.

Even though Ryck and Çağlar were among the last of the Marines loaded, it still was some time before the sudden acceleration surge let Ryck know they'd launched.

Operation Take Back was under way.

And then they waited. The *Danube Dream* had to be far enough out of the crowded inner space lanes to be able to launch the duck eggs and in the right position to align their entry. That made the trip in-system to earth orbit a long one: 23 hours. The drugs kept him calm, and he drifted with fleeting dreams that he could almost grasp. It took him a moment to notice the slight shaking that indicated the eggs were entering the atmosphere, and new drugs were injected to bring him to full alert.

The shaking became violent, and Ryck had to brace himself to keep from being slammed about. This was planned as the outer layer had to ablate away to release the four eggs.

Ryck could feel the difference when his duck egg broke free. The extreme violence abated a few degrees while a lower-frequency vibration increased.

This was when they were the most vulnerable. The eggs were highly shielded, but still, entering an atmosphere like this left visual signs as the superheated air flared around him. They were landing in daylight, but still, they could be picked up.

Which was why there had been a launch window. The operation was kicking off on August 18 at the height of the annual Perseid meteor shower. The hope was that as the duck eggs were picked up despite all the cloaking, they would initially be taken for meteors. By the time the loyalists figured it out, hopefully, it would be too late.

Ryck waited for the dull sound to grow as more of the duck egg was ablated away. This would be his warning. He felt Çağlar tense up, and he followed suit, bringing in his arms as tightly as he could and squeezing his legs together.

Ten seconds later, Ryck's side of the egg split open followed by Çağlar's a fraction of a second later. This tiny difference kept them from slamming into each other. The shock of hitting the atmosphere was huge, despite the ablative slowing of the capsule. Ryck had been ready, but his compacted body position was almost flung apart. He managed to keep tight, though, and within a few moments, he had stabilized. Slowly, he extended into the age-old freefall position and started his descent.

The deployment of the foil was done mechanically. There was an emergency ripcord, but if he had to resort to that, he would be hopelessly off course and beyond any hope of reaching the objective. He'd be too far off course to make it there on time. He kept waiting for the opening shock as the ground below him came into greater focus.

Ryck would rather have hit the objective just before dawn, but their target's schedule controlled when they had to hit it. It was now early morning, and below, a large metropolis began to take shape. Brussels' rush hour looked to be almost over as Ryck's foil deployed. He had the Center on his display, but he didn't need it. The large capitol building was very evident. All around him, he could see Marines as they began to converge on the Center.

For a few minutes, Ryck hoped they'd land undetected. The Marines had the best cloaking systems known to man, and the undersides of the foils had chameleon-cells to mimic the sky above them. But this was the center of the Federation government, and that was probably too much to hope for. Even with loyalist forces rushing to reach Hartford, they would not leave the Center undefended. At 2,000 feet, firing reached up from several points in the complex, and Ryck's display lit up as Marines were hit. Eleven Marines were killed before the first landed on the ground.

Ryck's foil was hit twice, which disrupted the circuit for his chameleon cells, turning the underside of his foil to a flat black. He felt extremely vulnerable as he descended the last 300 meters, sure he was about to take a round from below. But he made it down, ditched his harness, and took out his M99. The Marines had a variety of high-speed weapons, but Ryck felt comfortable with the '99, and so that is what he chose to carry.

Ryck couldn't help but feel a slight rush of guilt as he unslung that '99, though. For close to 300 years, Marines, or any military, for that matter, were prohibited from carrying arms on Earth, and that had been driven into his head since recruit training. Then he had to laugh at that. He was leading a full-out assault, and he was worrying about carrying a weapon?

Çağlar ran up to him with a questioning look as he heard Ryck laugh, which cause Ryck to laugh yet again. The gunny simply shook his head as the two Marines gathered themselves to move out.

Ryck might have inserted himself into the mission, but he was not going to be in the assault element itself. Çağlar grabbed him by the arm, and led him at a run to their first rally point: the alcove at the front of the Liberty Fountain.

With the Marines landing all around and firing at the security forces, civilians were in full panic mode. An elderly couple was shot down just on the edge of the fountain—whether from loyalist or Marine fire, Ryck couldn't tell. He forced himself to ignore the couple as he monitored the fight.

It took less than two minutes to breach the side entrance. The jimmylegs, most of them legacy guards whose fathers and grandfathers had served, were more ceremonial than anything else and augmented by FCDC professionals. The jimmylegs were brave, but they were no match for the Marines. They acquitted themselves well, though, taking down four Marines KIA and two WIA before the Marines were able to blow the door.

The immense, 14-meter tall, 10-meter wide bronze front doors were ignored. They were too massive, and the side doors on the left side were a much better choice. Ryck could almost imagine the FCDC officers shouting as they realized the front doors were being bypassed and trying to rally the guards to stop the Marines who were already in the building.

"Let's go, sir," Çağlar said as he led Ryck, along with six bodyguards, to the breach. As city-wide security began to react to the assault, it wouldn't be too smart to be caught outside. Although the Marines had managed a breach, the building itself was fairly secure and would be more easily defended than the front plaza.

Ryck rushed into the capitol building. He'd been in it several times before, mostly as an adornment for the then current chairman. This time, he intended to take it.

He was confident of that part of the mission. History was replete with cases of hotels, factories, and government centers being taken by armed groups, mostly militants and terrorists. None of them had the same capabilities as modern recon Marines. But in almost all cases, those taking the buildings had been eventually killed and the buildings recaptured. Ryck knew they could seize the capitol, but could they keep it? There were too many factors that would affect their ability to hold the building that even the AIs couldn't give a probability of success.

A second breach was accomplished—this one on the roof via the air-conditioning units. Forty-eight Marines had landed on the roof, and they had just broken through the air ducts. Within moments, Ryck expected them to rappel down to the rotunda floor and secure the main entrance to the Great Hall.

Ryck wished there had been a way to break into the Great Hall before anyone knew they were there, taking the Council by surprise. They hadn't come up with any viable plan to do that, though, so those in the hall had ample warning that something big was going down, and the FCDC troops and jimmylegs were able to retreat back to the hall and form a hasty defense. There was little likelihood that the dwindling number of guards inside the capitol building could hold off the Marines for any significant amount of time, but they didn't need to. All they had to do was delay the Marines until reinforcements from the city could arrive.

The Marine AIs had given estimates between 16 and 23 minutes before the first wave of reinforcements could launch a counterattack. The assault was now six minutes old, which was unbelievably quick, but it still comprised a significant amount of the cushion the Marines had. On the roof and in the plaza, Marines with crew-served weapons were setting up, but it was vital that the Great Hall be seized ASAP.

Ryck, Çağlar, and his phalanx of bodyguards were waved through the breach by a Marine. Five meters inside the door, the security scanner was still intact. Red lights flashed, and a siren sounded as the eight Marines ran through it. The two dead jimmylegs lying beside the detector weren't in any position to do much about it, however, Ryck noted.

Ryck's display gave a full picture of the ongoing fight. There was a pitched battle going on at the east entrance to the Great Hall. Rounds were skipping off the granite flooring and hitting the walls in the corridor, sending chips of stone flying in all directions. As

Ryck ran up to the nearest wall, a spent round came skittering down the passage spinning to a halt not a meter away from his feet.

"Sir, we need to move back," Çağlar said.

"No, we're here now," Ryck responded.

With his face-shield display turned to max resolution, the amount of data displayed threatened him with data overload, which in a combat situation could be deadly. But Ryck had years of experience with which to train his mind to be aware of his personal situation and any potential danger while still taking in the overall battle. Besides, he had seven Marines protecting him. He thought that was overkill, but he had bowed to the pressure from his staff.

Ryck looked at the display timer; it has been nine minutes since the first round was fired. He could see the avatars for the secondary breach team clumped together up ahead, but the curve of the corridor kept them out of his direct line of sight.

He needed to find out what was happening, but Kyle was heavily engaged in the firefight at the front of the hall, and Ryck knew he shouldn't be interfering with a commander in the midst of the fight. But he just couldn't stay in the dark, so he initiated contact with Sergeant Major Brasie on the P2P.

"What's the status with the breach?"

"Give them one mike, sir, and they'll be in."

"We're at nine mikes now. We don't have much time," Ryck said.

"Understood, sir. We're working on it," the sergeant major responded.

Ryck knew they were working on it, and he knew his questioning the sergeant major would not speed anything up, but it was just not in him to stand around quietly surrounded by seven Marines whose sole mission was to keep his skin intact. He was a warrior, not some fragile figurehead.

At last, the breaching device's avatar started flashing red as the breach team hightailed it back down the corridor, three of them coming into sight just ahead of Ryck.

"Fire in the hole, fire in the hole!" came over the general net.

A few seconds later, a huge explosion rocked the building as smoke and dust rolled down the corridor, reaching and passing Ryck and his team. Ryck hastily deployed his filter to clean the air so he could breathe.

No one had been quite sure how strong the walls to the Great Hall were, so the breach team had erred on the side of overkill. There were civilians on the other side of the wall, and should things go wrong for the mission, any Marine survivors could—undoubtedly would—be held accountable for casualties. But there were also security personnel inside who were willing and able to resist, and it was hoped that the blast would either knock some of them out of the game or at least temporarily stun them.

Immediately, a mass of Marines rushed the breach and stormed into the Great Hall. Energy beams lit up the dust as guards fired at them. Airborne dust, though, absorbed and reflected that energy, rendering the weapons far less effective. Return kinetic fire from the first wave of Marines took those guards out.

"Let's move it," Ryck said aloud, jumping to his feet and rushing forward.

Caught by surprise at their charge's rush, it took them a moment to follow. Ryck ended up leading his team over the rubble and into the Great Hall instead of them making sure it was secure enough for him.

A round of some sort pinged at Ryck's feet, but he paid no attention to it as he took in the scene.

Several small groups of guards, FCDC and jimmylegs, were making last stands refusing to surrender and being cut down where they stood. Marines were also falling, but it was obvious that the fight was won—for the moment. Ryck ignored these last life-and-death struggles as he focused on the front of the hall where a group of twenty or so men were standing and looking desperate. At a full run, Ryck charged down the nearest aisle as the first, then the second guard around the group fell to Marine fire.

He started sucking air as he ran, so he spit out the filter. Alongside him, the spectators and hangers-on were trying to retreat from the hundreds of Marines who were pouring in, but Ryck didn't give them a second thought. His attention was on the power brokers.

Two of the men in the front bolted. They didn't get far before being cut down, either by design or in a crossfire. Ryck hoped neither was someone vital.

By the time Ryck reached the front of the hall, the fighting was petering out. A dozen Marines surrounded the group, who were moving against each other in an attempt to reach the center, like a school of sardines surrounded by sharks.

Ryck slowed to a walk as he approached, looking for his target.

One man was pulled from the group by two Marines who began to hustle him to the aisle.

"Thank you for your help, sir, but now we've got to get you out of here," one of the Marines said loud enough for the rest to hear.

The Brotherhood ambassador started to protest, but he was dragged away before he could say much.

"Gentlemen," Ryck said as he came up taking off his helmet. "Cooperate, and no one else will be hurt."

All eyes locked on him as he was recognized.

"Well, well," the first minister said. "You're much more resourceful than some of us imagined. Not all of us, but some," he added, looking daggers at the chairman who nervously stood tall, trying to look defiant.

"If all of you can take a seat, please?" Ryck asked, expecting to be obeyed.

Backed up by the armed Marines, he was obeyed.

A final flurry of shots sounded out, followed by a moment of silence before murmuring broke out among the 200 or more men and women in the hall.

"You are now prisoners of the United Federation—"

"You are not the Federation! You are rebels! Traitors!" the chairman shouted as he came to his feet, his anger overcoming his prior apprehension.

The chairman was "assisted" back to his seat by a helpful Marine.

"As I was saying, you are now prisoners of the United Federation. Your resistance is at an end. More and more of your forces are laying down their arms, and the bulk of humanity has weighed in, declaring the provisional government the true government of the Federation."

"Bullshit!" the chairman said, halfway getting out of his seat before a glare and a wave of the muzzle of the weapon from the Marine standing by him made him think twice about standing up. "No major government has sided with you traitors," he said only slightly more controlled.

"Oh, like the Brotherhood? The ambassador of which so conveniently gathered you here this morning so we could sweep you up?"

Ryck could see comprehension dawn on half of the men sitting before him.

The Brotherhood ambassador had called for the meeting, but not to assist the provisional government. Five days before, Ryck had given Vice-Bishop Hadad what amounted to a surrender offer and asking him to get it couriered to Earth and the Council. Knowing that the Brotherhood would dearly want to be the force behind a peaceful cessation of hostilities, it was only a matter of following the proposed peace settlement. Once the meeting between the ambassador and the Council was set, the operation was launched. The ambassador had, in fact, gathered the Council and senior officials but without knowing the Brotherhood was being manipulated. And with him hustled out of the hall, he was not around to protest Ryck's assertion.

"Touché," the first minister said quietly, earning a glare from the third minister sitting beside him.

The man seemed to be enjoying himself despite the situation, a smile fixed across his face.

"So what's going to happen to us?" a man who Ryck did not recognize asked hesitantly.

"Aye, there's the rub, now, isn't it," Ryck said. "Well, for starters, just to clean up loose ends and to reassure the citizens, the chairman is going to sign a transfer of power, acknowledging me as the sole and legal chairman."

"The hell I will!" the chairman shouted, standing up before being shoved back into his seat."

"As I was saying, while it isn't really needed, the chairman will sign a transfer of power. As for the rest of you, after you swear allegiance to the Federation, which means me, you can be on your way and back to your duties."

"Unharmed?" the same man asked.

"Of course. Why would you be harmed? We need you back at your posts."

That seemed to cause a stir among the men. The air of apprehension started to shift into both relief and something more calculating.

The man asking the questions broke into a satisfied smile while others started to glance at the rest as if to gauge their reactions.

"And the Council?" Third Minister Geoff Forsyth asked.

"For now, you will return to your duties. A new temporary council will be formed, and some of you will be asked to serve on it."

Ryck glanced down to where he held his helmet. The display was still on, and he picked out 17 minutes gone. The reinforcements could arrive any moment now. He listened with half an ear for the sound of crew-served weapons opening up outside.

"And me?" Admiral Blankenship, the Chief of Naval Operations asked.

"You'll go back to your duties for now."

"For now?" the CNO asked sourly.

"You're slated to serve on the temporary council, if you're willing," Ryck said, trying to keep his throat from seizing up as he said the words.

"He's playing you, Jerry. You too, Geoff. Can't you see that?" the chairman said. "And what about me?" he asked Ryck. "No going back to my duties for me, right?"

"You're right. After you sign the transfer, you, your family, and anyone else who so desires will go into exile with the Brotherhood. You can change that as you wish if you can find another government to accept you."

Poker face, Ryck. Make them believe the Brotherhood is on board with this! he stressed to himself, trying to look natural.

"And what makes you think I'll sign? Any moment, reinforcements will come and free us."

"Because if you don't sign, I will cut off a finger. If you still don't sign, I will cut off a hand, and I will keep cutting off parts of you until you are no more. So for you, it's really a pretty simple decision. Sign and live a luxurious life within the Brotherhood, or get chopped to pieces."

Gasps greeted Ryck's words. The men had started to relax. Ryck had seemed reasonable, and it looked like they were in no immediate danger. To hear him so calmly discuss cutting the off the chairman's fingers had to be a shock to them.

"You, you wouldn't," the chairman managed to stutter out. "And what about the rest. You going to chop them up when the reinforcements arrive?"

Some of the men blanched at that.

"No, I won't chop them up. Just kill them—humanely, but they'll be dead none-the-less," Ryck said matter-of-factly.

"Bullshit! Look, he's not going to do that!" the chairman shouted at the other men. "No civilized person will do that."

"You better listen to him," the first minister said calmly as if they were discussing the latest agricultural reports.

Ryck looked deep into the chairman's eyes before he turned and shot the first minister right in the chest.

The first minister's eyes registered surprised shock as he slid off his seat to collapse in a heap on the floor. Several other men jumped up and away from the body as if his death could be contagious.

"But. . .why. . .but he liked you!" the chairman said, his voice incredulous.

"And I liked him. But if I can do that to someone I like, think what I will do to you," Ryck said, putting as much malice in his tone as he could.

The chairman blinked, his mouth gaping open and shut like a beached fish.

"Sign it, Charlie! Sign it you bastard! This is all your fault. This is because of Ellison!" the third minister shouted, taking a step towards the chairman.

The chairman stared at the first minister. The first row of seats was slightly higher than the front aisle, and the first minister's blood started to flow forward. The chairman had to step aside as the blood flowed up to his feet.

"Gunnery Sergeant Çağlar? The transfer?" Ryck asked.

Çağlar stepped forward, pulling the document out of his cargo pocket. The podium was up on the stage, and the seats of the chairs folded up when no one was sitting. Ryck hadn't thought of that problem.

"Turn around," he told Çağlar.

The big Marine turned and presented his back as a platform while holding out the stylus.

"Sign it!" several men shouted out.

In a daze, the chairman took the stylus and looked at the transfer.

"This won't hold, you know. It's under duress," he said.

"Whether it holds or not will be up to the courts, not us."

Ryck put his hand suggestively on the Buck combat knife at his side. The chairman stared at the knife for a second, then shrugged. He scribbled out his name where indicated.

"Your scan?"

The chairman gave the slightest of smiles and looked into the scanner. As soon as the green acceptance light signaled, Ryck took the stylus and signed his name. He held the document up, and within a moment, his retina was scanned.

It was done.

The chairman looked resigned, as if he knew he was a dead man walking. Ryck so much wanted that to be true, but his word had been given, and more than that, other governments frowned on the executions of heads of state, even ex-heads of state. Ryck would need their support if he was going to pull this off.

As if in counterpoint to his thoughts, the chatter of a machine gun reached him from above.

"Do I have full authorization as Chairman of the United Federation?" he queried his AI.

As soon as the transfer of power was completed, the entire AI system should have noted that, giving Ryck the full author granted to chairmen.

"Affirmative. You have full authority."

"Open the general military and security net," he ordered his AI, then, "All hands, all hands, cease firing. This is the Chairman of the United Federation. All hostilities have ended. I repeat, all hostilities have ended. Remain in place until further orders."

He followed that with the authorization code given to him by the AI. This code would clear his message as authentic.

Above Ryck, the machine gun chattered away.

Shit! What's wrong?

He started to give the order again when the firing above petered out. Silence took over.

He caught the former chairman's eyes. There was resignation in them and more than a little anger.

"Gunnery Sergeant, please have the former chairman escorted to his quarters. Ensure that no harm is done to him or his family. And get a corpsman to ziplock the first minister."

Ryck didn't care one way or the other whether the first minister was resurrected or not. He was too numb at the moment, but he knew he was under the spotlight, and benevolence might go a long way in calming the high officials for the short term and until they started plotting against him.

Ryck should have been feeling elation, joy, pride—something. The battle was won, against all odds. But he knew the war wasn't. One-and-a-half fleets were still out there, fleets loyal to the old chairman. There were hundreds of thousands of FCDC troops just on Earth, and while Ryck may have stayed their hands for the moment, that didn't mean they wouldn't raise them again. If the Navy or the FCDC decided to fight, then the war had just begun.

Chapter 43

The loyalist military and FCDC didn't fight it, though. Maybe it was because fighting the transfer of power meant it had lost the war if not all the battles. Maybe it was because the letter of the law was clear, even if it was enacted under duress. Maybe it was because Ryck promised no one would be charged with war crimes, and no one would be dismissed from the service. Maybe it was because they understood the will of the people.

And the will of the people was pretty clear. Survey after survey showed that, with numbers running as high as 80% in some planets that the former government had to go. Most local governments had not openly declared for the evolutionaries with the shadow of the loyalist Navy hanging over them, but what many forgot was that the Navy was made up of the same people, and the individual sailor's leanings were not much different from that of the population at large.

Twenty-two ships declared their defiance of the "illegal transfer of power" and fled Federation space. As long as they didn't carry on the fight, Ryck was happy to let them go. Some independent world would undoubtedly welcome them—and the ships, as those 22 now constituted the 8th largest human navy.

The promise of no prosecution for military personnel was a tough one for Ryck to swallow, but it had been necessary. No one, not even Commander Xhosa of the *Kravitch*, who had been willing to follow Admiral Kurae's order to drop the planet buster on Ellison, would face charges. The Federation was in disarray and needed its Navy, and history was pretty clear that when defeated armies were discharged en masse, trouble was always the result. For the good of the Federation, Ryck had to let go of his personal desire for retribution.

The next three weeks were non-stop work with Ryck consolidating his hold on power and getting ready for the future. Even Hannah's arrival, which was deemed vital by the newly elevated Zeke Montero, didn't do much to calm Ryck down. He was grateful for her presence beside him in appearance after appearance, but he felt the weight of the Federation on his shoulders, getting heavier and heavier by the minute.

The members of the CAC quickly made their way to Brussels, ready to start taking over the responsibility of actually running the Federation, something Ryck was anxious to let them do. He was a warrior, a fighter, but not a bureaucrat.

To his welcomed surprised, the CAC had already worked out an outline for a new Federation after they had prevailed. Ryck had been so involved with the military aspects of the fight since his escape that he'd neglected his duties as chairman, but the members of the CAC had kept working.

While the provisional government had already done so, the Federation Charter was to be officially amended, first abolishing the restrictions placed on women by the Fourth Amendment, and then with the Sixteenth Amendment, strengthening the protection of civil liberties for all citizens, no matter their gender, race, creed, or nationality—or species. With the Trinoculars and Klethos now known, the door was being opened to them or any other species yet to be discovered.

Ryck thought that last was a little pie-in-the-sky, but it did set the tone for a new, accepting Federation where equality and freedom were paramount.

The new Council would be set to nine individuals: representatives being appointed from the military (alternating between the Navy and the Marines), FCDC, and the Bureaucratic Corps, and five members being elected from the population at large. The ninth member would be the chairman, who would be elevated from within the Council by the other members and who would vote only to break a tie.

An interim council was put in place with the four surviving members of the CAC along with a fifth member who had not yet been appointed, a military member (the Chief of Naval Operations, which Ryck initially wanted to fight and put in Liam Hanata, but finally relented), the FDCD Commander, and the Assistant Minister for Foreign Affairs. Ryck kept the position of chairman. This council would serve for one year before a permanent council would be formed and sworn in.

Already Ryck could see the political game being played as new council members and others aspiring for the permanent council started to maneuver to position themselves for the future. Ryck had naively hoped that the Machiavellian political game of thrones would somehow disappear, but he realized it was probably something embedded within the human DNA.

Three days after the formal transfer of power, and two days after the chairman and his entourage (which had turned out to be much smaller than anticipated) had started their exile, martial law had been lifted. Goods started to immediately flow, with the Confederation taking advantage of its favored nation status. Ryck was grateful for the Confederation's help, but he wasn't about to let the Federation become subservient to the smaller alliance. He quickly offered all alliances, planets, nations, and registered trade groups a six-month holiday from tariffs and duties. If he informed the Juliette Group of this a few days before the general release, well, that was just a "bureaucratic slip-up."

Additionally, if Propitious Interstellar received a number of new contracts, displacing IGA Corp, well, that was because the interim council had to act quickly to get the Federation back on its feet. That was what was being told in response to inquiries from reporters, at least.

After a whirlwind three weeks of nonstop work, and after a long night discussing the situation with Hannah, Ryck was ready for the next step. He summoned the other members of the interim council to the Government Building's knave, where he had the Charter Table set up. The original Federation Charter had been signed on the table, and Ryck knew its significance. The old table simply reeked of gravitas.

Ryck looked out at the other eight members of the interim council. Arrayed behind those worthies were staff members and representatives of various branches of the government and three news teams who were recording everything. He surreptitiously reached one hand behind him, which Hannah took and squeezed, giving him her support.

"Citizens of the United Federation, we have just gone through a difficult period, probably the most difficult in our history since the signing of the Charter. During this schism, we were split into 'loyalists' and 'evolutionaries.' But neither term was appropriate. We were all loyalists, loyal to what we perceived to be the very basis upon which our great Federation was founded. And the Federation has always been evolving, trying to improve itself. Unfortunately, the difference in which way we wanted our federation to mature caused a temporary schism, a temporary split, which to our mutual horror, led to bloodshed. That is behind us now, and we can't let that interfere with the way forward. We must, I repeat must, forgive. Not forget those who gave their lives for a cause, but forgive.

"When I agreed to serve as the co-chairman of the provisional government, it was with the understanding that it was to be a temporary measure. We are a federation of a broad and diverse population, a population of many strengths and capabilities. One small part of the United Federation is its Navy, its Marine Corps, and its FCDC, second to none not only within human space but within the known universe. And I have been proud to serve as a Marine for the past 38 years.

"But I feel that the military, as vital as it is, should not *be* the government. It should serve the people, not issue orders. Over the last 300 or so years, the military has slowly increased its hold on power. I believe this has been with all the best intentions, but as I have learned, the skills learned on the battlefield do not necessarily translate into running a federation the size and complexity of ours.

"I only answered the call of the office because it was my duty. I did not lead the provisional government in order to seize power for myself. Consequently, I will be signing over a new transfer of power, naming Michiko MacCailín as your new chairman."

The surprised expressions facing him warmed his heart. They hadn't seen this coming. After staring at Ryck in disbelief, the council members immediately started covert glances at the others standing around them. Only Michiko kept her eyes locked on Ryck's.

If the others think they can elbow her out of the way, he thought, *or marginalize her, I think they'll have a tougher time than they'd imagined.*

"In front of me, I have the transfer of power. Chief Justice, will you please examine it?"

There was a glint in Justice Goldman's eye as he picked it up. It was no secret that the man was terribly upset with the change in government, and Ryck knew the old man thought Ryck's resignation could only help the old loyalist cause. Ryck also knew the old man was wrong. Michiko was far more politically savvy than Ryck could ever hope to be.

The chief justice made a show of examining the document, undoubtedly conscious of the holocams, if the way he twisted himself so they could pick up his profile was any indication.

"I find this document to be legal and valid," he said in a dramatically stentorian voice.

"Very well. Councilman MacCailín, if you would come here?"

Ryck had previously asked her what her title should be: councilwoman or councilman. She had immediately said councilman, stressing that equality is also shaped by language.

Michiko approached the table, then took the transfer of power from the justice and read it over before placing it back on the table before Ryck.

"Will you accept this transfer?" Ryck asked.

"I will."

With nothing else left to be said, Ryck took the stylus, and without hesitation, signed his name. He stared at the sensor until it flashed green, accepting his retinal scan. He pushed the document and the stylus to Michiko who signed it and recorded her scan as well.

Ryck felt a huge surge of relief. It was done.

"Chief Justice, if you will administer the oath?" Ryck asked, even if he no longer had the authority to do so.

Ryck could see the man was happy to be in the spotlight, and his stage presence took over.

"Use this one," Ryck said, handing a small card to the justice.

Justice Goldman glanced at the card, then looked back up at Ryck confused.

"Just use it," Ryck assured him.

The chief justice nodded, then cleared his throat.

"Raise your right hand," he told Michiko, "and repeat after me."

"I, Michiko MacCailín," he started, stumbling over her first name.

"I, Michiko MacCailín," she repeated.

Do solemnly swear to be a servant to the United Federation of Nations and her citizens. I will defend the Federation from all her enemies. I will defend the rights of the citizens, ensuring freedom and liberty for all without exception. I swear this with the last breath of my body and with every cell of my being. So help me God.

Every other office in the Federation had a long and much more formal oath of office. The new chairman's though, put together two nights ago by Ryck and Hannah and signed into law only this morning, was far more direct and to the point. The chairman was the servant of the people, the protector of the people, not a tyrant. Ryck felt the powers of the simple words as he listened to Michiko. Or Chairman MacCailín now. He was confident that she would abide by that oath.

Ryck stepped back, taking Hannah's hand in his.

Go with God, Michiko. Go with God, he prayed.

Chapter 44

"Are you sure about this?" the new Chairman of the United Federation of Nations asked two hours later after Ryck had briefed her on what he could after his own short stint as the chairman of the reunited Federation.

"Yes, ma'am," Ryck answered easily.

"And you, too?" she asked Hannah.

"Hannah took Ryck's hand in hers and said, "Yes, we be in this together. We made our vows to each other for eternity, and this, well, this will just be the next step for us."

"It just doesn't seem right," Michiko said, more to herself than to the other two. "Look, I was surprised that you transferred the chairmanship to me. Oh, I knew your heart wasn't in it, and I hoped someday to fill the position, but now?"

"I told you, I did it for the Federation. Yes, my heart wasn't in the position. But I've done many things in my career for which my heart wasn't in it. But I was a liability as chairman, waiting for things to boil over."

"But you never really explained that."

"I am an oathbreaker. People can never truly trust an oathbreaker."

"But it was for a good cause. You saved a planet."

"That doesn't eliminate the fact that I broke my oath. Sandy said I should have stayed and faced the consequences of my actions."

"Yes, your friend, Sandy, Pe-Pel—"

"Sandy Peltier-Aswad. He didn't break his oath."

And I killed him for that, with my bare hands.

"But if you had turned yourself in, what would that have accomplished?"

"It would have kept 30,000 civilians on *Prometheus Station* alive. It would have kept 11,000 civilians alive on Watershed. It would have kept untold numbers of sailors, troopers, and Marines alive."

And Ben!

Hannah's squeezed Ryck's hand tight, and he knew she was thinking the same thought.

"But now we're free. In the long run, you have saved lives, not just those from Ellison."

"Maybe. That will be up to you and those who follow you. I hope you're up to the task."

"You could have led the way, you know. There is time for me later," Michiko said, seeming sincere to Ryck, not just a politician making nice.

"No, I couldn't. Before too long, people would remember the 11,000 on Watershed. They would remember how I coldly killed the first minister just to cow the old chairman."

"He's in regen," Michiko countered.

"But I did it. And those who are now serving would wonder when I'll kill them the same way. No, it's best like this. You are relatively untouched, and this gives you a clean slate."

"And there's another thing, Chairman," Ryck said, his voice quieter and more introspective. "I said my heart wasn't in it. That's somewhat of a lie. Oh, my heart wasn't in the day-to-day running of the Federation. But, I've gotten use to the power, and it has already started to fill my heart, to change me. If—I mean when—the people started to remember the deaths, remember that I'm an oathbreaker, would I be tempted to use my power to crush any resistance to my hold on the office?" He reached out and Hannah took his hand. "I think I'd be able to refrain, but as they say, 'power corrupts, but absolute power corrupts absolutely.' As a Marine, I tend to see things as right or wrong, black or white, and I wouldn't want to be tempted. No, I'd rather step out now before that happens."

"And what makes you think I'll be any better?" the chairman asked.

"Because I think you can handle it better. And I, well we," he said as Hannah took a step forward to stand beside him, "trust you."

The chairman looked at Ryck for a long moment as she contemplated him.

"I appreciate that," she finally said. "But in all candor, while I don't think I'll be consumed by the power, we won't know for sure, now, will we? Until I'm faced with a situation.

"But this plan of yours, why? You could go back to Tarawa and stay on as commandant. You could even retire and go back to Prophesy. Why so drastic an action?"

"Because if I'm around, as commandant, or even as a gentleman farmer back home," he said, "I'll be a weight around your neck, a shadow that reminds people of what we had to do. You'll suffer for it. It will be better if we're just memories."

"But this? I can't in all good conscience let you do it."

"It's not your choice," Hannah said. "It's our choice, and we lost our own flesh and blood to ensure we have the freedom to do what we want. We told you simply as a matter of courtesy. You may be the chairman, but you do not have a vote in the matter."

"But you, too? Why?" Michiko asked Hannah.

"Do you really think I can live without Ryck, growing old in an empty home?" Hannah asked.

"But you still have two children. Don't you want to see your future grandchildren?"

Hannah's voice got steely cold. "And that be none of your business. Until you marry someone, until you fall in love with someone, do not presume to understand."

The chairman blanched under Hannah's glare. "Apologies. I do not mean to presume. And if this is your choice, yes I believe you have sacrificed enough to earn that right. I will clear the ship for arrival and arrange for transportation to the spaceport. If there is anything else you need, please let me know."

She stood up to leave, then hesitated. "General, I hated you once. But you still saved my life, and I am indebted to you. And I know you have saved so many more, and at a very steep cost. I am a free woman because of you, and I intend to use my freedom—and the position you have ceded to me—to make sure you are properly honored. Thank you."

The Chairman of the United Federation stepped up to Ryck and hugged him, long and hard. She finally let him go, then spun around and walked out the door where her staff was already clamoring for her attention.

Four hours later, Hannah and Ryck were waiting in the government VIP lounge at Brussel-Zaventem. Their ship was in its final approach. Ryck reached out and grabbed Hannah's hand.

"Are you sure about this?" he asked her.

"If you be asking me if I want this, then no. But do we have to do this? For the good of the Federation, then yes."

"But the sacrifice."

"It be far less of a sacrifice than that of all those who died, Ryck."

"Like Ben?"

"Yes, like Ben. Do you want to waste that, Ryck? Do you want all of what we've done to collapse?"

"No, of course not. But what about the twins?"

"They're old enough, Ryck. They're adults now, and they have their lives to live. They'll be fine."

"You don't have to do this, you know?"

"What I told the chairman was true, Ryck. I can't go through the rest of my life without you. I'd rather spend every remaining moment I have at your side."

Ryck had expected that answer, but he'd had to ask. He had to be sure she was going through with this willingly.

The two sat in silence, lost in their thoughts. Ryck had almost forgotten what it had been like when he was not a Marine. His mother dying, then his brokenhearted father dying—killing himself, Ryck was sure, so his kids could get the insurance money. Myke leaving Lysa and him, his intention of joining the Navy, but ending up a Marine with Joshua—and how Joshua led him to the love of his life. He looked over at Hannah, realizing how lucky he'd been in love.

As a Marine, he'd lost so many friends: Joshua, Donte, Hecs, Bert. He'd killed so many men, two with his bare hands: Coltrain Meyers and Sandy. There was an immediacy to that which would never fade. He could feel their blood on his hands even now, and Coltrain sometimes came to visit him in his dreams.

Ryck had lived a full life, but one he was now willingly leaving.

He startled when Çağlar opened the door to the lounge and said, "It's time, sir."

"Well, I guess this is it," Ryck said, standing up and offering a hand to his wife. "Let's get this over with."

Çağlar led them outside to where a small hovercart waited. He offered them the back bench seat before slipping in beside the spaceport driver. In silence, they rode to where a stubby yacht was fueled and ready for launch.

"Wait here," Çağlar told the driver as he led Hannah and Ryck to the small lift. It was crowded with all three, but it was only ten meters to the lock. Çağlar entered the code; the lock opened, and he led the way inside.

The yacht was not a luxury model. It was a workhorse with signs of hard use. Çağlar showed Ryck the controls, not that Ryck would be flying it. The yacht was self-navigating.

"Sorry that the fabricator isn't working," Çağlar said, pointing at the small unit.

"Well, it's not like we're going to be using it," Ryck said with a forced laugh.

"Is that the—" Ryck asked, pointing to a large switch, obviously just added to the yacht.

"Yes, sir. Just flip it to red, and it's activated.

"Sir, are you sure about this?" the big Marine started.

"We've gone over this. This is the way it has to be," Ryck assured his friend.

A few tears began to roll down the gunny's eyes. Ryck stepped up and pulled Çağlar down to his level and hugged him.

"You've been a good friend, Hans, and I love you from the bottom of my heart. Fair winds and following seas, my friend."

"I love you, too, sir. I've been honored to serve with you."

Çağlar broke the hug and stood up, almost hitting his head on an overhead bin. Hannah reached up and took him by the collar, pulling him down and kissing his cheek.

"Thank you for watching over my Ryck all these years. You've been like a son to him, but you were his guardian angel as far as I be concerned."

Gunnery Sergeant Hans Çağlar stood staring at the two for a moment, his mouth working, but nothing coming out. He suddenly wheeled about and stumbled to the hatch. A moment later, and he was gone. They were alone.

Traffic control would launch the yacht, and then the ship's AI would take over to get it out of Earth's orbit, so the two strapped into adjoining seats.

"Flight 20ZD75, please prepare for take-off," the spaceport's AI informed them.

Ryck's hand reached over to take Hannah's in his. They sat there in silence, holding hands, as the countdown commenced.

"I love you," Ryck said as the ship rumbled to life.

Forty-five minutes later, out beyond the orbit of the moon, a bright light flared in a brilliant flash before disappearing.

Fifteen minutes after that, the government issued a news release that General Ryck Lysander, Commandant of the Marine Corps, and his wife, Hannah Hope-of-Life Lysander, were killed when the yacht taking them back to Tarawa exploded. An investigation would be conducted to discover the cause.

TARAWA
November 10, 43 Years Later

Epilogue

The old couple slowly made their way up the uneven walk leading into the pub. The man was well-dressed, his brown spider-silk coat and hand-tied bowtie a rarity anymore. The frail woman, dressed in a fine blue camisole and blossom skirt, leaned heavily on the old man's arm. His weather-lined face bespoke years out in the sun, but he beamed with pride with his love at his side.

He held open the door for her, waiting patiently for her to make it through.

"Thank you, kind sir," she said, her voice barely a whisper.

He didn't have any problem hearing her as he answered, "Of course, my lady."

The Globe and Laurel was an old establishment, loved by generations of Marines. On the walls were three centuries of photos, holos, and displays. The pub was a virtual museum to the Marines.

With the Transium Emergency, most of the Marines on Tarawa were deployed, and those that were still on the planet were celebrating the Marine Corps birthday pageant, so the pub was almost empty. It would fill up later, after the ball. In the back, though, an elderly man sat, nursing a beer. He was a big man, and age hadn't diminished much about him. He looked up as the couple came in, but kept his seat.

The old man escorted his lady to an overstuffed chair by the real wood fireplace, an extravagance quite rare anymore. He sat her down and tucked a blanket around her legs.

"I'll be back shortly," he told her.

"Take your time. I'm not going anywhere," she said as he leaned over to kiss her cheek.

The old man straightened up and made his way to the back of the pub where a double set of wooden doors led to another room.

As he reached for the doors, a voice called out, "Excuse me, sir, but you can't go in there now."

The old man turned around to see a young man, behind the bar.

"That's OK Mr. Geiland. He can go," the other patron said from his table.

"But Sergeant Major Çağlar, that's for—"

"I know, and it's OK."

The old man peered into the dark corner where the sergeant major sat, and a smile slowly crept across his face. He lifted one hand in a half-salute, and despite the disproving look on the young man behind the bar's face, opened the door and entered the back room.

The room was dark, the ancient incandescent lights turned off. The only illumination came from the two emergency exit lights. The old man blinked several times as his eyes adjusted. Slowly, he made out a figure sitting alone at a table against the near wall.

"Sorry, Mr. Geiland, but I'm not done yet," the gravelly voice spoke out.

The old man cleared his throat, and the other man, also old, but short with extremely broad shoulders turned around to see who had disturbed his solitude.

"I'm sorry, sir, but this is a private affair. Could you please give me some time here?" the short man asked.

The old man seemed to ignore the request. He shuffled forward and took a seat at the adjoining table.

"You seem to be alone, so I'd appreciate it if I could just sit for a while."

At his words, the short man looked up as if recalling something. Finally, he shook his head, unable to make the connection. He hesitated, and then waved a hand at the seat the oldster had already taken.

"It's not tradition, but then again, it's not tradition that Derrick and Jericho chose to pass within a few days of each other. So stay if you want. But I won't be good company."

There was a bottle of sherry on the table in front of the short man, unopened. Both men sat in silence, their minds going to wherever old men's minds wandered when the memories became too intense.

"Jorge Simone," the short man said when the silence got too loud.

The old man said nothing.

Finally, Jorge asked, "And you are?"

"Donte."

"Hmph. I knew a Donte once. We toasted him in this very room, a long time ago."

"I know," the old man said.

That phrasing caught Jorge's attention, and he looked closer at the man, trying to distinguish something about his new companion. Something seemed to be registering with him.

"You seem familiar. You remind me of someone I once knew," Jorge said.

"The universe is a big place. We all have doppelgangers, I'm guessing," the old man replied.

"You don't look like him, though. It's your voice and cadence that remind me of him."

The old man shrugged in the dim light.

"Where you from, Donte?"

"Fresh Beginnings. I'm a farmer there. Good land for farming."

"The independent world? Not much in the way of a government there, right?"

"Right enough. The corporations run most things, but they tend to leave the immigrants alone."

"I thought you sounded Federation. When did you leave?"

"You've got a good ear, Jorge. My wife and I immigrated 43 years ago. I would have thought I'd assimilated by now."

"Forty-three years? Right during the evolution?"

"Thereabouts."

"Did you serve?"

"I'd have to admit to that."

The two men sat in silence for another minute, before Jorge asked, "Don't mind me being nosy, but most men who emigrated then fought for the loyalists. I'm guessing you didn't."

"Everyone knew you were a perceptive man, Jorge," the old man said, not confirming nor denying the statement.

"You know, I saw Sergeant Major Çağlar out there when I came in. He was just sitting there, like he was waiting for someone."

"I've heard of him. One of the best Sergeants Major of the Marine Corps, if what I read was right."

"That's true. He served when General Ling was the commandant, and together, they changed the Corps to what it is today. I wonder, though, why he's out there."

"I doubt he was asked to meet anyone," the old man said.

"You know, about that time, even some evolutionaries needed to make fresh starts. Do you think it would be possible for someone, say someone pretty important, to fake their death, say in a ship explosion? Then with help, maybe from someone on the inside, and maybe with help from someone in the Confederation, escaped, underwent plastic surgery, and started a new life?"

The old man smiled and said, "*Quid visum accipias est.*"

"Ah, 'Accept that which you see,' Donte. I said that once to a very good friend. A friend who I lost 43 years ago, and have missed every day since."

"I think all of us have had to make sacrifices. All of us lost someone in those days."

"Donte, I'm here because I am the last living member of Class 59-2 of our Naval Officer's Training Course. It is tradition that the last two members meet here on the Marine Corps birthday and share a bottle of sherry that we saved back so many years ago. Unfortunately, my two surviving classmates, Jericho Freemason and Derrick Ohu chose to pass last month, just a few days apart from each other. So I am alone. I've been sitting here looking at the sherry, and we all know that old men with memories should not drink alone. I would be honored if you would join me and lift up a glass to our classmates."

"It is I who would be honored, Jorge," the old man said.

Major General Jorge Alfredo Guzman Simone, UFMC (Ret) took the bottle of 302 Massandra and carefully peeled back the foil, releasing the cork. The flowery bouquet of the fine sherry filled the room, bringing atrophied senses back to life and triggering so many memories.

There were three glasses in the class box, and Jorge poured half a glass of sherry into each. One was left on the table for fallen comrades, and the two men carefully lifted the other two glasses and lightly clinked them.

"In retrospect," the two intoned together.

There wasn't much else to say as they slowly sipped the sherry, each lost in his own thoughts.

Finally, the old man struggled to his feet.

"I want to thank you, Jorge, for allowing me to share this moment with you. If you ever get to Fresh Beginnings, please look me up."

"What are you doing now?" Jorge asked. "The ball is tonight, and I would love to have you as my guest."

The old man hesitated, tempted, but with a sigh, he shook his head. "I appreciate the offer, but my wife is waiting for me outside. And we really need to get back to the farm."

"Your wife? Ha—"

"My wife, *Rachel*," the old man said with finality.

With that, the old man turned and headed for the door.

"Fair wind and following seas, my friend," Jorge said.

The old man hesitated, then pushed the door open. His wife looked up as he emerged into the main pub and started to rise, but the old man waved her to relax. He walked over to the retired sergeant major, who was still nursing the same beer.

"Sergeant Major, happy birthday."

"I was hoping you'd come, sir. I made sure the obituaries reached you."

"Thank you, but I'm not who you think I am. I've, I've changed. I'm just a farmer, living a quiet life. And it suits me."

"A man does not change, sir," the sergeant major said. "And you will always be who you were, no matter what you're doing now."

"I was never able to tell you thanks before. For everything," the old man said.

"It was my honor, sir," the retired sergeant major said. "If I may ask, though, will you see your great grand. . .I mean, anyone else while you're here?"

"We discussed it, but too much time has passed, too much water under the bridge. It's probably better if we left things as they are."

"I understand," Çağlar said. "But if I came out to Fresh Beginnings one day, to see where we captured the Ferret, for example, do you think I could perhaps stop by and say hello?"

The old man hesitated. He owed the sergeant major so much. He and Major Pohlmeyer had arranged everything and had given his wife and him 43 more years together. Without them, the old man and his wife would have had to do in actuality what had only been staged. Yet, secrecy had been so much a part of their life that to even give the slightest chance of discovery was anathema to him.

He looked at his wife, who was sitting watching him. She was in failing health, and that killed him. It probably wouldn't be long now for her.

Hell, I'm the one with recurrent bouts of the Brick, and I'll outlast her. It isn't fair.

The thought of being alone petrified him. He looked back at Çağlar, then back at the door to the back room where Jorge still was. He missed them. He missed the Corps. He couldn't go back to the Marines, but the Corps was not the organization, not the uniforms, but the men and women who made it up. And he came to a sudden decision.

"Grubbing hell right you can, Hans. I would appreciate it."

He shook the sergeant major's hand, then turned and walked to his wife, the love of his life.

"Come on, Hannah," he said, as her eyes widened at the first time in 43 years he'd used her real name. "Let's go home."

Author's Note:

I want to thank all of you who have read this series. When the idea of Ryck and the UFMC hit me in early 2014, I never realized how much I would enjoy writing the series and the overwhelming response it has received. This was a labor of love, but unless others read the books, then they have no purpose. So from the bottom of my heart, thank you.

I also want to thank those of you who have helped me along the way. You've made me a better writer, and the correspondence I have received has been a welcome part of the process. And for those of you who have let me "borrow" your names as characters in the books, thanks again.

This is the final book in Ryck Lysander's saga. Ryck has been a huge part of my life over the last year-and-a-half. I hope you enjoyed watching him grow as much as I enjoyed writing about his journey. There will be more books in the UFMC universe, though. I currently have four planned and more are bubbling around somewhere in the dark recesses of my brain. Some characters you already know will be in the forefront, and some issues, such as the Klethos, will be examined in more depth. I hope you will give these books a shot.

The next series is about Ryck's children, Esther and Noah. The first book in the series is *Legacy Marines*.

Jonathan Brazee
25 December 2015
Bangkok, Thailand

As always, I welcome a review on Amazon, Goodreads, or any other outlet.

If you would like updates on new books releases, news, or special offers, please consider signing up for my mailing list. Your email will not be sold, rented, or in any other way disseminated. If you are interested, please sign up at the link below:

http://eepurl.com/bnFSHH

Other Books by Jonathan Brazee

The United Federation Marine Corps

Recruit
Sergeant
Lieutenant
Captain
Major
Lieutenant Colonel
Colonel
Commandant

Rebel (Set in the UFMC universe.)
Behind Enemy Lines (A UFMC Prequel)
The Accidental War (A Ryck Lysander Short Story Published in *BOB's Bar: Tales from the Multiverse*)

The United Federation Marine Corps' Lysander Twins

Legacy Marines
Esther's Story: Recon Marine
Noah's Story: Marine Tanker
Esther's Story: Special Duty
Blood United

Coda

Women of the United Federation Marines

Gladiator
Sniper
Corpsman

High Value Target (A Gracie Medicine Crow Short Story)
BOLO Mission (A Gracie Medicine Crow Short Story)
Weaponized Math (A Gracie Medicine Crow Novelette, Published in *The Expanding Universe 3,* a 2017 Nebula Award Finalist)

The Navy of Humankind: Wasp Squadron

Fire Ant (2018 Nebula Award Finalist)
Crystals
Ace
Fortitude

Ghost Marines

Integration (2018 Dragon Award Finalist)
Unification
Fusion

The Return of the Marines Trilogy

The Few
The Proud
The Marines

The Al Anbar Chronicles: First Marine Expeditionary Force--Iraq

Prisoner of Fallujah
Combat Corpsman
Sniper

Werewolf of Marines

Werewolf of Marines: Semper Lycanus
Werewolf of Marines: Patria Lycanus
Werewolf of Marines: Pax Lycanus

To the Shores of Tripoli

Wererat

Darwin's Quest: The Search for the Ultimate Survivor

Venus: A Paleolithic Short Story

Duty

Semper Fidelis

Checkmate (Originally Published in The Expanding Universe 4)

The Bridge (Originally Published in the Expanding Universe 5)

Golden Ticket (Originally Published in Hope is Not a Strategy)

The Lost One (Originally Published in Negotiation)

THE BOHICA WARRIORS

(with Michael Anderle and C. J. Fawcett)
Reprobates
Degenerates

SEEDS OF WAR

(With Lawrence Schoen)
Invasion
Scorched Earth
Bitter Harvest

Non-Fiction

Exercise for a Longer Life

The Effects of Environmental Activism on the Yellowfin Tuna Industry

Author Website

http://www.jonathanbrazee.com

Made in the USA
San Bernardino,
CA